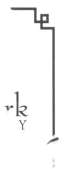

A STRANGER ON THE PLANET

ADAM SCHWARTZ

A STRANGER ON THE PLANET

A NOVEL

SOHO

Portions of this novel appeared in altered form in the *New Yorker* (July 18, 1988) as "The Grammar of Love"; in *Wigwag* (February 1990) and in *Writing our Way Home* (Schocken Books 1992) and in *Coming of Age in America: A Multicultural Anthology* (The New Press 1994) and in *Growing Up Jewish* (William Morrow 1996) and also in *An Introduction to Critical Reading* (Harcourt Brace 1999) as "Where is it Written"; in the *New Yorker* (June 22, 1992) as "This Bed" and in *Doubletake* (Winter 1996) as "Dancing with Earl."

Published by
Soho Press, Inc.
853 Broadway
New York, NY 10003

Library of Congress Cataloging-in-Publication Data

Schwartz, Adam, 1956–
A stranger on the planet : a novel / Adam Schwartz.
p. cm.
ISBN 978-1-56947-869-1
1. Mothers and sons—Fiction. 2. Mentally ill parents—Fiction.
3. Family secrets—Fiction. 4. Domestic fiction. I. Title.
PS3619.C48555S77 2011
813'.6—dc22

2010032477

10 9 8 7 6 5 4 3 2 1

For my mother,

Carole,

and

my daughter,

Annie.

"Friend, I need your part of the story in order to complete my sense of self. . . ."

—JAMES ALAN MC PHERSON, *Elbow Room*

PART

ONE

SEA OF TRANQUILITY

My mother met Eddie Lipper in the Catskills on July 4, 1969, and married him in Las Vegas sixteen days later. She claimed they were pronounced man and wife at the exact moment Neil Armstrong set foot on the moon. I didn't believe her, but I was twelve years old that summer and would have welcomed just about any man into our lives. My mother was thirty-five, and I know the same was true for her.

We were a family of four: me; my mother, Ruth; my twin sister, Sarah; and our younger brother, Seamus—a name recommended to my mother by our neighbor Mary Murphy from County Cork. My name is Seth. Seth Shapiro. Ruth said she selected all of our names because she wanted our initials to represent how strongly we were connected: SSSSS. She called us her chain of love. She was right, of course—the four of us were deeply and painfully bound together—but over time I have come to see these letters as an ideogram for silence.

• • •

My parents met at NYU. My mother was an undergraduate there, and my father was in the medical school. Throughout her teenaged years Ruth had been overweight and mentally unstable. At sixteen she was hospitalized after an especially bad psychotic episode. She regressed into an infantile state, blathering in baby babble and covering herself in her own feces. Four years later, she had lost fifty pounds and learned to keep herself calm with cigarettes and tranquilizers. For her second date with my father, she brought him home to Long Island for a Sabbath dinner. He proposed one month later. By the fifth year of their marriage, my mother had given birth to three children. In the seventh year of their marriage, my father made an important medical discovery that gilded his career. His photograph appeared in a *Life* magazine story about one hundred outstanding young Americans. He was an overnight star and left my mother for a young woman from France who had come to Boston to spend a year as a postdoc in his lab. My mother was twenty-nine.

At that time we were living in a small house in a Boston suburb. After the divorce, my mother moved us to a four-room apartment in New Jersey in order to be closer to her family. She began dating not long after we moved. I'm sure she was in no condition to look for another husband, but her sister and father viewed my mother's divorce as a shame, an embarrassment. I felt exactly the same. Not having a father around, I was as self-conscious as someone with two noses. My mother was usually fixed up with men by her older sister, Rhoda—a depressing assortment of widowers or odd, bland, thoroughly second-rate men. Still, I viewed every man she went out with as a potential father, and I watched her get ready for her dates with hope and amazement. She always enlisted my help in fastening her girdle-and-brassiere contraption. I didn't like this job, but I was the only one with the strength to do it. I didn't like how the thing felt so stiff and heavy with metal components.

I didn't like the columns of flesh that formed down the length of my mother's back as I placed each clasp in its eyelet. I needed all my strength for the last couple of clasps, by which point her back would look like a Torah scroll. Sometimes when she called for my help I would catch my mother admiring her breasts in the mirror. They were pendant shaped and enormous, mapped with bluish veins beneath skin so pink and shiny that it appeared translucent. She would cup them, lift them, lower them, then say with a sigh, "Jesus, I have great breasts."

The next morning I would pump her for news about her date, but she was always indifferent. One man might have been too old, another not well educated enough for her. She would give me these reports as she studied a crossword puzzle through a haze of cigarette smoke. The real problem, we both knew, was that any man was too far a step down from my father—a handsome, vital, successful doctor.

One weekend, Rhoda and her husband went to a Catskills resort. Eddie was the recreation director, and Rhoda handed him Ruth's phone number. Two weeks later, my mother drove up to the Catskills on a Friday night to meet him. My brother, sister, and I stayed with Rhoda and her family. I loved Rhoda's ranch house. When I opened her refrigerator, I was dazzled by the bounty of bright fruit—cherries, grapes, peaches, oranges, and bowls of melon balls. The pantry was neatly lined with enough food to last for five years. They had owned a color television since 1965, built right into the brick wall of their family room. Their finished basement was furnished with ping-pong and billiard tables, and the closets were brimming with toys. Someday, I vowed, I would live this way.

When my mother returned on Sunday night, she was in an exuberant mood. She and Rhoda were sitting at the kitchen table; I was two steps below them, in the family room, sitting on the shag carpet with my siblings and cousins, watching *The Wonder-ful World of Disney*, but I tuned in to what my mother was saying. "Oh, Rhoda, let me tell you, he's the right man. I know it! He told me he's always wanted boys to raise." I knew how much my mother wanted her older sister's approval, and I felt a little bad for her when Rhoda said in a cautious-sounding voice, "Well, that's nice for you, Ruth. That's nice." But I understood Rhoda's wari-ness—my mother's enthusiasm was completely unmodulated, like the voice of a person who's hard of hearing. Barry, Rhoda's hus-band, studied my mother over the top of his Ben Franklin glasses.

"Just be careful, young lady, " Barry said.

"You don't have to worry about me," my mother said. "I can handle myself just fine."

"We know," Barry said. "You're a good girl, Ruth."

My mother downed her iced tea in one long gulp, like a shot of some bracing moral tonic. "Of course I am," she declared. "I've always been a good girl."

On the way home my mother told us that Eddie had asked her to marry him.

"After one weekend?" Sarah exclaimed.

"I think he'd be a good father."

"How do you know?" she said.

"Because he told me he always wanted boys to raise."

"You're both out of your minds," Sarah declared.

My mother and I exchanged looks in the rearview mirror. Her eyes were apprehensive; we both understood that there was very little connection between our words and our true feelings. In two days my brother, sister, and I were going to spend two weeks with my father and his family at a summerhouse he had recently bought on Cape Cod. My mother had been deeply unsettled by my father's invitation, and I sensed her high excitement about Eddie was a reaction to our upcoming visit with my father. He had shown only minimal interest in my siblings and me since the divorce, but I still loved him beyond reason and fairness, which drove my mother mad. On the three weekends a year I visited him, my mother would call at six o'clock on Sunday mornings, telling my father that it was urgent that she speak to me. My father would call out to me in an angry voice that my mother was on the phone. I knew she was doing this to create tension between my father and me, and I would berate her for calling so early. She would respond by reminding me what a bastard my father was. She still loved him too, of course, loved him as unreasonably as I did, and all we could do about it was pummel each other for our illusions.

"How come you didn't tell Aunt Rhoda he wants to marry you?" Sarah asked.

"Because I wanted my children to be the first to know."

"No, you didn't," I countered. "You were afraid Aunt Rhoda and Uncle Barry would tell you to wait."

"Oh, for God's sake," Ruth exclaimed, "stop raining on my parade."

Then she tried to get me more enthused about Eddie by saying that he was friends with all the famous ballplayers.

"Which ones?" I quizzed her. I looked at her face again in the rearview mirror as she tried to puzzle out an answer to my question.

"Sandy Koufax."

"Sandy Koufax?" I said. "Yeah, sure."

EDDIE WAS COMING THE NEXT evening to meet us. My mother had told us that Eddie had spent the day in the city looking for a job, using his father's contacts in the garment industry. At the end of the day, the four of us—me, my mother, Sarah, and Seamus—sat on the steps of our apartment building waiting for him.

The commuter bus from New York stopped at the far end of the street. At six thirty we saw a flotilla of exhausted-looking men coming our way. "Oh, there he is!" my mother cried out, dramatically waving her arms. Eddie waved back. I thought he looked like a bowling ball—corpulent, low to the ground, his face darkened by a heavy five o'clock shadow. He was bald, but his liquid black eyes gave him a youthful appearance. As he approached, my mother brought a hand to her brow as if to shield her eyes from the light, but the sun was setting behind us.

Eddie's mouth formed itself into the shape of a sickle, his teeth showing only on the side of his mouth that scythed upward—a smile that immediately reminded me of Jackie Gleason's. Eddie placed a hand against my mother's cheek and said, "Nice to see you, baby." In the months to come, I became more certain that Eddie had styled himself after Jackie Gleason: the exaggerated "Nooo"; the eyes bugged out in a fit of apoplexy; the way he called my mother "baby"; his light, almost dance-like steps and the cha-cha-cha hand motions.

Eddie knelt down, drawing level with Seamus's face. "I'm very happy to meet you, little man."

Seamus turned his face into Ruth's arm.

"How are you, beautiful?" he said to my sister.

"My name is Sarah," she replied, and kicked our mother in the back.

Then Eddie rose and shook my hand. We were the same height, but he probably outweighed me by one hundred pounds. "I've heard a lot about you, kid," he said, adding a wink, as if we were already on familiar terms.

Upstairs in our second-floor apartment, my mother settled Eddie onto the couch. She was affected and off-key, like a bad actress auditioning for a role as a 1950s housewife.

"Are you comfortable, Eddie darling?" my mother asked as

she positioned a fan right in front of him and helped him off with his shoes. Eddie unbuttoned his shirt and handed it to her. When he stretched his arms behind his head, I could see oval stains the color of pee on his white undershirt. "Can I get you something to drink?" she asked. "Water? Pepsi?" Then, in a fit of improvisation, she added, "A martini? Is that something you'd like?" My mother wouldn't have known a martini if she'd fallen into one.

"Pepsi is fine, baby," Eddie replied, as he stretched out on the couch and opened a copy of the *Daily News*. Sarah, Seamus, and I all huddled together in the kitchen.

"Why is he calling you 'baby'?" Seamus asked.

"Because he's bogus," Sarah answered.

My mother ignored her and turned to me. "Seth darling, would you bring this Pepsi out to Eddie?"

"Do I have to?"

"Don't you want to spend some time with Eddie?"

"No."

"Seamus, honey, would you bring this out to Eddie?"

He fastened himself to her leg and shook his head.

"Sarah?" she asked.

"No chance."

Our mother looked at us in exasperation, as if we were a failed experiment.

"Jesuschristalmighty! I'll do it myself."

Eddie came to the table in his undershirt. He swigged his Pepsi straight from the bottle. When he caught me staring at him, he gave me another huge wink. "So, kid, I hear you're a star athlete."

I immediately stared at my mother, but she sent back an innocent look, as if she couldn't imagine where he might have heard such a thing.

"I'm just OK," I replied.

"He hits a home run nearly every time up," my mother said.

"No, I don't. I've never hit a home run. I didn't even start for my Little League team."

"Don't worry, champ," Eddie said. "We'll make a ballplayer out of you."

My mother smiled at me as if she had proven some contested point. Then I asked her if I could have a Pepsi too. She told me no, reminding me that we weren't permitted to have soda at meals.

"Why can Eddie have one and not me?"

Eddie squeezed my arm. "Didn't you hear what your mother said, goddamnit!"

I was stunned; tears sprang to my eyes. Sarah's eyes widened with shock. My mother put her hand on my arm and said to Eddie, "He's not used to having a man around. He doesn't have a father."

"I do too have a father."

My mother cast me a reproving look, as if I had revealed some well-kept family secret. Then she asked Eddie how his job interviews had gone.

"Fine. Ted Heller at Safir Swimwear said I had a job for the asking." Eddie didn't sound very enthusiastic.

"Well, that's wonderful," my mother exclaimed. "So we have two things to celebrate."

Eddie said he had even better news. "Just before I came down to the city, I asked Mr. Cousins, the owner of the hotel, for a substantial raise. I explained to him that I had a family to support now, and he said he would seriously consider my request."

My mother's face seemed to have lengthened by about six inches.

"You don't support us," I said. "My mother does. My mother and my father."

My mother pinched my leg under the table.

"Eddie," my mother said, "we agreed that you'd look for a job in the city. We can't move to the Catskills."

"Ruthie," Eddie replied, with that sickle smile, "when Mr. Cousins offers me a raise, I'll use it for leverage with Ted Heller."

"Oh, Eddie darling, I'm not sure that's such a good idea."

Sarah said, "Why would someone who sells bathing suits care how much you earn for leading calisthenics in the Catskills?"

Eddie ignored her and said to my mother, "Let's just see what Mr. Cousins offers. Mr. Cousins said to me, 'Eddie, if I give you a raise, I know you'll spend it on your family. That Bernstein still has the first dime I paid him.'"

"Does Bernstein make more money than you?" I asked.

"Mr. Bernstein has been at the hotel a lot longer than I have," Eddie said.

"So he's more important than you," I said.

My mother pinched me again.

Then Eddie announced that he had some great news for me. "I spoke with Mr. Cousins about having your bar mitzvah at the hotel, and he said he would rent me the nightclub at a nominal charge."

"What about Sarah?" I said.

"What about her?" Eddie said.

"My bat mitzvah, that's what," Sarah said. "Seth and I are sharing the haftarah, and I'm not doing it at some hotel."

"Me neither," I chimed in.

Eddie gave us an incredulous look.

"Our cantor and rabbi have been preparing Seth and Sarah since last spring," our mother explained. "They can't go up to the Catskills to officiate a bar mitzvah."

"That's no problem," Eddie said. "We can hire the rabbi in town. He does all the bar mitzvahs at the hotel." Then Eddie continued to lay out his grand vision for the event. We would hold the ceremony in the ballroom, where the hotel held High Holiday services. Then after the service we would go to a private room in the dining hall for lunch, and in the evening we would have the nightclub set up for a sit-down dinner. Eddie said that through his connections he could hire some top-of-the-line entertainment—a small band and a comedian.

"A comedian?" I repeated.

"I think we could get a Corbett Monica, or maybe even a Dick Shawn."

"I'm not having a comedian at my bar mitzvah, and I don't want a band either."

My mother tried to explain to him that we were just interested in a simple religious ceremony.

"I've never heard of a kid who didn't want a band at his bar mitzvah," Eddie said, with a snort of disbelief.

AFTER DINNER WAS OVER, Eddie went back into the living room to watch baseball. Seamus and I helped our mother and Sarah clear the table, though the two of us had never lifted a finger to help before.

"Go and sit with him," my mother whispered to me.

"I don't want to."

"Do it for me then. Just do it for me, all right?"

I went into the living room and sat next to Eddie on the couch. He was leaning forward, one hand on the channel dial. He kept changing back and forth between the Yankee game on channel eleven and the Mets game on channel nine.

"Stay with me, kid, and you'll never miss a pitch," he told me. I had already missed dozens of them, but I didn't say anything.

After Ruth finished cleaning up in the kitchen, she and Seamus joined us on the couch. Sarah went into the bedroom she shared with our mother to read her book, *Planet of the Apes*. Eddie supplied a running commentary about the games. Tom Seaver was about to pitch low and away. Cleon Jones was going to tag up. When the players didn't do as he had predicted, he called them bums and sons of bitches. My mother feigned interest for a while, then excused herself to put Seamus to bed. When she returned, she sat next to us on the couch and opened an Agatha Christie mystery. The year before, my mother had taken us to see a doubleheader at Yankee Stadium and had spent the afternoon sitting in the bleachers reading *Pride and Prejudice* from cover to cover.

At ten thirty, my mother told me it was time for bed, but Eddie told her I ought to stay up because Tom Seaver was pitching a perfect game and we were witnessing history. Then one of the Cubs finally got a hit in the ninth inning. "Son of a bitch!" Eddie exclaimed.

"Does this mean it's not historic anymore?" my mother asked.

"That's right, baby," Eddie said, and sent me another wink, as if only he and I understood how hopeless women were when it came to sports.

"All right, sweetie, bedtime," my mother said to me.

"Good night, son," Eddie said, and tousled my hair.

A couple of minutes after I had changed into my pajamas, my mother came into the room and sat on the side of my bed. Seamus was asleep on the other side of the room.

"That was nice," she said, "all of us watching the game together. Just like a family."

"I guess so," I replied.

She told me she was glad I approved of Eddie.

"Are you really going to marry him?"

"Yes. I think he'll be a good father."

I knew Eddie was all wrong, but I didn't see a way out. More than my sister and brother, I was the one who truly missed having a father. I was the most difficult of my mother's three children—the most unhappy, the most surly, the most headstrong, the poorest student. My mother and I both believed that all my faults could be fixed by having a man in my life. My deepest longings had set these events in motion, had brought Eddie into our lives, and I felt powerless to do anything about it.

I asked my mother if she and Eddie were going to have more children.

"No, darling. No more children."

"Does that mean you're still going to have sex with him?"

"Yes," she said. "Men and women still have sex when they're not trying to have children."

"I know," I replied defensively.

"Seth, honey. I just want you to know one thing. I still consider you the man of the house."

My mother had conferred this title on me when I was six, right after my father had left. The words hadn't meant anything to me then, and they didn't mean anything to me at that moment. I doubt they meant much to my mother either. But she probably thought it was something she ought to say, like a prayer you recite but don't believe in.

THE NEXT MORNING MY MOTHER drove us to the airport for our flight to Boston. Seamus was crying because he didn't want to leave our mother for two weeks. I tried to cheer him up by telling him about all the wonderful things we would be doing on Cape Cod. We'd go sailing and swimming and waterskiing. Of course I was also saying this to agitate my mother.

"Tell me something," she said to me. "Why doesn't your father buy a house for you and your brother and sister to live in before he buys a second house for himself?"

She was right. My father lived in a ten-room house in Cambridge with his wife, Hortense; their child, Francois; and a nanny. We lived in a four-room apartment.

"But this house is for us," I answered. "That's why he invited us for two weeks."

"That's right," she retorted. "I'm sure he was thinking of you and your brother and sister when he bought this house. That's why he never calls you or writes. Because he's always thinking about you so much."

Sarah was glum about the trip because she would have preferred to go to sleepaway camp with her friends. She was also much more realistic than I was when it came to our father. Like me, she was hurt by the fact that he paid so little attention to us, but she didn't harbor any illusions that he secretly loved us, that, if not for Hortense and my mother, he would love us openly, unconditionally. When Sarah and I were very young, we had communicated in our private twins' language; after our father left and I retreated into myself, missing him with a searing sadness, we gradually lost our private language until, at age twelve, with our hormones humming like an electrified steel fence, we barely communicated at all.

As we approached the airport, Sarah said, "Mom, I don't want you to marry Eddie. I don't want him for a stepfather."

"Fine. Then you can go live with your father. All of you. I'm sure he'll be thrilled to have you."

Seamus began crying, saying that he didn't want to go live with our father.

THE HOUSE IN WELLFLEET HAD three small bedrooms. My father and Hortense shared one; Francois shared another with his nanny, Mathilde, an old woman from France; Sarah, Seamus, and I were assigned to the third. "Jesus Christ!" Sarah said to me. "We're twelve years old. Doesn't he understand that we need our privacy at this age?" Sarah was zealous about maintaining her privacy, and not just because she was twelve and her body was changing. Her vigilance was a reaction against our mother, who left her bloodstained panties hanging from the shower rod, who changed her clothes in front of all of us, who, three months before, had come into the bathroom when I was showering, pulled back the curtain, and exclaimed, "Oh, look, you have pubic hair too! So does your sister."

We settled into a routine at the house in Wellfleet right away. Seamus and I woke up every morning at around seven. We'd go into the living room and play board games and read for about an hour. Now and then Seamus would cry out, "Seth, I'm bored here. I want to go home!" I was just as bored and lonely as my brother, but I'd tell him to keep quiet, afraid that our father would send us home if he heard our discontent.

At eight o'clock Mathilde and Francois would come down and have breakfast with us. Mathilde kept her iron gray hair wound in a tight bun. She always wore nylons, heavy black shoes, and a sweater, no matter how hot the weather. Mathilde spoke to me in high-speed French and treated me like a six- or seven-year-old, as if my age were lost in translation too.

"No, no," Mathilde exclaimed the first morning, as I poured milk over my cereal. She seized the bottle and tipped a tiny amount over Francois's cereal. "Comme ça," she said to me.

"I'm sorry," I replied, reclaiming the bottle of milk. "Je ne parle pas français." Then I emptied half the bottle into my bowl. The Cheerios floated up to the top and over the rim like tiny corpses.

Mathilde raised her arms and admonished me in furious French. "Cochon! Vous causez seulement des problèmes! Je dis votre père à ce sujet."

"I'm frightfully sorry," I said in an affected British accent, "but you may not see my penis." Hearing the word "penis," Seamus

laughed convulsively, spraying milk and cereal across the table—
an action three-year-old Francois immediately imitated.

Mathilde became apoplectic. "*Vous petit juif sale! Avez-vous
été élevé dans une gouttière?*"

"No, no, no," I said. "I'm dreadfully sorry if you've never seen
a penis. But it's impossible. Quite impossible."

At about ten o'clock I would hear water coursing through the
pipes. This was my signal to go upstairs and jump in the shower
with my father. Hortense was maniacally frugal and couldn't bear
to think of what their water bill would be if all seven people in
the house showered individually. I was glad for this arrangement,
because it was a chance to spend time alone with my father for
ten minutes. He would be almost done with his shower when I
stepped into the back of the tub; after a minute we'd trade places.
I would shower rapidly, then wrap a towel around my waist, and
sit on the rim of the tub, watching my father shave. Our conversation was always the same: He always asked me if I had played
nicely with my brothers that morning, and I always told him yes,
and he always said, "That's nice." Then I would wait expectantly
for him to ask me more questions, to inquire about my life, hoping that the close, steamy, shaving-cream-and-toothpaste-scented
air of the bathroom would provide a medium for greater intimacy
between us. But he would just regard his face in the mirror, looking to see if he had done a satisfactory job of shaving himself.

One morning I told him that I thought my mother was going
to remarry.

"I know," he replied, sighing heavily, as if the mention of my
mother placed a burden on him.

"How do you know?" I asked.

"I just do," he said.

I wasn't surprised that he knew about Eddie, especially if my
mother planned to marry him. It gave her an excuse to get my

father's attention, to remind him that she still existed, to impose a little chaos on his nice, orderly life.

"I met him the day before we came here," I said. "I didn't like him."

My father was still regarding his face in the mirror.

"He yelled at me and twisted my arm."

My father finally turned around and looked at me.

"Did he hurt you?"

"Not really."

"I see," he said. "I see."

WE ALL SPENT THE AFTERNOONS at the pond behind our cottage. My father and Hortense would read *The New York Times* and the *Boston Globe* from cover to cover, then they would open their books and medical journals. Sarah would isolate herself on a blanket about twenty yards from us, reading, writing letters, or swimming far out into the pond. Occasionally my father would look up and gaze out at her, as if trying to decide whether or not he should be concerned. Seamus and I had our books to read, and sometimes we played cards or Monopoly. An old canoe was beached near the house. One day I asked my father if Seamus and I could paddle around the pond in it. He said no, explaining that it wasn't safe without life jackets. Then I asked him if we could buy life jackets in town.

Hortense looked up from her book. "No, no," she said. "You are here for only ten more days. We are not going to spend money on life jackets."

"This is the most boring place in the world!" Seamus complained.

"Good. Then next summer you can stay home," Hortense said.

My father asked Seamus what he would like to do.

"Seth said we were going to go sailing and waterskiing. All we do is sit here and read."

"We are here to relax," Hortense told him. "Your father and I work very hard and we need to relax."

"Why don't we go to the ocean?" I suggested, thinking waves might be more interesting than a placid pond.

My father gave me a pained expression. "We have this nice pond all to ourselves. Why do we need to drive to the beach and get sand in everything?"

"How about miniature golf?" I suggested, recalling a number of courses I had seen on Route Six.

"Yeah!" Seamus exclaimed. "Let's do that!"

My father turned to Hortense. "Horty, my love, would you like to go miniature golfing?"

"No," she said very decidedly, without looking up from her book.

"Hortense doesn't want to go," my father translated. "Can you think of something we'd all enjoy?"

"I just did," I replied.

He pressed his lips tightly together. "Look how nicely Francois is playing. Can't you two go play with him?"

Francois was playing in the nude along the shoreline among a bright scatter of beach toys, singing children's songs in French. Mathilde watched over him, barefoot but still clad in her heavy sweater.

"He's only three years old," I pointed out.

"Besides," Seamus added, "they don't even speak English."

Hortense glared at us over the top of her book. "Thank God!" she declared.

My father laughed uproariously.

Over the next week I grew more and more sullen. Hortense was becoming livid at all the food I left on my plate. At dinner one night she handed me the same plate I had used at breakfast that morning. The plate was gravelly with filaments of old toast; a mound of leftover jam solidly adhered to the rim. I asked for a clean plate. Hortense told me I could have a clean plate when I finished my jam. I replied that I didn't like jam for dinner. "Too bad," she said. I helped myself to one of the hamburgers my father had cooked on the grill. At dinner the next night Hortense banged down the same plate in front of me. Next to the two-day-old jam was a congealed disk of ketchup and my leftover burger, glazed with a white, waxy membrane of fat. Again I requested a clean plate. Hortense ordered me to finish my hamburger. I refused, declaring it no longer edible.

"It's fine," she insisted. "I'm sick and tired of you wasting good food. We don't have money to throw away."

"What's the big deal?" I said. "You're both doctors."

"We are researchers. We have very little money."

"Then how come you bought this house?" Sarah asked.

"What's the difference whether I eat the hamburger or not?" I added. "You've already paid for it."

"Elliot!" Hortense exclaimed. Usually Sarah and I exchanged smiles when Hortense said our father's name; her pronunciation of it rhymed with idiot. But at that moment my sister and I just looked down at our plates. My father was concentrating on his food. He wanted no part of this. "Seth, just eat what's on your plate," he said.

A platter of plump, bursting hot dogs was next to Hortense, out of my reach.

"I'd like a hot dog, please," I said, my hands folded primly in my lap.

"No," Hortense responded. "You finish what you have."

"I'd like a hot dog, please," I repeated.

I was ready to forgive my father everything—his indifference, his abandonment of me—if he told Hortense to give me a clean plate with a hot dog on it.

"Look, Seth," he said, "just eat what's on your plate. Then you can have all the hot dogs you want."

Sarah, sitting next to Hortense, plucked a hot dog off the platter and put it on my plate. She pushed her chair away from the table and went out the door. I cut one piece of the hot dog and chewed it very slowly, looking directly at Hortense. Then I declared myself full and left the table.

I went outside to look for Sarah but didn't see her anywhere. It was after seven thirty, and I could already see a star in the twilight. I dragged the canoe down to the water, stepped in it, shoved away from the shore, and paddled until I reached the middle of the pond. Then I let the canoe drift and fell into one of my most consoling reveries—that Hortense would leave my father. She always railed about living in the United States, and she was so devoid of love or humor or happiness—certainly it seemed possible that she might leave him and return to France with Francois and Mathilde. My father would be shattered. I would go live with him, nurture him with love and solace, and he would finally recognize me as his true family, the one person in the world who would love him unconditionally and never leave him. I fantasized in this fashion until the sky was almost black. The stars were massing, the trees turning into a dark ring around the water. I was waiting for my father to come look for me, to shout out my name. This was my chance to hear concern in his voice, hear him express grief and panic over me. But all the lights in the house gradually went off, and I knew I could stay out on the pond all night and my father would sleep undisturbed for his usual ten hours. Then I tried to imagine his reaction if he came down to the beach in the morning and found my drowned corpse on the shore. Would he collapse to the ground in sorrow and regret? Or would he turn my body over with his toe, studying it disapprovingly?

Finally, I did hear a voice calling me, but it was Sarah's, not my father's. As I paddled into shore, I saw Sarah sitting on the ground, her knees pulled up to her chin. She put her head down and began crying.

I stepped out of the canoe and pulled it up onto the land. I wanted to put my arms around Sarah, to comfort and console her, but I was too self-conscious. Physical affection was a foreign language to us. I sat down next to her and asked her why she was so upset.

"I just had my period. My blood is all over the sheets. I don't want Hortense to know."

"She's a woman. She'll understand."

Sarah, still agitated, began rocking back and forth. She could see that I didn't get it. I had recently read Anne Frank's diary and remembered how Anne rejoiced in getting her period, calling it her "sweet secret." I couldn't reconcile Sarah's reaction with what I had read about Anne Frank.

"This is my first time. It's supposed to be a big deal between mothers and daughters," Sarah told me. "Mom is going to have a fit if she knows that Hortense had to help me."

"Do you want to hide the sheets?" I asked.

"Yes, but where? You know Hortense is going to find them."

"Not if we paddle out to the middle of the pond and drop them overboard."

"All right," Sarah said, laughing with relief. "Let's do that."

She went back in the house and returned with the sheets in a pillowcase. As she sat facing me in the front of the canoe, I gave it a shove, jumped in, and paddled back out to the center of the pond. Sarah dropped the pillowcase over the side. For a moment it billowed out under the surface of the water, looking like a drowned ghost. "Oh, shit!" Sarah exclaimed. "Maybe I should have put some rocks in it." But then it gradually became heavy with water and we watched the sack containing my sister's bloody sheets disappear down into the blackness.

Paddling back in to shore, I asked Sarah what she was going to do about Mom.

"What about her?" Sarah replied.

"Isn't she going to know that you've already had your period?"

"Not if I don't tell her. Next month I'll just pretend it's my first time."

"Do you think Mom is really going to marry Eddie?" I asked.

"Jesus, I hope not," Sarah said. We had not received a letter from her in the nearly two weeks we had been on Cape Cod, and we knew this was a bad sign, as if she was hiding something. We looked at each other, then away, realizing that our mother was probably doing something mad. We could help each other in small ways—she could pluck a hot dog off a platter for me, I could help her dispose of her bloody sheets—but we both felt helpless and alone floating in the middle of that vast black pond.

Back in the house, Sarah went into the bathroom and took some of Hortense's sanitary pads. But in our room we were faced with the problem of a bed without sheets—something we hadn't thought about in our excitement. Still feeling heroic, proud that my idea of drowning the sheets had relieved Sarah of her sadness, I offered to put my sheets on Sarah's bed and deal with the flak from Hortense.

"What are you going to tell her?" Sarah asked, as I removed the sheets from my bed.

"I'll tell her I had a wet dream."

Sarah laughed as she helped me fit the sheets onto her bed.

"A really massive one," I added. "I'll tell her that I was dreaming about Mathilde and just couldn't control myself."

"Seth, stop it," Sarah protested, laughing even louder. "You'll wake Seamus."

"Oh, Mathilde, you don't know how those heavy black sweaters turn me on!" I said, pulling the sheet tight on my end. Sarah fell onto the bed and put both hands over her mouth to stifle her laughter. I lay down next to her and said in a faux French accent, "Oh, *chéri*, you get me so hot when I watch you roll down your pantyhose at the beach."

Seamus woke up looking stunned and puzzled, then joined us in our laughter.

The next morning I looked in the refrigerator and didn't see my old plate. Hortense didn't call for me to shower with my father. After he and Hortense ate breakfast, he summoned Sarah and me into the living room. We sat on the couch; he sat facing us in a hard-backed chair from the kitchen. I was certain he had already discovered that the sheets were missing, but apparently that wasn't the case.

"Hortense and I have been very disappointed in your behavior," he said to us.

Tears immediately welled up in my eyes. Sarah looked away; perhaps she couldn't bear to be reminded of how much I loved our father, a love, we both knew, that would never be returned.

"Haven't you been enjoying yourselves here?" he asked.

"No," I said.

"Can you tell me why?"

"You don't pay any attention to us."

He stared at me for several seconds, his expression teetering between exasperation and concern, as if weighing what it would cost him to acknowledge my pain.

"What about you, Sarah? Do you feel the same?"

"Yes. You're cold and distant. I don't know why you wanted us to come on this vacation."

"I see," he said. "'Cold and distant.' I see."

Sarah and I just stared at him. "All right then," he said, placing his palms on his thighs, as if something had been settled. "We can all try to do a little better."

Later that morning, when we went down to the pond, my father called me over to look at the newspaper with him. That night, men were going to set foot on the moon, and my father showed me illustrations in the paper to explain the science of the moon walk. He told me about how the lunar module would detach itself from the spaceship and then orbit the moon thirty times before it landed in the Sea of Tranquility. He explained that the moon had no atmosphere and very little gravity. "A boy like you would weigh only about twenty pounds on the moon." I knew this was his way of responding to my complaint that he didn't pay attention to me, but I wanted love, not scientific explanations. I kept looking away.

"Aren't you interested in this?" he asked.

"No."

"No?" he repeated, incredulous.

"I'm not interested in science."

"Fine," he said, lacing the word with anger. He snapped the paper open to another page.

For a couple of moments I gazed out across the pond. On the far side was a small white sandbar. At that moment the sandbar looked like an oasis, a strip of white beach, unexplored terrain where I could be completely alone, away from everything. I went over to the canoe and began dragging it down to the shoreline.

My father asked me what I was doing.

"Going to the moon."

He told me to stop, that I wasn't allowed to use the canoe.

"Too bad," I said. "I already have."

He banged his newspaper down and came over to me, yanking

me away from the canoe by my ear. "I've had it with you," he yelled. "I've had it with this thoroughly dreadful behavior." I headed straight for the pond, dove in, and began swimming away. Except for the ringing in my ear, I felt strong, easily capable of reaching the sandbar. Usually, I had very little awareness of my body, but as I continued to swim I enjoyed the sensation of feeling muscular and light. At some point I heard Seamus crying for me. The dread and panic in his voice echoed across the water. I wanted to turn around to see how far I had come, but I knew that if I saw my little brother, I would feel too guilty to continue. I didn't look back until I reached the sandbar. They were all so small and far away. My father was standing on the shoreline, his hand to his brow, monitoring my swim. When he saw that I had reached the opposite shore he went back to his chair. I sat down on the sandbar for a couple of minutes, thinking about the one detail of the space mission that had morbidly interested me: When Apollo 11 was returning home, the spaceship had to reenter the earth's atmosphere at a very exact angle, with no margin for error; if the spaceship missed, it would either be vaporized or boomerang back into space, with no hope of reentry. I couldn't stop myself from dwelling on the second scenario, imagining the astronauts entombed in their spaceship, knowing they could never go home, just waiting to die.

On the other side of the sandbar was a smaller pond. I decided to explore and began tracking the bend of the shoreline. Up ahead, about twenty yards away, I saw a girl in a bikini lying on a blanket and reading a book. She waved me over. As I approached her, I noticed a NO TRESPASSING sign. I asked the girl if it was all right for me to be there.

"No problem," she said. "That's my stepfather's sign. I'm not into private property. I don't believe in being territorial."

She was certainly older than me. Her hip arced gracefully up from her rib cage and gradually tapered down to her shapely legs. She asked me if I had a cigarette. I patted my pockets as if this might be a possibility.

"Sorry. I left them at home. I just swam across the pond."

I asked her what she was reading. She held up her copy of *On the Road.*

"I've read that," I said. I hadn't liked it very much, but when she told me she was reading it for the third time, I said that it was my favorite book too. She asked me what other books I liked. I told her that in the past year I had read *Of Mice and Men*, *The Grapes of Wrath*, *David Copperfield*, *The Metamorphosis*, *The Catcher in the Rye*, and *Look Homeward, Angel*. My reading habits were the one vanity I allowed myself. I was a poor student but prided myself on being able to read anything that was fiction.

She asked me what grade I was in.

"Ninth," I said. I had just completed sixth grade. I didn't like to lie and exaggerate—those were my mother's traits. I wanted to model myself after my father. I believed his life was happier than my mother's because he was more realistic and circumspect, because he didn't hope for things he couldn't have. But I was afraid she would send me back where I had come from if she knew I was only twelve.

She told me her name was Zelda, that she was going into the eleventh grade, and that she lived in Cambridge, Massachusetts.

"My father lives in Cambridge too."

"Are your parents divorced?"

"How did you know?"

"Because you told me that your father lives in Cambridge. That means you live somewhere else."

"Oh, right," I replied.

She laughed affectionately. "Do your parents get along?" she asked.

"Not at all."

"Neither do mine. My mother still has credit cards in my dad's name, and she runs up thousands of dollars in bills. Then she and my dad get into huge fights over it. My psychiatrist said that my mother's spending habits are her way of acting out her sexual claims over my father."

"Yeah, I think my mother has the same problem."

Zelda asked me if I wanted to come in and get high.

"Sure . . . but what about your parents?"

"Oh, my mother and stepfather are at some moon-walk party in Provincetown. They probably won't even come home tonight because they'll get falling-down drunk."

"How come they didn't bring you with them?"

"I didn't want to go," she declared. "I'm against spending all that money on sending men to the moon when so many people right here on earth don't have enough to eat."

I told her I completely agreed with her.

Then Zelda stood up, whisking the sand off her beautiful limbs—nut brown and matted with a fine golden down. A sexual shiver went from my gut to my groin. I said that sending men to the moon was the most immoral thing our country had ever done.

Zelda's room was on the second floor of a breezy old ship-captain's house, low ceilinged with wide pine floorboards. She handed me one of her stepfather's bathrobes, then pulled out a white halter top and a Band-Aid box from her bureau. She pulled on the top and I put on the bathrobe. Then I watched her reach behind and undo her bikini top. It fell to her feet, enchaining her ankles. When she bent over for it, I caught a glimpse of her breasts, white as lightbulbs against her tanned body.

"Don't you want to get out of that wet bathing suit?" she asked me.

"Oh, sure," I said, and shimmied out of the suit underneath the robe.

She went over to her turntable and put on a Jefferson Airplane record. Then she sat next to me on the bed as she opened the Band-Aid box and extracted a skinny cigarette pinched at the ends. She lit it and inhaled a deep mouthful of smoke, looking as if she was trying to set a record for holding her breath. Then she held the joint out to me. I imitated exactly what she had done, but the smoke scalded my lungs and I coughed it all out. We passed the joint back and forth. It only made me a little dizzy and dreamy; I was far more powerfully affected by staring at her legs, by the sexy blend of scents in the room: lotion, talcum powder, and the marijuana, sweet and pungent. I had never kissed a girl before—I expected a silvery movie screen-kiss—but when my mouth met Zelda's, I was shocked at how wet and groping a real kiss was. She moved her tongue around inside my mouth. I slipped my hand underneath her halter top and slowly inched it upward, as if the goal was to reach her breasts without her knowing what I had in mind. When my hand finally cupped one, I squeezed and fondled it as if I were testing the ripeness of a cantaloupe. Zelda sat up and removed her top. We embraced each other, her breasts pressing against my partly exposed chest. "Oh, this feels nice," Zelda murmured.

"Yes," I agreed. My mouth moved to her breasts, kissing and suckling until my lips were numb. Then I remembered that I had another hand, a free hand, and I began to move it down Zelda's belly. She caught it just as I reached the elastic of her bikini bottom.

"Bummer," she said. "I'm having my period."

For a moment I was perplexed as to why she was telling me this; then I caught on: Her bottom wasn't coming off.

I wasn't sure what came next, so I said, "My sister is having her period too."

Zelda looked at me strangely, wondering why I would share that information with her.

"It's probably the moon," she said.

Then she pointed at my erection tenting the bathrobe.

"Oh, I don't think this is because of the moon." She smiled coyly, opened up the robe, and studied me approvingly. "Far out," she declared.

"Thank you," I said.

Zelda bent down and kissed the tip of my penis.

Stunned and slightly scandalized, I said, "Oh, that's all right. You don't have to do that if you don't want to." I immediately regretted my words, wondering why I always became polite at all the wrong moments.

Zelda raised her head, looking at me through her hair, which had partly fallen over her face. Then she moved a mass of it behind her ear, a gesture that filled me with more yearning than I would have thought possible. She moved close to me and kissed my cheek. "You're sweet," she said, and placed her hand on me. Until that moment, my experience of sex had come from masturbating to photographs from *Playboy* or to certain passages in D. H. Lawrence, but that did nothing to prepare me for the wonder of the real thing. It was as if I had been studying a planet through the wrong end of a telescope and someone had simply, kindly turned it around for me. I wanted Zelda to kiss me, or at least look into my eyes, but she just watched herself stroke me. I closed my eyes, felt a tremor in the back of my legs, then heard Zelda whisper in my ear, "Yeah, come, come." I opened my eyes and saw a pearl white thread glistening across my belly. "That was nice," she said. I apologized for being so loud. Zelda cupped my penis, but it began to feel like a strange, woolly appendage, a little mouse corpse Zelda was cradling in her palm. As I gradually shrank up, I felt myself becoming shy. I turned over onto my side. Zelda cuddled up next to me.

"Do you feel sad?" she asked.

"No," I replied a little defensively, but that's exactly what I was feeling.

"It's all right if you are," she said. "Sometimes that happens. Afterward you get sad."

Zelda and I spent the rest of the afternoon and night together. We played Monopoly and passed another joint back and forth. She told me that she was pretty much a prisoner at the summerhouse because her mother had discovered she had been seeing a twenty-two year old Vietnam vet she had met in Harvard Square. The vet's name was Zack, and her mother had found out about him after Zelda had withdrawn five thousand dollars of her bat mitzvah money from the bank and given it to Zack so he could privately print copies of his novel to sell in the square. She told me his novel was about a group of Vietnam vets who try to stop the capitalist war machine by bombing factories. So Zelda was grounded for the summer, only allowed off the property to see her psychiatrist, Dr. Feingold, who was spending the summer in Wellfleet too. I wanted to tell her stories about myself that were just as lurid, so I told her all about my cruel and bizarre stepmother and then moved on to my mother. I was going on and on about my mother's most lunatic episodes, but I began to sense that telling Zelda stories about my mother wasn't enhancing my sex appeal.

For dinner we ate some cold roast chicken her parents had left for her. At ten o'clock, despite our moral objections, we turned on the television to watch the moon landing. I reached over to hold Zelda's hand. She didn't respond—didn't squeeze it to signal affection, didn't look at me meaningfully or lean against my shoulder. I understood that Zelda was only spending time with me because she was bored and lonely, but that didn't stop me from imagining that I might go live with my father in Cambridge and that Zelda would be my girlfriend. After school, we would go to her house and have sex and on weekends we'd go to movies at the Orson Welles theater. Certainly her parents would prefer me—a nice, polite, well-read boy—to Zack, and I was certain that she would come to appreciate my refined literary sensibility. She would read *Catcher in the Rye* and *Look Homeward, Angel* and see me as I saw myself—an exquisitely sensitive and romantic composite of Holden and Eugene. I'd like to say that I was inspired by the historic event I was watching on the television: If men could actually travel to the moon, then how far-fetched could it be to believe that my father would invite me to live with him and that Zelda would be my girlfriend. But I was so involved in imagining my great new life that I was barely aware of Neil Armstrong setting one foot on the moon and declaiming his famous words. I think the moon landing had the opposite effect on Zelda—it gradually brought her back to reality. She removed her hand from mine and told me I better get going.

"Do you think your parents will come home tonight?"

She looked down and shook her head. Then I noticed tears slanting across her face. I leaned over and began kissing her; she returned my kisses, sweetly, softly. This was the type of kissing I had imagined—boyfriend and girlfriend kissing. We made out for about ten minutes. My bathrobe had fallen open, and I pressed my erection against her.

"Look what's happened to you," she said.

Feeling bolder, I asked, "Can you do what you did before?"

"You mean this?" she replied, and put her hand on me.

"No, before that."

"Can you say it?"

I had no idea what the term was, no words for what I wanted

her to do. I looked at her helplessly. Then she whispered in my ear, "*Blow job.*"

"Blow job," I repeated.

She commanded me to lie down on the couch. Then she knelt down next to me and said, "You're a very lucky boy. For your information, I happen to give the best blow jobs in the world. Zack told me I was better than the professional girls he had been to in Nam." Then she put me in her mouth, sucking and yanking heedlessly, zealously, as if trying to vanquish my hard-on. When it was over, she kissed the rim of my ear and whispered that I better get going.

"I love you," I said.

"You better go now."

Before leaving, I wrote down my address for Zelda. I couldn't leave with hers because I had arrived and was departing in my bathing suit. I didn't really think she would write to me, but three months later, near the end of October, I came home from school one day and found a ten-page letter from Zelda in the mailbox. She apologized for not writing sooner, but so much had happened to her. In August, Zack had ridden down to Wellfleet on his motorcycle to help her escape. When her mother and stepfather were out, she'd jumped onto Zack's motorcycle and they'd split, heading north for the concert at Woodstock. On the New York State Thruway they got caught in a massive traffic jam. Then the rain came. She had never been so miserable in her life. She was cold, wet, hungry, exhausted, and Zack was being a complete asshole. He told her to stop complaining so much, that she sounded like a bourgeois bitch, that this was nothing compared to what he had experienced in Nam. When they finally reached the town in which the concert was being held, she had ditched Zack and just begun walking down a street. Someone was selling water for a dollar a glass, and she bought three glasses because she hadn't had anything to eat or drink for more than twelve hours. Zelda was about to buy her fourth glass when a woman in a house across the street began yelling at her neighbor for exploiting these poor young people. She told Zelda to come into her house and that she could have all the food and water she wanted. Zelda said the family was great to her, except for their twelve-year-old daughter, a girl named Mara, who seemed angry at her parents for bringing Zelda into their house. The girl sat in a chair and read a book about astrophysics as if to show Zelda how superior she was. But after dinner Zelda told the girl all about Zack and she became a little nicer. She said that Mara really tripped out when she realized Zelda was Jewish too. Zelda said it was like Mara wanted to be her but looked down on her at the same time. Mara reminded her of me: super straight, very curious, and judgmental (I was stunned that Zelda had seen right through my poses). Zelda spent the night at the family's house, and the next day her mother drove up to get her. Her parents decided to send her to an all-girls boarding school in Connecticut, which was where she was writing to me from. The school wasn't so bad, Zelda concluded. Some of the girls were bogus, most were sex maniacs, but a couple of them were a real trip.

By the time her letter arrived, my mother's marriage to Eddie was already bleeding out. She had married him, of course, and of course it was a calamity. Eddie had opened up his own garment factory with money borrowed from my mother, but the business was in trouble from the beginning. After a time he simply stopped going in to the city, staying in the apartment all day, not bothering to shave or change out of his bathrobe. His eyes were chronically bloodshot from his violent bouts of crying. At night, my mother whimpered and moaned on the floor. Eddie stamped around the apartment like a lovesick elephant. "Ruthie, baby," he would cry, "please come to bed. Oh, baby, please come to bed!" Sarah and I shared a bunk bed, but she spent nearly every night at the house of her best friend, Cheryl Edelstein. I would lie on the top bunk, wanting to escape my body, praying that I would die during the night.

But Zelda's letter saved me; it provided me with a passport out of myself when I needed it most. Every night, I reread her letter in bed, thrilled that she was safely ensconced at an all-girls boarding school, hoping and praying that days and nights would pass rapidly until I was old enough to come for her.

AFTER KISSING ZELDA GOOD-BYE ONE more time, I walked back to the sandbar. The water felt silken against my body. When I reached the middle of the pond, I turned over onto my back and looked up at the sky. At that moment I *was* inspired by the moon landing. Floating in the middle of that vast black disc of water, reveling in my own sweet secret, gazing up at the stars and the moon, I felt that I had traveled millions of miles away from my life and had my found my own uncharted spot in the universe, a place where anything was possible, a place where I was free from the gravity of my other life. I imagined that the astronauts felt exactly the same way, bounding weightlessly, joyfully across the surface of the moon.

My euphoria subsided as I swam closer to the house and noticed that all the lights were blazing. It hadn't occurred to me until that moment that my father and Hortense might have been concerned when I didn't return after dark, and, full of dread, I tramped up to the house. When I opened the door, I heard my father call out my name. "Yes," I answered. My father, Hortense, and Sarah were sitting at the kitchen table. Sarah burst into tears when she saw me. My father stared at me with a mixture of anger and relief. I crossed my arms over my chest to warm myself up. I could have controlled my shivering, but I let myself vibrate violently in an attempt to quell my father's anger.

"Are you all right?" he asked.

I told him I was cold.

"Sarah, go get your brother a towel." Then he asked me where I had been.

"I met someone. We were watching the moon landing."

"You were watching the moon landing!" he repeated incredulously. "Do you know we called the police? Do you know there were divers looking for you in the pond?"

Sarah returned and handed me a towel. I draped it around myself but kept shivering in order not to answer.

"I mean, didn't it occur to you to call us?"

"I don't know the phone number here."

"Look, I have to call that police lieutenant and tell him you're all right."

My father went over to the phone and dialed a number on a card. I tried to get a sympathetic look out of Sarah, but she refused to return my gaze. I heard my father telling someone that I was back and that I was all right. He said that I had been at someone's house watching the moon landing. Then I heard him say, "Yes, all right. I understand." He put the phone down and looked hard at me. "Do you know that I'm going to have to pay for the rescue effort? Do you know how much that's going to cost?"

I didn't answer.

"Hundreds. They dragged the pond. They brought in divers. This is going to cost hundreds of dollars." Then he pointed his finger at me and said, "I'm sending the bill to your mother. She can pay for this." He kept staring at me, expecting a response. When I remained silent, he said, "All right, Horty, let's go to bed."

I went into the bathroom and changed into my pajamas. Sarah was in her bed, turned to the wall, when I returned to the bedroom.

No one had replaced the sheets on my bed. I lay down on the bare mattress and told Sarah that I was sorry. She didn't answer.

"Sarah?"

"I'm never talking to you again," she said. "For as long as I live."

SEVENTEEN YEARS LATER, she told me what had happened. The police had found the bloody sheets when they were dragging the pond looking for my body. As a diver brought them up from the bottom of the pond, one of the men on the boat cried out that they had found something. The boat sped back to shore and a policeman laid the bloodstained sheets on the ground. Hortense said that the sheets belonged to her. A policeman asked my father if I might have tried to hurt myself. "I don't think so," my father said. Then he added, "I don't know." The policeman told my father that he might have to prepare himself for bad news and they would continue to drag the pond. Then Sarah realized she needed to explain.

"Why?" my father asked her.

"I don't know," Sarah replied.

"Everyone has accidents," he said. "Didn't your mother teach you anything?"

Sarah told me all this in 1986, a couple of days before her marriage to Aaron Zelman. I was treating her to a celebratory dinner. As adults we had become extremely close; we had recovered our private language, mainly through the medium of our mother. She was the main topic of our lives: her madness, her habits, her demands, her crude, sad, and comic life. As close as we had become, though, we were both discreet and shy with each other about our sex lives. But at dinner that night we got drunk and exchanged sex stories like two old friends. She told me that the best sex she ever had was on July 4, 1976, when she and Aaron had made love on the beach in East Hampton. She said he was a true maestro, so much better than any of the teenaged boys she had fucked, boys who always came too fast and kept their eyes shut. Aaron gazed into her eyes the whole time, she said. Then I boasted that I had received my first blow job the night Neil Armstrong set foot on the moon.

It took Sarah a second to do the math. Then she screeched, "You got a blow job when you were twelve years old!" The people at the next table turned and looked at me.

"Sarah! Shhh," I said.

"Seth, I never would have guessed that about you."

I felt a little guilty, as if I had revealed to Sarah that I had access to a private bank account during our childhood.

"Well, I did have to wait seven years until my next one."

I didn't tell her that it took me nearly that long to get over the blow job Zelda had given me, that throughout my adolescence it cast a spell over me as potent and paralyzing as any kiss from a princess with magical powers. I replayed the act over and over in my imagination, believing that only someone who recognized me as her true soul mate would do such a thing for me. I didn't understand, of course, that Zelda was just a mixed-up fifteen-year-old who had been left alone for the night by her parents, a girl who was just trying to feel in control of things, and the only way she knew how was through sex. Sarah demanded details. Who? How? When? I told her it happened that day in Wellfleet when I swam across the pond and everyone thought I had drowned. Sarah's eyes filled with tears, remembering all those hours when she had thought I was dead. Then she told me about the bloody sheets. I was mortified and apologized profusely. I imagined her humiliation, her secret so publicly exposed, everyone staring at the sheets, at her, our father's thoughtless comments. Sarah made light of it. "Seth, did you really think we could hide those sheets at the bottom of the pond and not have Hortense discover them?" We both laughed, but then she began crying. Tears welled up in my eyes too. Sarah tried to laugh my tears away, saying, "Why are you crying, asshole? Some fifteen-year-old girl was going down on you!" But of course we were crying because we were seeing ourselves as children, remembering how sad and strange our lives were during the summer of the moon landing and Woodstock, remembering how we had haplessly, hopelessly tried to rescue each other.

SOS

On July 4, 1976, my mother, sister, and I celebrated the bicentennial at the Long Island summer home of Abe Zelman, a sixty-year-old married man who had been trying for years to get my mother into bed. We found ourselves in this position because back in March I had told Hortense to go fuck herself. Of course I had wanted to say that to her for as long as I had known her, and I finally had the opportunity after my wisdom teeth were pulled. I told the oral surgeon to send the $175 bill to my father, but when the bill arrived at his house, Hortense opened it up and immediately phoned me, demanding to know why my college health insurance didn't cover the expense. I told her I was only covered if I went to the University of Chicago clinic. Hortense asked me why I hadn't done that. I explained that the procedures were done there by residents in oral surgery and I had wanted to go to a real oral surgeon, adding that my friend had gone to the clinic and the resident had pulled the wrong tooth. Hortense told me that she was sending the $175 bill to my mother; they were already spending enough money on my tuition. I reminded her that my father was required to pay all of my medical expenses until I was twenty-one. Hortense pointed out that she had been to France only three times in fifteen years because of all the money they had spent on me and my siblings. I replied that maybe she ought to have thought of that before she began having an affair with a married man with three young children. Hortense said she would have her revenge against me when I had my own ungrateful children. Then she added that I was too much of a child myself ever to have children anyway. That's when I told her to go fuck herself.

The next day my father called and told me that I needed to apologize to Hortense. I refused, insisting that Hortense owed *me* the apology. My father replied that Hortense didn't owe me any apologies, and, if I looked at things honestly and dispassionately, I would realize that Hortense had always wanted the best for me. "Really?" I said. "What about that time she refused to give me a clean plate until I ate my leftover jam?" My father said that he had no idea what I was talking about.

At the end of May, I received a letter from the bursar's office informing me that I would not be permitted to enroll for classes in September until my outstanding tuition bills were paid in full. The total came to $4,800. I called up my father and asked him why he hadn't paid my tuition. "When you apologize to Hortense, then I'll pay your tuition," he answered. I told him that he was required to pay it. "That remains to be seen," he said.

I had a 4.0 GPA. Surely the university would give me a scholarship once I explained my circumstances to the dean of admissions, a man I believed was keenly invested in my success. In high school, I had been a C student, and my SAT scores were mediocre. I had no realistic chance of getting into the University of Chicago, but I applied anyway, hoping for an intervention of divine justice. I idolized Saul Bellow, and for my one-page personal statement

I had written a ten-page essay about how I had fallen in love with Chicago through its literature. I had read *The Adventures of Augie March* in tenth grade, which led me to the novels of Theodore Dreiser, James T. Farrell, Meyer Levin, and Richard Wright, and the poetry of Carl Sandburg. I concluded my essay by stating that, although I had never seen Chicago, the city's great literary tradition had provided me with a map of the city's soul. By the end of March of my senior year, I had already been rejected by a number of colleges, including Rutgers, the school my father was hoping I'd get into because the tuition was so much lower than at the other schools where I'd applied. Then, on April 1, I received a letter from *Scholastic Magazine* informing me that my story "Two by Two" had won first prize in their national high school short story contest. I still hadn't heard from Chicago, so I immediately called the admissions office to let them know about my prize and put a copy of "Two by Two" in the mail to the dean of admissions. Three days later the dean called me. He told me that the fiction prize was a great achievement, but they were in a quandary about my application. Everyone on the committee felt my essay and my story were brilliant. Could I help them understand the gap between my mediocre grades and my other achievements? "I don't know," I replied. Actually, I did know, but in a way that was too inchoate and personal for me to easily articulate. How could I explain to him that nothing felt real to me except the novels I read—not the other books I was supposed to read for school, not the grades I received, not the things I said to people—that something was always lost in translation between my feelings and actions, that, except for books, everything about my life felt alien to me. Then the dean asked me what my home life was like. "My home life?" I repeated. The dean said that he noticed on my application that my parents were divorced and that certainly couldn't be easy. "Oh, right, my home life," I said, finally understanding.

she and Jeremiah had had oral sex, she said yes, but told me that she wasn't into oral sex anymore when I proposed that we graduate from hand jobs to blow jobs.

Jane was sympathetic to the fact that I was still a virgin at age nineteen. When I proposed to her that we have sex just one time, she told me she would consider it, but I had to remember that it would be a one-time deal, that it was something she would do for me as a *friend*. Encouraged, I said, "Of course! In fact, I think I it would be easier for us to be friends if we had sex just one time."

The night I told Jane about my conversation with the dean of admissions, I was so despondent, and Jane was so clearly appalled by my father's cruelty, that she told me to take off my clothes and get into her bed. She went over to her bureau and extracted a small box from the top drawer. Then she lay down next to me and rolled off her jeans and underpants, keeping her top on. I had never seen her nude below the waist, but this business was too gynecological for me. She removed a diaphragm from the box and squeezed jelly from a tube around its rim. Then she hiked her legs up in the air and inserted the thing into her vagina, a look of intense concentration on her face as she felt for the right fit. "All right. I'm ready," she said.

I lay on top of her and she guided me in. Just as I was registering the divine sensation of being inside her, I felt a sudden spurt from the center of my body.

"Did you come?" she asked.

"I think so."

"See," she said, "it's really not that big of a deal."

Still, for the next couple of days, I let myself feel hopeful. If Jane became my girlfriend for real, if I could look forward to having sex with her all the time, I wouldn't care about what happened with my father or with school. I'd support myself through my job at a Hyde Park bookstore. I'd rent a small room, become a famous writer by twenty-one, and marry Jane. I wouldn't need my father or anyone. But reality set in after a week. Not only was the sex not that big of a deal, I realized, per our agreement, that it really was a one-time thing, and that, before I became famous and married Jane, I would have to tell my mother that I might not be returning to school in the fall. I had put it off because I knew she would try to emotionally leverage this falling-out with my father. So I called up Sarah in her dorm room at Rutgers and asked her if she would tell Ruth for me.

"Not a chance," she replied.

"Sarah, I'll do anything for you if you call her for me. I'll write every one of your English papers until you graduate."

"Seth, don't you think it would be easier just to apologize to Hortense?"

"I know, I know, but I can't do it. It's difficult to explain."

"You'd prefer to live at home with Mom than apologize to Hortense?"

"SOS," I said, using our secret code: "Save our Shapiro." Sarah and I would say it to each other when our problems became too overwhelming, when one or both of us felt we were going under emotionally.

"I'm not calling Mom for you, but I'll call Dad and see what I can do."

Sarah called me back the next day.

"Dad said he's happy to pay your tuition after you apologize to Hortense."

"What did you say?"

"I told him that Mom would probably get a lawyer to enforce the divorce agreement, that he would have to pay your tuition eventually, and that the only thing all this would accomplish would be to cause you to miss a semester or two of school."

"You told him Mom was going to get a lawyer? What did he say to that?"

"He said that if you're so concerned about missing any school, you can transfer to Rutgers and pay your own tuition."

"Do you think that's why he's doing this? To get me to transfer to Rutgers?"

"No, I think he really believes you owe Hortense an apology."

When Sarah and I had been applying to colleges, our father had tried every means of persuasion and pressure to get us to go to Rutgers, where the tuition was so much lower than anywhere else because we were residents of New Jersey. Sarah was admitted to a couple of small liberal arts colleges—Macalester in Minnesota and Union in upstate New York. Our father had pointed out that Rutgers was just as good academically as either of these schools and half the cost. Sarah had told him that she preferred a small liberal arts college and that she really wanted to get out of New Jersey.

"What's so bad about going to college in New Jersey?" our father had said. "I went to college in New Jersey. In fact I had to live at home when I went to college because money was tight."

"But aren't you happy that I have more options?" Sarah had asked. Then he offered Sarah a deal: If she went to Rutgers, he would give her five thousand dollars when she graduated. She could use it for anything she wanted—graduate school, a trip to Europe.

"But wouldn't you pay for graduate school anyway?" she replied.

"That remains to be seen," he said.

WHEN I CALLED MY MOTHER to explain my situation, she crowed with delight after I told her what I had said to Hortense. "I tell you, Seth, I surely did something right with you children!"

My mother had said the same thing—"I surely did something

right!"—when I received all As my first quarter at the University of Chicago. I had asked Sarah, "Do you think it would be too cruel to remind Mom that I had to get one thousand miles away from her before I finally did well in school?"

"What about that dean of admissions?" my mother asked now. "Maybe he can do something for you?"

"No, Mom, he can't do anything."

"Why not? I'm sure you're quite a feather in his cap."

"He just can't. I know."

"What about Saul Bellow? Can he do anything for you?"

"Mom, I've told you a hundred times: I don't know Saul Bellow."

At the beginning of winter quarter, I had landed a job at the most popular bookstore in Hyde Park. One day my prince came in to buy some books. As I was ringing up Bellow's purchases, the great man asked me if I was a student at the university. Then he asked me what I was studying and where I was from. A zillion things were going on in my mind. Bellow could tell I was starstruck, and I appreciated the kindness and the attention. I badly wanted to tell Bellow that I had written my college application essay about *The Adventures of Augie March,* but I didn't want to frighten him off. Would his mood suddenly curdle if I mentioned one of his novels? I wanted to tell him that if I had not read *Augie March* and *Herzog,* I would probably be at some third-rate college, not at the University of Chicago. Actually, seeing Bellow I was reminded that I owed him a much more direct debt for my admission to Chicago, but it was a connection I felt extremely self-conscious about. My prize-winning story, if not exactly plagiarized from, was deeply influenced by a Bellow story titled "The Old System." "Two by Two" was based on an incident from my own life—when I was ten, my grandfather had used me as a go-between to let my mother and aunt know that he had decided to be buried next to his second wife, Rose, not next to his first wife,

Esther, the mother of his two daughters, and a huge family uproar
had ensued, a drama of poisoned feelings and betrayal—but the
style and most of the premise was directly borrowed from "The
Old System." In Bellow's story, as in mine, the Jewish soap opera is
filtered through the memory of a geneticist named Isaac, a relative
of the feuding parties. I had been vaguely aware of being under
the spell of "The Old System" when I was writing my story, but
seeing Bellow in person, I became conscious of how directly I had
appropriated it. I felt as if I had something belonging to Bellow in
my pocket, something he didn't even know he was missing.

Then I noticed a small, delicate, iridescent feather pleated
into the band of Bellow's fedora. *A feather in his cap.* I finally
understood that dumb expression my mother always used. It was
a vanity, a sign of pride, the famous author in all his splendid
plumage. As I was handing him his change, knowing it was now
or never, I readied myself to tell Bellow that his novels had literally changed the course of my life. "Mr. Bellow, I like your hat,"
I said. Bellow put his head back and laughed. "Thank you very
much. So do I."

I was so excited about the encounter that I told everyone I
knew, including my mother. By the time Ruth had finished telling
everyone *she* knew, I had become Bellow's protégé.

"Seth darling," my mother continued on the phone, "I just want
you to know that everything's going to be all right. Maybe we can
get a loan from the bank, and I know Abe Zelman will be happy to
help with legal advice. I'll do anything I can to help you."

"Thanks, Mom."

"I love you, darling. We'll get that bastard."

When he decided not to pay my tuition, my father didn't really
anticipate how much my mother would welcome the chance to
nettle him, to impose herself in his life—and he couldn't have
known about Abe Zelman. My mother had met him when she

needed a lawyer to handle her divorce from Eddie. She was a second-grade teacher and deeply in debt from all the loans she had co-signed for Eddie. Abe had offered her a summer job in his law office at a surprisingly generous salary, and she had worked there every summer since. As part of his campaign to get her into bed, Abe gave her bonuses and bought her expensive gifts. She accepted the money and gifts, though she had no intention of sleeping with him. She had an on-and-off-again lover, Jimmy Conroy, the married principal of the school where she taught. Besides, she found Abe physically repulsive—he had a pug nose, elephantine ears, and fingers like sausages. When Ruth told Abe about my father defaulting on the divorce agreement, he immediately drafted a letter, threatening my father's with various legal actions, including charging fourteen percent interest on the unpaid tuition. He also said that he had reviewed the thirteen-year-old divorce agreement, and its terms were thoroughly unacceptable to his client.

My mother was so thrilled with the letter she read it to me over the phone.

"Mom, don't you think this is a little excessive? Suing to change the terms of the original divorce agreement? Charging interest on the unpaid tuition?"

"Look, thirteen years ago your father played hardball with me. Now it's my turn. Besides, Abe's not charging me for his services."

"Don't you think he's going to expect something in return?"

"Honey, I appreciate your concern, but I can handle Abe. I've been doing it for years."

The year before, my mother had told me about Abe's most ludicrous attempt to seduce her. She and Abe had been the last two people in the office at the end of the day. Abe had gone into the bathroom and come out completely naked. He had opened his arms and said, "Please, doll, just one kiss." Ruth had burst out laughing. She told me his penis looked like a snail, barely visible beneath his huge belly. I was scandalized when my mother told me this, but she said that Abe was harmless.

After my mother told me about Abe's letter, I received another letter from the bursar's office informing me that my tuition had been paid in full. I knew I would have to call my mother and share the news with her, but she beat me to it.

"I tell you," she said, "that Abe Zelman is some lawyer. Honey, you really ought to write him a letter to thank him."

"Sure," I said.

"You know, sweetie, Abe would like very much to see you. He's so proud of your success, and he hasn't seen you in years."

"All right," I said.

"Abe's invited us all to his summerhouse for the Fourth of July. I told him I didn't know if you could come, but it would mean a lot to him if you did."

"Sure, I'll come."

"Oh, sweetheart, that's wonderful! Absolutely wonderful! I'll send you the money for the plane fare tomorrow."

"Thanks, Mom."

"You won't forget to send him a thank-you note?"

"No, Mom."

I was more thankful for the plane ticket home than I would have ever admitted to Ruth. Ten days before, Jane and I had gone to a party together, and she had left with another boy. A boy with an earring! The next morning I knocked on Jane's dorm door. I decided to pretend that everything was normal, that Jane and I would go to breakfast in the dining hall as usual. She didn't answer the door, but I knew—I just knew!—she was in there with the boy from the night before. I went back to my room, waited an hour, and then knocked on Jane's door again. No answer. I went to the dining hall and saw the two of them at a table together. When we finally talked that evening, Jane told me that I was too needy, that she wasn't attracted to me, and that she didn't think of me as her boyfriend. I began crying and told Jane how much I loved her. She looked at me sadly and apologized for hurting me.

"Just tell me one thing," I said.

"All right."

"Did you have oral sex with him?"

For the next two weeks I barely slept. Lying in bed at night, I couldn't stop myself from imaging Jane having sex with the boy from the party. *Oral sex.* I tried everything to dull my thoughts. I masturbated five times a day. I drank from a bottle of vodka until my bed was whirling around the room like Dorothy's in *The Wizard of Oz.* But nothing helped. My mind was deteriorating. I couldn't read, couldn't write my papers, couldn't think. My 4.0 GPA was in the toilet. My brain was emptied of everything but the image of Jane going down on the boy with the earring.

ON JULY 1, SARAH, RUTH, and Seamus met me at Newark Airport. I surmised that Seamus had come at my mother's request so that she could foster the illusion of a close, happy family. Sarah had come because I phoned her the night before and pleaded with her, claiming that I was in no condition to ride alone with our mother in the car for thirty minutes. Then I asked her if she could get me a job at the telemarketing company where she was working for the summer. "Sure," she said. "You want to spend the summer at home, though?" I told her I needed to get out of Chicago for the summer. "You love Chicago, Seth. Is everything all right?" I said I was fine. Just fine.

Sarah drove home from the airport. I sat next to her in the front. Ruth was in the back, the hand holding her lit cigarette in the vague vicinity of the window. Seamus was sitting next to her, a knitted kippah bobby-pinned to his head. Since his bar mitzvah, Seamus had become more and more observant. Our mother began keeping a kosher house to accommodate him, but my indifference to the rules of kashrut created tension between us. On my last visit home, he had discovered me eating a slice of pepperoni pizza on a dairy plate and had stood over me like a yeshiva-boy version of the Grand Inquisitor, his arms folded tightly across his chest, his eyes welling up with tears but still blazing with condemnation. Later he had removed the plate from the drainboard and dropped it in the garbage.

Seamus and I did have one thing in common: He wasn't speaking to our father either. Six months before, Seamus had read in the local paper that Elliot Shapiro was scheduled to deliver a lecture at a hospital just down the road from our apartment. Seamus was sure he would call and had waited all day by the phone, but never heard from him. The day after the lecture, Seamus called our father at home and asked him why he had not bothered to visit when he was only five minutes away. Our father replied that he had come to town just to deliver the lecture. He had gone directly to the airport after he was done. Seamus told him that was no excuse and then proceeded to deliver his own lecture about what a bad parent he was.

For about five minutes no one in the car said anything. Then Ruth said, "Seth, you're very quiet. Is everything all right?"

The ashtray in front of me was overflowing with lipstick-stained cigarette butts.

"I have a deal for you, Mom. If you can go the next two months without a cigarette, I'll answer any question you want to ask me about my life."

"Ha, ha, very funny," Ruth said, and took a deep drag on her cigarette. She exhaled the smoke out the side of her mouth in the direction of the window. In the rearview mirror, I caught Seamus glaring at me. He didn't approve of the way I treated our mother. I rolled my window all the way down, and the sudden blast of air lifted Seamus's kippah. He clapped it down with one hand.

"Seth, please close your window," he said.

"I'm being asphyxiated up here," I replied.

"All right, I'm putting it out," Ruth said, dragging deeply on her cigarette one more time and then letting it jet away out the window.

"So how's your girlfriend Jane?" Ruth asked.

"Fine."

"Why don't you invite her out to visit this summer? You can see some Broadway shows, go to museums."

I didn't say anything.

"The two of you can share a room if you want," Ruth added. "You know I'm very open-minded about these things."

I was still silent.

"What's the matter? Did I say something wrong?"

"No, Mom," I said. "Besides, I'm not sure Reb Seamus would approve."

"I'm going away. Remember?" my brother said.

In two days Seamus was going to Israel for a month with Young Judea.

"So you'll invite her to visit then?" Ruth repeated.

"We'll see," I said.

"You're not still a virgin, are you?"

"Jesus Christ, Mom!" I exclaimed.

"Your sister is still a virgin, but I think it's different with girls."

Sarah turned around and looked hard at Ruth. "You just said something wrong."

"Look at the road, for God's sake," Ruth said.

Ruth lit another cigarette. "Why? Why did I say something wrong?" she said defiantly. "You and Seth tell each other everything."

Actually, I hadn't known—and didn't particularly want to know—whether or not my sister was a virgin. I felt extremely uncomfortable, as if I had accidentally seen Sarah in the nude.

"I think it's wonderful that you and your brother are so close. That's one of my proudest achievements as a mother."

I SPENT MOST OF THE next three days watching television and drinking my mother's liquor. None of us were drinkers, but Ruth kept some dust-coated bottles of scotch, gin, and brandy behind the steel-wool pads in the cabinet under the kitchen sink. Sarah worked from 6:00 p.m. until midnight. On my second night home she came in at twelve thirty. I was sitting on the couch, watching an old movie, and drinking a bottle of B&B brandy. I asked her if she'd like some of it.

"I don't like the taste of alcohol," she replied.

"Neither do I," I said, "but this is different. This bottle is over thirteen years old. Mom told me it was left over from her wedding. Try a sip."

I held out my glass to Sarah.

"Oh, this *is* amazing!" she exclaimed. "I've never tasted anything like it."

"Go get a glass."

Sarah sat next to me on the couch and I poured her a drink. She asked me when I had begun drinking so much. I told her that Jane had left me.

"Oh, Seth, I'm sorry. Did you see it coming?"

"Yes and no. We had some problems, but she had invited me over to her house in Highland Park for Passover and her family really loved me, especially her mother."

"Did you ever think that might be the problem?"

"What do you mean?"

"Most nineteen-year-old girls don't want nice, safe boys their mothers would love."

"Maybe so."

I knew that Sarah was right, but we shared the impulse to court other families as if we were hoping to be adopted by them. Both of us, in our own ways, had spent our lives looking for substitute families. In high school, Sarah had put a great deal of energy into being popular—it was her ticket out of our apartment and into the houses and lives of the many wealthy families in our town. Virtually every weekend she slept over at a friend's house, sleeping in their clean, comfortable homes, swimming in their pools, eating their expensive food. Of course she knew her friends' families had their own problems—divorces, bankruptcies, wayward children—but any family seemed like a reprieve from our own.

"Jane was too beautiful for me anyway. Girls that beautiful don't want to go out with boys who are just average looking."

Sarah pursed her lips, as if she wanted to disagree with me but knew I was right and was perhaps relieved that I was being realistic.

"If you're average looking, then what am I?"

"Prettier than me."

"Thanks," Sarah said, laughing.

"Do you think I'm too needy?" I asked her.

"Everyone is needy."

"As needy as Mom?"

"Don't do that to yourself, Seth. No one is as needy as Mom."

We laughed, but of course we were both terrified by the possibility that one day we might be as needy as our mother.

"God, I'm really dreading going to Abe Zelman's tomorrow," she said.

"Why?"

"Because his son, Aaron, is going to be there. Mom once tried to set me up with him, and I told her I wasn't interested, but she gave him my phone number anyway. When he called me up, I lied and told him that I had a boyfriend."

"What did he say?"

"He was actually very nice. He apologized and said that his father and my mother probably misunderstood each other. I said, 'Oh, I don't think so.' He laughed and said, 'Probably not.'"

"So don't go," I said. "I'm the one who has to go, not you."

"No, I have to go," she said. "When I told Mom I wasn't going, she began crying, telling me that I needed to do this for her, that Abe really wanted me to meet Aaron, and that she would be so embarrassed if I didn't go because of all the free legal help that Abe had given her."

"Sorry," I said.

"Forget about it."

"Look . . . Sarah . . . about what Mom said in the car the other day."

"What? About my being a virgin? I don't care."

"Neither do I. I guess that's all I'm trying to say."

We sipped our brandy, looked at each other, then away. I was actually surprised that she was still a virgin. I knew she'd had lots of boyfriends and had presumed she had slept with some of them.

"How did she know anyway?" I asked.

"How does she know anything? She asked me."

"You told her?"

Sarah yawned. "Sometimes it's just easier that way."

WE SET OUT FOR EAST HAMPTON after lunch the next day, July 4. Seamus had left for Israel the day before. After we crossed the George Washington Bridge, Ruth told us that she had some news: Abe was pursuing a suit against our father to change the terms of the thirteen-year-old divorce agreement.

"Mom," Sarah said, "we got what we wanted. He paid Seth's tuition. I don't see the point in being vengeful."

"Oh, and he wasn't being vengeful when he refused to pay Seth's tuition?"

"Maybe he was," Sarah answered. "But we still need to have a relationship with him. How can we do that if you're suing him?"

"Say, look here," Ruth said, "I'm doing this for the two of you."

"Mom," I chimed in, "can't you at least be honest and admit you're doing this for yourself? Suing Dad is just a way for you to get your jollies."

Ruth lit a cigarette. "Fine, then why don't you go live with your father for the summer?" she replied, exhaling smoke in my direction. "I'm sure he'd be happy to have you sit around all day and drink."

I turned around and looked at Ruth. "Mom, can you tell me, on your word of honor, as God is your witness, that in the past two weeks you have not used the phrase 'I have that bastard by the balls' or some variation thereof?" She didn't answer. "See," I continued, "this is about your interest in my father's balls. Nothing more."

Since returning home from Chicago, I had felt ill in the heart over demolishing my relationship with my father—and all because I couldn't bring myself to apologize to Hortense. After years of indifference, he had finally begun paying attention to me during my senior year of high school. When I was writing "Two by Two," I had called him for help with some of the scientific details I was using in the story. Of course he had been happy to discuss science with me. I sent him a copy of the story after I won the Scholastic Award. He wrote back a letter that began: "EXTRA-ORDINARY!" Despite his lobbying so intensely for Rutgers, he was actually very proud when I was admitted to a prestigious university, and I could sense he regarded me differently afterward. I sent him copies of the papers I wrote for my classes with the high grades and the professors' comments on them, and he wrote back with his own comments and questions about the essays. During the winter quarter, he had come out to Chicago to give a lecture at the medical school, and the two of us went out to dinner at Morton's. Sitting among the businessmen, enveloped in the manly scents of cigars and charred beef, sharing an expensive bottle of wine, we had talked for hours, mainly about my studies and the books he was reading. I realized that my father hadn't paid attention to me until I was well credentialed, but I excused it by rationalizing that he simply wasn't interested in children, and now that I was on my way to becoming an accomplished adult, he could appreciate and love me as his son. After dinner, we went to see Ryan O'Neal in *Barry Lyndon* at a movie theater in Water Tower Place. Throughout the movie he kept his hand on my knee, and I felt like a boy again: Alone, just the two of us, with no Hortense, no Ruth, and no siblings, he was finally free to love me, as I had always believed he would. Less than two months later, I had told Hortense to fuck herself.

WHEN WE ARRIVED AT THEIR HOUSE, Abe and his wife, Marcy, kissed Ruth on the cheek. Sarah extended her hand to avoid a kiss, but Abe just looked at her hand and said, "What? No kiss?" Sarah leaned in and let him kiss her on the cheek.

"How's the genius?" he said to me, and pressed my hand.

"What? No kiss?" I said to him.

Ruth looked stricken, but Abe burst out laughing.

"I'll give this handsome boy a kiss," Marcy said.

Abe and Marcy gave us a tour of the premises: It was more like a compound, with a huge main house, a guest cottage, an in-ground pool, and tennis courts. The three of us each had our own room in the guest cottage, which also included a living room and a small kitchen. Abe told us to put our suits on and meet them at the pool.

As we walked toward the pool, Ruth asked me if I had remembered to thank Abe.

"Thank him for what? Suing my father?"

Abe and Marcy were sitting at a table by the pool, both of them in their bathing suits and deeply tanned. Abe's huge brown belly was as round and tight as a balloon; Marcy's hair was an unnatural shade of black, and her lips were smudged with electric pink lipstick. Her nails were painted the same color. A gold Star of David was enshrined deep within her seared and corrugated cleavage. Sarah and I wore T-shirts; Ruth had on a terrycloth bathrobe she had found in the guest cottage. Abe asked us what we would like to drink.

"I've already had two scotches and I'm feeling no pain," he said. Ruth said that sounded good to her.

"Me too," I added. Sarah said she'd have a ginger ale. On the table was a platter of shrimp, colossal and gleaming. *Rich people's shrimp*, I thought. I immediately helped myself to one. Ruth said that both of them looked like they had been enjoying the sun.

"Oh, I know," Marcy replied. "Don't you think my hands look just like a Negro's?"

She showed us her white palms and then the brown backs of her hands.

"You could definitely pass for Sammy Davis's sister," I commented, and helped myself to another shrimp.

"Sarah," Marcy said, "I'm so glad you're finally going to meet Aaron. He just graduated from Harvard Law School and is joining Abe's practice at the end of the summer."

"You know, I do have a boyfriend," Sarah said to her.

"Since when?" Ruth exclaimed. "You didn't tell me you had a boyfriend!"

"Oh, well, Aaron has a girlfriend too," Marcy said. She placed her electric pink fingernails on the table and leaned forward conspiratorially. "A Puerto Rican girl," she said. "But we don't think it's serious, thank God."

"Just what every nice Jewish boy wants," I said, "a not-so-nice Puerto Rican girl."

"Seth, let's go for a swim," Sarah said.

"I'm a little dizzy from this scotch," I answered. Sarah stood up and pulled her T-shirt over her head. "Come on," she commanded. "You'll feel better once you get in the water."

"Your daughter has some body," Abe said to Ruth.

Sarah dove into the water and stayed under as long as possible, no doubt to drown out any more comments about her body. She surfaced at the far end just in time to hear Abe declare that her breasts were going to make some young man very happy one day. I reluctantly got up and took off my shirt. My mother stared at me, her eyes already a little bloodshot and woozy. "All my children have beautiful figures," she said.

I swam over to Sarah at the far end of the pool. "Try to keep a lid on it," she said quietly.

"I'm only providing cover for you."

"Bullshit. You don't like them because they're rich and obnoxious and suing Dad. Besides," she added, "we wouldn't be here right now if you had apologized to Hortense."

I dunked myself under the water and stayed there until Sarah yanked me up.

"What are you doing?" she exclaimed.

"Drowning myself in guilt."

Just then we heard a car drive up. "Aaron's back," Marcy said.

The prodigal son kissed Ruth and Marcy, then stripped off his polo shirt. His body was golden and muscular. Sarah looked at the grotesque bodies of his parents and then back at Aaron as if she had missed something. He dove into the pool and swam over to us. I stood straight up and shook his hand; Sarah stayed crouched under the water and gave him a little wave.

· · ·

DINNER WAS SERVED OUT ON the deck overlooking the ocean. The setting sun turned the sea a beautiful shade of lilac. Aaron brought out a kettle of steamed lobsters and placed one on each person's plate. Marcy served corn on the cob and a salad made from Jersey tomatoes. Abe poured everyone wine. Apparently, Sarah had suddenly developed a taste for alcohol, because she drank the wine with a smile on her face.

Sarah and I were studying our lobsters.

"Do you like lobster?" Marcy asked Sarah.

"Yes. Thank you."

Neither of us had ever eaten lobster before, and we were furtively looking at the three Zelmans to see how it was done.

"Of course she likes lobster," Abe said. "What nice Jewish girl doesn't like lobster?"

"Aaron, honey, help Sarah with her lobster," Marcy said. Then, turning to Sarah, she added, "Aaron's an expert at this."

Sarah and I both watched Aaron break the back of her lobster; with a long two-pronged fork he skillfully extracted the plump white tissue from the red carcass. Then he used a nutcracker and a fork to break the claw and slither out a pink slab. "Would you like me to help you with yours, Seth?" he asked.

"I've got it," I said, and tried to fit my nutcracker around the torso of the lobster.

"Darling, let me help you," my mother said.

I squeezed the nutcracker and the lobster went skidding into my lap. My mother laughed uproariously. Eating her lobster, Sarah looked as if she was in ecstasy.

As Marcy blathered on about yachting into New York Harbor to see the tall ships, I finally extracted a morsel, dipped it in butter, and nearly swooned—it was the most luscious, sweetest, richest thing I had ever tasted. Then Abe told me how proud my mother was of my academic success at Chicago. Ruth kicked me under the table.

"Abe, thank you very much for your help recently," I said.

Marcy asked me what I was studying.

"English."

Ruth, who had already drunk three glasses of wine, said, "He's going to be a famous writer someday."

"Oh, what do you write about?" Marcy asked.

"Things," I mumbled.

Marcy said that she was the educational director of the Temple Emanuel Sisterhood and was planning to set up a class for young people to write stories and poems about the Holocaust. Would I be interested in helping her?

"I'm pretty busy this summer," I said.

Ruth swigged down her fourth glass of wine. "Do you know that Seth is studying with Saul Bellow?" she exclaimed.

"Seth, that's amazing," Aaron said. "I love his novels. What's he like in person?"

"Who are you talking about?" Marcy asked.

"Saul Bellow, Mom," Aaron explained. "He's the most important Jewish writer in the country."

"Oh, then I certainly want to read something by him. Seth, what would you recommend?"

"*Pride and Prejudice.*"

"*Pride and Prejudice,*" Marcy repeated. "Is it about the Holocaust?"

"Absolutely," I said.

I looked around the table. Abe was staring into his glass, an unhappy expression on his face; my mother looked distraught; Sarah glanced at Aaron and he gave her an understanding smile. Ruth raised her glass. "I'd like to propose a toast to Abe. You've done so much for my son. I don't know how I can ever thank you for all your help. "

"Oh, I'll think of something," Abe said, with a big wink.

"Here, here," Marcy said, raising her glass.

I was watching my mother sullenly, but mainly I was angry at Sarah. I felt abandoned by her. I could see she liked Aaron, liked the Zelmans' expensive food, their wine, their stunning views. I knew she was thinking that this would be a nice family to belong to, and I didn't blame her: If the Zelmans had a beautiful daughter who had just graduated from Harvard Law School, I would have had Abe and Marcy crowning me as the Nicest Jewish Boy in all the land. But they didn't have a daughter, they were suing my father, and I wanted Sarah to be as resentful as I was.

"Honey, do you know that Abe offered to pay your tuition if your father didn't come through in time?" my mother said to me.

Marcy added, "I'll never understand how a parent can turn his back on his own child."

I turned to Marcy and said, "You're talking about my father."

Ruth put her hand on my arm. "Oh, sweetheart, you don't know half the things that bastard did to me."

I yanked my arm away and stalked off. Behind me, I could hear my mother apologizing for my behavior.

I WENT BACK TO THE GUEST COTTAGE and got into bed. In the distance, I could hear fireworks going off, but I was happy to be by myself, alone with a book. At about ten o'clock I heard my mother go into her room; I was just drifting off to sleep an hour later when I heard the door to the cottage open again. I presumed it was Sarah, but after a minute I heard Abe's voice in my mother's room. I could only decipher the odd word or two—they were keeping their voices down—but then I heard the sound of bedsprings screeching, then moaning and sighing. I lay very still for about five minutes, debating whether or not I ought to go out, wondering if they would hear my door open and shut, until I heard the door to the cottage open again. The sound of the bedsprings had become rhythmic, as if someone were jumping up and down. A few minutes later, Sarah opened the door to my room.

"Seth?" she said softly.

"I'm awake."

"Can I come in?"

"Sure."

She lay down on the opposite side of my double bed.

"Thanks. A mouse is skittering around in my room."

We lay silent for a moment, the bedsprings in our mother's room screeching incessantly.

"You can hear them in here too," I said.

Sarah reached for my hand. The tangy scent of sex rose from her body like the shimmer of heat from hot asphalt. Reflexively my nostrils pinched in and then flared out. She knew I could tell that she had been having sex with Aaron, but she also knew I wouldn't say anything about it. She understood that the last thing I wanted to think about was my sister having sex. Was this the only normal thing about our family?

"Oh, Abe, I can't breathe anymore! At least let me get on top."

"Doll, I'm coming. I'm coming."

"This is all my fault, isn't it?" I whispered.

"No," Sarah whispered back.

But from the other side of the wall, I heard the true cost of my words to Hortense.

"Oh, Abe, this is really getting painful."

"I'm almost done. Oh, God, I'm almost there. Almost . . ."

Sarah and I were born with our umbilical cords twisted around our necks, and my mother loved to tell the story of our traumatic births. Sarah and I had titled it "Was Anybody Praying?" Neither of us were breathing when we emerged from the womb. We were on respirators for ten days and it was touch and go. But a rabbi came to pray over us, and our grandmother tied a red thread around each of our wrists. Finally, on the tenth day, Sarah and I were able to breathe on our own. "I thanked the doctor," Ruth would say, "but the doctor said, 'Don't thank me. Was anybody praying?'" When my mother told this story, Sarah and I always joked that we had probably tried to strangle each other before we were born. But lying next to her now, hearing Abe fuck our mother, I wondered if it was actually a suicide pact. Perhaps, floating in the briny ether of our mother's womb, we had been able to hear some cruelty or coldness out in the world, a world where children were abandoned and women were debased.

Finally we head Abe's orgasmic victory cry: "*Yes! Yes! Yes!*"

"A regular Molly Bloom," I commented.

"Who?" Sarah said.

"Never mind."

"Look, Seth, you do need to apologize to Abe about that *Pride and Prejudice* business."

"I know . . . but I can't stand it when Mom lies like that about me. You don't know how many times I've asked her not to tell people I know Saul Bellow."

"She's just proud of you."

"You're not going to tell me I have to apologize to Hortense too, are you?"

"No, you don't owe Hortense any apologies."

"Well, that's a relief."

"Aaron told me he had seen a copy of Mom and Dad's divorce agreement. Apparently Mom really did get reamed. According to Aaron, Dad hired the top divorce lawyer in Boston, who thoroughly kicked the ass of the mediocre lawyer Mom had hired."

"Jesus," I said. My father had committed adultery and had left a wife and three young children. I always presumed a judge would have awarded my mother anything she asked for. "I mean, I believe it, but still. . . ."

"Seth, why do you think we had to live in a tiny apartment and he's lived in that huge house?"

We were both silent for a moment or two. Abe said something and my mother laughed. I thought I heard her say, "*I love you too.*"

"Do you ever wonder how Mom and Dad could have possibly gotten married?" Sarah whispered to me.

"All the time," I replied.

When I thought about how my parents might have come together, I imagined their second date, a Sabbath dinner at my mother's home on Long Island. My father's mother had died when he was twelve, and when he crossed the threshold of my mother's childhood home that night his orphan's heart was probably no match for the scene that greeted him: a dining-room table set with a white linen cloth, beautiful china, a braided challah, a silver kiddush cup. The Sabbath candles illuminated my mother's adoring gaze and my grandmother's radiant warmth. I imagined my grandfather, unctuous and conniving, calling him "Dr. Shapiro."

Like me, like Sarah, my father was looking for another family he could belong to.

"I think that's why it's so hard for me to get my bearings in life," I said. "They pull me in such opposite directions. Maybe that's why I don't know how I'm supposed to act most of the time."

Between the distant poles of my mother and father, I felt as if I were trying to navigate my way in the middle of some vast white tundra. I only had my sister, my polar opposite, my North Star, to guide me.

"I know exactly what you mean."

"So, are you going to see Aaron again?" I asked.

"Not after what I just heard his father doing."

"Too bad. I can tell you like him. He seemed nice, not like his parents."

"Not a big deal," she said.

I didn't believe her—not any more than I believed that she had a mouse in her room, or that she had been a virgin before that night.

"What are you going to tell him if he asks you out?"

"I'll think of something. I always do."

I might have been the writer in the family, but my sister was the most accomplished liar. It was the way she kept the peace, and inoculated herself against the meanness of the world.

VIRGINS

• JANUARY–JUNE 1979 •

Rachel and I became lovers during the winter quarter of our senior year. We were enrolled in a seminar on Tolstoy and sat next to each other on the first day of class. Professor Krzyzowski announced that we were in the right city but the wrong season to read Tolstoy. "We ought to study Tolstoy in the spring and Dostoevsky in the winter," he said ruefully. Chicago was the right city, of course, because of its Slavic spirit—the green-domed Catholic churches with ornate spires, the pierogies and pastries, all those Polish, Croatian, Ukrainian, and Russian names crowded with consonants, the broad blond faces one saw throughout the city.

During the first month of the term, we continued to sit next to each other, exchanging smiles and small talk before and after class. I knew that Rachel had been anointed as the top English major in the college. She had won every department award and was Professor Hall's research assistant. The author of a famous book of literary theory, Edmund Hall was the most prestigious professor in the English Department. So I wasn't surprised when I went to a department meeting for students interested in graduate school and saw Rachel sitting on a couch. She beamed radiantly at me; I went over and sat next to her.

The professor who ran the meeting tried to dissuade us from going to graduate school. The job market for PhD's in English was at its lowest ebb in the history of the profession, he explained. He told us to expect to spend six or seven years completing our degrees without any guarantee of a decent job. He also strongly advised against applying to graduate school at Chicago. We ought to study with different professors; the department was looking for new blood; moreover, he reminded us, Chicago, unlike the other top graduate programs, didn't hire teaching assistants or provide support for every PhD student. Despite everything I heard, I was still planning on applying to the graduate program at Chicago. I was also applying to the program in religion and literature at the Divinity School, where admission was not as competitive and financial aid was more generous. I loved the university, loved Hyde Park, loved Chicago; I couldn't imagine a better life than cocooning myself in Regenstein Library and sitting around seminar tables in classrooms with dormered windows on the upper floors of Cobb Hall for another six or seven years.

When the meeting ended, I asked Rachel where she was applying. She told me Stanford and Berkeley.

"Not here?" I had heard rumors that Professor Hall had appealed to her to stay on, promising her a prestigious fellowship.

"No, I don't like Chicago very much."

"Why did you come here?"

"A scholarship I couldn't turn down. How about you?"

"Where am I applying, or why did I come here?"

"Both."

I told her I was applying to Harvard, Yale, and Chicago. Then I told her the story of how I had been an average-to-poor student in high school but won first prize in the *Scholastic Magazine* high school short story contest.

"That's amazing," she said. "You say really smart things in class. Why do you think you didn't do well in high school?"

"I guess I didn't take myself very seriously."

"What do you think changed?" she asked. She had pulled her knees up under her chin and was facing me, one arm extended in my direction along the back of the couch.

"I put a thousand miles between my mother and me."

Rachel laughed. "I had to put two thousand miles between me and my mother."

"Yeah, but you were probably a star in high school too."

"Well, I think it's far more interesting to be a misunderstood creative type."

"I bet your mother isn't nearly as bad as mine," I said.

"My mother punched out my stepmother at my bat mitzvah. Can you top that?"

"When I was twelve my mother married a man she had only known for two weeks. Their marriage lasted four months. He broke my nose and stole my mother's car and jewelry."

"Let's call it a draw," Rachel said, a smile lighting up her face. Then she asked me if I still wrote stories.

"Not so much," I said. "My sophomore year I took Kadish's introductory course in creative writing. In the margin of my story he wrote, 'This sentence is a disgrace to you, the university, and to the country.'" I laughed but Rachel looked appalled.

"What an ass!" she exclaimed.

"Oh, he's not so bad. He's had to labor under the shadow of Saul Bellow, and I think he feels that his life is a bad imitation of Bellow's. His surliness is just part of his serious writer act."

"I wouldn't be so sympathetic to a professor who wrote something like that on one of my papers."

"Well, I'm actually very close friends with his daughter, Wendy, so I know what he has to deal with. She's a student here too."

Actually, the main reason I was sympathetic to Kadish was because I had read his novels. I thought they were artful miniatures, but not the grand canvases created by Saul Bellow. Kadish, so brutally honest, had to know that he would never be as famous as Saul Bellow when he faced the blank page every morning.

"When I was in Kadish's class, Wendy and I went out briefly. Now that was strange. To be sleeping with your professor's daughter. Maybe I ought to enroll in his advanced creative writing class and write a story about that."

"But you're still close friends with her?" Rachel asked, as if that interested her more than my idea for a story, or the fact that I had slept with a professor's daughter.

"Yes. Very close."

"That's so unusual."

"Really?" I said. "To tell you the truth, it's actually easier for me to be friends with girls than to be their boyfriend." I immediately wanted to kick myself for saying that, for neutralizing myself.

"I'm the same way," Rachel replied.

"It's easier for you to be friends with girls than to be their girlfriend?"

I smiled but she didn't smile back.

"No, with men."

Everyone had left the room. Rachel and I were alone. I wanted to ask her out, but if she said no—if she said something about having a boyfriend or being too busy—I'd still have to sit next to her three times a week for the remainder of the term. She put her coat on, getting ready to go.

"I'd really like to read one of your stories sometime," Rachel said.

"Where are you going now?" I asked.

"I think I'll get some lunch. How about you?'

"The library. . . . Well, I guess I'll see you in class," I said.

"I really enjoyed our conversation," she replied.

That night I tried phoning her in her dorm and was relieved when the person who answered the phone said she wasn't in. The next afternoon I noticed Rachel sleeping in one of the comfortable reading chairs by the windows in Regenstein. I sat in the chair opposite her, opened my biography of Tolstoy, and waited for her to wake. After about twenty minutes she opened her eyes and looked at me happily, as if she had been hoping to see me when she awoke. I asked her if she wanted to go to the coffee shop in the basement of the library.

Over coffee, we found ourselves in an intense discussion about Sonya Tolstoy, the great writer's muse, collaborator, and sacrificial wife. Rachel said that Sonya was a classic example of a woman who had subordinated her creativity to enable a male artist. I countered that Sonya certainly had a genius for life—managing the books, the estate, the hordes of children; transcribing her husband's manuscripts; serving as a literary midwife for the great novels. Rachel replied that this showed that men's and women's creativity was differently gendered. *Gendered?* I didn't know whether we were arguing or agreeing. Besides, did I really want to go out with someone who used the word gender as a verb?

"Look," I said, "would you like to go out on Saturday?"

Rachel's face relaxed, as if she were relieved that I had changed the subject. She said she would love to go out with me.

On Saturday night we went to Theresa's, a blues bar in a blighted neighborhood only minutes from the grand houses of Hyde Park and Kenwood. The place was dim, hazy, and crowded. I counted only four other white people—probably also students from the university—but everyone was solicitous and friendly.

The barmaid who brought our drinks offered us chili dogs, free of charge, and the musicians, most of them elderly black men, asked us every now and then how we were enjoying the music. Rachel had suggested coming to Theresa's, and I was glad for it. We didn't have to discuss literature or our mothers. We drank beer, slow danced, and held hands as we listened to the music.

Back in her room, Rachel and I kissed on her bed for about ten minutes. Then I began to unbutton her shirt. She smiled shyly at me and unbuttoned mine too. We kissed and fondled in the nude, but I felt as if I were sipping a soda without any fizz. Then Rachel yanked my penis like a cow's udder.

"Not so hard," I said, placing my hand on hers.

She gave me a plaintive look. "I've never done this before," she said.

I was surprised, shocked, really. She was attractive and sociable, a daughter of liberal parents, a child of Berkeley, circa 1969.

"Any reason why?" I asked.

"I never met anyone I liked enough." I stared into her eyes and she looked away; we both knew her answer didn't explain why she was in bed with me on our first date. I surmised that she didn't want to be a virgin when she graduated, before she returned to Berkeley, and had decided that I was her last, best chance.

"I suppose I'm honored," I said. She looked up at me, placed a hand against the side of my face.

"I felt I could trust you," she explained.

"Thank you," I said.

"You think it's really strange that I'm still a virgin," she said.

"No, not really," I lied.

"I do," she replied.

"Why?"

"Because how can I pretend to know anything about litera-ture or life if I've never been in love or had sex? I feel like a fraud discussing and writing about *Anna Karenina* when I've never experienced any of those feelings."

"Experience is overrated," I said. "I'd rather discuss *Anna Karenina* with you than with anyone."

"Even Professor Krzyzowski?"

"I'd rather discuss *Anna Karenina* with you *in the nude* than with anyone," I said.

Rachel laughed and kissed me on the mouth. She went under the covers and put her mouth on me. I was completely flaccid, and Rachel wasn't moving her head, just keeping her lips suctioned over the head of my penis. I tapped her on the shoulder.

"It's all right," I said. "We can just go to sleep tonight."

"Was I doing that the wrong way?" she asked.

I didn't have the heart to tell the truth. "No, that felt nice. I just think I've had a little too much to drink."

She cuddled up next to me. "Next time you can show me what to do."

"I'm happy we could get nude and talk," I said.

"Me too," she said. "I like talking to you in the nude."

Rachel bought some condoms the next day, but in bed that night I said we ought to wait a couple of weeks before having intercourse, wait until we were really comfortable with each other's bodies; the experience would be nicer that way, I explained. Then I put my hand between her legs and parted the inner terrain very lightly, as if handling the petals of a rose. "I like to be touched this way too," I said to her. Of course, I hadn't known how to touch a woman until Jane had shown me, until she told me that I didn't need to try to fit my whole hand into her vagina.

"Thank you for being so nice about this," Rachel said.

I felt like a phony. The truth was that I had never had sex with a virgin and couldn't bear to think about the blood and the pain. I had read *The Bell Jar* when I was a senior in high school and had literally become ill over the scene in which Sylvia Plath hemorrhaged after she lost her virginity. The morning after reading it, still thinking about that scene, I became so light-headed in the shower that I had to drop to one knee before I fainted completely and fell through the glass door.

Two weeks after we began sleeping together, Rachel and I still hadn't had sex. Until I met her, I had just presumed that I could happily live out my life without ever having sex with a virgin. Reluctantly, I called Sarah at Rutgers.

"Hello, Sarah."

"What's two plus two?"

"Um . . . five?"

"Hi, Seth."

This was the game Sarah and I always played when I called her: My voice sounded exactly like our father's, and she always gave me a math quiz so she would know whether it was me or him on the other end.

I told her I had a new girlfriend.

"Nice," she replied.

I could already sense the vibe between us was weird. Usually we phoned each other only to complain about our parents, almost never to discuss our love lives, especially since the night we had heard Abe Zelman fucking our mother.

"She's still a virgin."

"Is that a problem?"

"Yes."

"Why? Is she fifteen or something?"

"No! She's my age."

"Is she ugly?"

"No, she's very attractive."

"Is she from Alabama or someplace like that?"

"No, Berkeley."

"So, what's the problem?"

"I've never had sex with a virgin before."

"Congratulations then."

"I think I have some type of phobia about having sex with a virgin."

"Why?" Her voice was a little more sympathetic.

"Did you read *The Bell Jar* in high school?"

"Seth, every girl my age read *The Bell Jar* in high school."

"Well, that scene when Sylvia Plath hemorrhages after sex really traumatized me. I'm afraid of all the blood and pain."

"Seth, you're not the one who's going to be bleeding or in pain."

"Look, when you lost your virginity, how bad was it?"

"Not so bad. More uncomfortable than painful."

"Did you bleed very much?"

"Not so much. Nothing like in *The Bell Jar*."

I was silent for a moment.

"Feel better?" Sarah asked.

"Yes, somewhat. . . . Since we're on the topic, I've always wondered whether you were really a virgin that time we spent the Fourth of July at the Zelmans' summerhouse."

"No, I wasn't."

"So why did you tell Mom you were a virgin? I don't think she would have been upset."

"I don't either. It was just the opposite. I knew she would have wanted to hear all about my sex life."

"You don't think I'm being like Mom now, do you?"

"No, Seth, you're not like Mom." She enunciated her reply with exaggerated slowness. These words were like a personal catechism between us, something we always needed to say to each other in order to be reminded that all was right with the world.

"So you never saw Aaron Zelman again?"

77

"No. I wrote him a letter and told him I didn't feel right about seeing him since he was suing my father."

"Do you think he believed you?"

"I don't know. But what was I supposed to say? I don't fuck men if their fathers are also fucking my mother?"

"Yes. I think it would have made him feel better to know the truth."

"You're being like Mom."

"You're so cruel."

"You're so strange."

"I know. You've told me that about a zillion times."

"No, I mean really, really strange. Every man I know would be foaming at the mouth over the chance to have sex with a beautiful, well-educated virgin, but you're acting like a drama queen about it."

"Are you saying I'm gay?"

"No, if you were gay, you wouldn't be so strange."

THREE WEEKS INTO OUR RELATIONSHIP, Rachel and I finally made love. I had never used a condom before—the other women I'd had sex with all used diaphragms or had been on the Pill—and I practiced putting one on without Rachel around so I would know what to do when the time came. I spent a long time going down on her, hoping that she would bear the pain of my penis more easily if she was really wet and close to an orgasm. She barely let out a sigh or groan when I finally did enter her. Actually, she never made much noise at all during sex, even when I brought her to orgasm with my tongue, which I had become quite skilled at during the three weeks I had been avoiding intercourse with her. Usually I knew she had climaxed when she shuddered slightly and then told me I could stop.

"Does it hurt? Are you all right?" I asked as I eased myself in.

"I'm fine," she replied.

"Really?"

"Seth. Quiet."

I came a minute later. When I pulled out I was afraid that my sheathed penis would be gleaming with bright red blood, but I only noticed white viscous matter; the condom had slipped about halfway up my penis.

"Oh, God, I hope I used the condom the right way," I said.

"What's the matter?" Rachel asked.

I turned on the bedside lamp and aimed it at my penis. I directed her attention to the unsheathed part.

"Do you think this whitish substance is from you or from me?"

"I don't know," she said, but she didn't seem especially concerned.

"Maybe you better do a pregnancy test just to be safe."

"Seth!"

"What?"

"Could you try being a little more romantic?"

"Oh, sure," I said. I turned off the light, and she cuddled up next to me.

"Do you feel any different?" I asked.

"Not especially," she said.

"Do you feel like you have a deeper, finer understanding of *Anna Karenina*?"

Years later, I had a girlfriend who told me I was the only man she'd ever slept with who became more talkative after sex.

"Seth, can we just go to sleep now?"

RACHEL WAS MY FIRST SERIOUS GIRLFRIEND. We spent every night together, though we had sex only once a week, usually after a movie on a Saturday night, as if it were a requirement to complete the evening. Our sex life reminded me of painting by numbers: uninspired, technically satisfying, vaguely therapeutic. Most nights we lay next to each other in her single bed reading and discussing *Anna Karenina* until well past midnight. As winter turned to spring, and the scent of lilacs wafted in through the open Gothic window of Rachel's dorm room, I read the chapter in which Levin has spent all day scything hay in the meadow with the peasants. At the end of the long day, Levin hears their songs and laughter, their joy in life, and realizes that he has found his purpose, that he is ready to renounce all his other wants—marriage, social reform—for this pure and simple life. I found myself powerfully moved. Rachel and I were soul mates, and what could be more divine than lying next to her in the nude every night and reading Tolstoy out loud?

"I feel exactly like Levin. I couldn't be happier than I am right now," I confessed.

"Yes," Rachel said, "but in the next moment Kitty rides by in the carriage and Levin realizes that he's deluding himself. He can't be happy without her love."

EVERY NOW AND THEN RACHEL SAID she wanted to read some of my fiction, but I still hadn't showed her anything and the winter quarter was nearly over. I was embarrassed to admit I hadn't written another story as good as "Two by Two." I had attempted to write stories during the summers, but I felt uninspired, every sentence echoing the sentences of the writers I loved. Writing essays for my classes was easier. I loved shaping arguments, and locating the right tone and language for a paper was not nearly as difficult as writing fiction. Most of all, I loved receiving high grades and high praise.

When I finally confessed to Rachel that I hadn't written anything better than "Two by Two," she replied, "So let me read that!"

"But I wrote that in high school."

"So? It has to be decent if you won that prize."

I finally relented and gave her a copy one day in my room. She read the story sitting on my bed; I was at my desk, my back to her, trying to read a book, but I kept turning around to look at her. When she finished, she just stared at me for a couple of seconds. "Seth, this is really good," she said.

"Really?"

"Yes!"

"You're just saying that because you're my girlfriend," I replied, though I was actually disappointed she wasn't more ecstatic.

"I'm being completely straight with you. I was so concerned I wouldn't like it and wouldn't know what to say. I think it's funny and moving. I love it. You ought to be writing fiction."

"Do you think my fiction is better than my essays for class?"

"That's comparing apples and oranges."

We had been exchanging drafts of our papers throughout the term. I had been curious to read Rachel's essays. Would I really be able to tell the difference between my papers and the papers written by the person regarded as the brightest star in the English Department? I knew the answer after reading just one paragraph of one of her essays. Her ideas were more sophisticated and argued with greater authority and clarity. I didn't feel competitive with her; in fact, I liked being the boyfriend of someone so smart and accomplished, but reading her essays reminded me of my limits.

"Come on. I need you to be honest with me." I had just shown her a term paper I had written for my seminar on the modern British novel: "Voyages In and Out: A Comparison of the Forms of Female Heroism in To the Lighthouse and Middlemarch." I had received an A on the paper. "Do you think this story is better than my To the Lighthouse and Middlemarch paper?"

"I enjoyed the story more."

"So you're saying that a story I wrote in high school is better than a senior seminar paper I wrote at the University of Chicago?"

"I'm just saying I enjoyed the story more."

• • •

At Rachel's urging, I signed up for Kadish's advanced creative writing course in the spring quarter. On the first day of class, Kadish read a story titled "My First Fee" by an early twentieth-century Russian writer named Isaac Babel. No one in the class had heard of the story or of Babel. The story was about a twenty-year-old proofreader and would-be writer who goes to an older prostitute named Vera for his first sexual encounter. But when they get to Vera's room, the young man becomes despondent when Vera removes her clothes and he sees she's not nearly as beautiful as he had imagined. Vera senses that he's lost interest, and the young man explains himself by inventing a story about having been a boy prostitute. Vera is visibly moved by the story and pays him a high compliment: "So you're a whore. A whore like us bitches." The young man bows his head and replies, "Yes. A whore like you." Kadish had read those lines with great emotion and laughed at other lines in the story as if he were sharing a private joke with the writer. No one in the class seemed to understand the story except for one girl, who laughed along with Kadish. She had a mass of tousled hair, dark circles under large, round eyes, and full lips. She fidgeted and sniffled a great deal. Kadish asked the class what we thought of the story. No one said anything. Then the girl who had appreciated the story along with Kadish raised her hand.

"Yes, miss. . . ?"

"Katz. But you can call me Cat."

"Miss Katz."

"I love the way Babel compares writing to sex."

"Yes. How so?" Kadish queried her.

"Well, the boy in the story gets his cherry popped. For real, with Vera, but also as a writer, right?"

"He does indeed," Kadish said.

Every student in the class was required to submit two stories during the term. I decided to use "Two by Two" for my first work-shop. I wanted to buy myself some time and to protect myself from Kadish's annihilating comments by turning in something that I knew was decent. I did wonder whether it was ethical to turn in a story I had already written, so I consulted Rachel.

"Does the syllabus say that you need to turn in stories written expressly for the course?" she asked me.

"No."

"Then I think you're fine."

EVERYONE WAS SITTING AROUND the seminar table with purple mimeographed copies of my story, waiting for Professor Kadish. Tall and bedraggled, he typically showed up to class five minutes late, half his shirt outside his pants, his necktie crooked, and look-ing vaguely annoyed, as if he had been having sex and suddenly remembered that he had to teach a class. He found his copy of my manuscript, moved his enormous eyeglasses to the crown of his head, and examined the story for a couple of minutes with a look of brutal concentration. Then he moved his glasses back down over his nose and said, "Well, Mr. Shapiro, consciously or unconsciously, is clearly paying *hommage* to Saul Bellow. But this story is more imitation than inspiration." Kadish began all the classes this way. He would deliver his verdict and then let the students say what they wanted.

For a couple of seconds the class was silent. Then one of the students said that he agreed with Professor Kadish. The story was too old-fashioned. "It's like he's trying to write in the style of a different era." Two or three more students raised their hands.

"I think the story is too Jewish."

"How so, Mr. Cantor?" Kadish asked.

"The names. Abraham. Isaac. *Chaya?*" Some of the students laughed. "I mean, isn't that a character from *Fiddler on the Roof?*"

The whole class was laughing.

"I agree," said another student. "The Old Testament references are so jejune."

Then one of the students commented that she didn't find Isaac very likeable, and that criticism opened the floodgates. Nearly everyone in the class said that they felt the same way about Isaac, that they didn't like him very much and couldn't sympathize with him. None of the characters were all that likeable except for the grandmother, said a number of students. Then Cat shot her hand up.

"Yes, Miss Katz," Kadish said.

"I think this business of whether or not we like a character is bullshit," she declared. "We're supposed to be interested in characters, not like them. I mean, I think that's the problem with most of the stories we read in this class. Everyone is trying too hard to create characters we'll like, and that's just boring. This is the only story we've read in this class where I really wanted to turn the pages. That's important, don't you think, Professor Kadish?"

Kadish nodded his head. "Yes, the story is extremely well told. Mr. Shapiro, do you have any questions for us?"

I was seething, but cautioned myself to hold it together. "*Hommage? Jejune?*" I said. "I think I might find the criticism more useful if people expressed themselves in English."

All the students stared at me, but Kadish actually smiled, and then Cat nearly keeled over laughing.

When I received my manuscript from Kadish, I turned to the last page to see his comments. *Poor man's Bellow. Technically capable but try writing in your own voice for the next story. B.* I went back to my room and reread "The Old System." I hadn't read the Bellow in four years, and each page sent waves of relief and shame through me—relief that the judges who awarded me the Scholastic Prize had probably not read "The Old System" and shame that my achievement was totally fraudulent. I had read the Bellow story so many times when I was in high school and had so thoroughly internalized the story's prose rhythms that the result was just the same as if I had been typing "Two by Two" with one eye on an open copy of "The Old System." Perhaps I ought to have felt relieved that Kadish hadn't brought me up on charges of plagiarism, for surely he had read "The Old System." Then I would have been facing expulsion just before I graduated. The university would never grant me a degree if they found out that I had been admitted on the basis of a plagiarized story.

I met Rachel for dinner in the dining hall. She asked me how my workshop had gone.

"Bad."

"But I thought you were going to submit 'Two by Two.' How could anyone not like that story?"

"Well, they all hated it," I said angrily, as if it were her fault. I showed her the manuscript with Kadish's comments.

"He's an asshole. Anyway, didn't you tell me *his* life and writing was a bad imitation of Saul Bellow's? He's definitely projecting his own self-loathing onto you."

"He's right about my story, Rachel."

"Seth, don't do this to yourself."

"Come to my room. I want you to read something."

Back in my room, I gave Rachel "The Old System" to read. I sat anxiously at my desk while she lay on my bed and read the story. I felt as if I were revealing my deepest, most shameful secret to her, a feeling that became more intense as I looked over my own story. I could hear Bellow in every sentence.

Rachel closed the book and said she liked my story better.

"Oh, come on, Rachel. I virtually plagiarized that story."

"I can see the similarities, but you write about women much more sensitively. The women in Bellow's stories are all grotesques, opening up their vaginas to intimidate small boys or bending over and showing off their pudenda."

I stared at her, wondering for the first time whether we were really right for each other.

"Thanks. I didn't think of it that way."

"Seth, stop punishing yourself. You didn't do anything bad. Come here," she said, patting the bed.

I went over to her. She began unbuttoning my shirt, reminding me that I didn't do anything wrong. "You're a really good person, Seth," she said, as she unbuckled my belt.

IN LATE MARCH, we heard from graduate schools. Rachel was admitted to Berkeley and Stanford and offered a full scholarship and stipend for both programs. I was rejected by Harvard and Yale and accepted to the University of Chicago graduate program but without any financial support. The Divinity School had admitted me with a full scholarship and stipend. I tried to look on the bright side—I was graduating from the University of Chicago magna cum laude; I would be supported for another four years of study at the university I loved—but this view didn't hold up for very long. My rejection from the top graduate schools validated Rachel's judgment of my potential as a scholar, and despite her praise of "Two by Two," I knew I had been admitted to the university on the strength of a plagiarized story. I felt like Cinderella at five minutes to midnight. At graduation, I would change back into the person I had always been—mediocre, average, a nobody.

One night, not long after we had heard from all the graduate schools we had applied to, Rachel and I were lying next to each other in bed, and I asked her what was going to happen to us after graduation.

"I don't know," she replied.

"We can spend Christmas vacations and summers together," I said. "I could transfer to a graduate program in California."

"Seth, baby, we have three months before we need to have this conversation. Let's enjoy the time we have." She touched my cheek. "You're going to look so handsome when you're older," she said.

"Don't you think I'm handsome now?" I exclaimed.

"Of course I do," she said. "I just mean when you're a hotshot professor, and married with children, you'll look especially handsome."

What an odd thing to say, I thought. But I understood she was conceding the limits of our relationship, the limits of her love for me.

I STILL NEEDED TO WRITE another story for Kadish's class, and the next night at dinner I asked Rachel about a story she had told me not long after we met. When she was twelve she had wanted to leave her mother and live with her father. Her mother, Joan, a therapist in Berkeley, was impulsive and irresponsible, and Rachel couldn't bear living with her anymore. She wanted some boundaries and normality in her life. Her father was a suburban rabbi and had remarried a woman much closer to him in temperament. Her mother didn't want to let Rachel go, and Rachel's parents had waged a custody battle over her. As the case was drawing to a close, the judge presiding over the case had interviewed Rachel privately in his chambers. After questioning her for about twenty minutes, the judge had asked Rachel whom she really wanted to live with. "My mother," Rachel replied.

"Why do you think you changed your mind so suddenly in the judge's chambers?" I asked her.

"I just felt I belonged with my mother. Why?"

"I think it's a great premise for a story."

"Seth, you are not writing a story about that!"

I was shocked by the vehemence of her response.

"Why not?"

"It's the most painful episode of my life, that's why. I don't want you to write about it."

"I wouldn't be writing about *you*. I'm interested in the moral and psychological complexities of a twelve-year-old child suddenly changing her mind in the judge's chambers. I mean, it's very Jamesian, don't you think?"

"Seth, please. I would consider it a violation of my trust in you if you wrote a story about that."

I began writing the story anyway. After all, I was just completing an assignment for a class, and Rachel didn't need to see it. I changed the girl to a boy, set it in New Jersey, and forgot all about Jamesian complexities. I remembered when I was twelve and had wanted to leave my mother too, remembered how a child can feel emotionally responsible for a lunatic parent. The boy in the story was me, or some version of myself, and the mother was a version of my mother. Rachel's story had provided me a medium through which to tell my own. I had never felt so pure and inspired about anything I had written. I only felt guilty about lying to Rachel. I had never lied to her before, but now I lied to her every time she asked me how the writing was going. "Not great," I'd tell her. "It's bad. Really bad."

FOR THE SECOND TIME THAT TERM, all my classmates were sitting around the seminar table with purple mimeographed copies of a story I had written while we waited for Professor Kadish. No one made eye contact with me except for the girl who called herself Cat. When she came into the room, she said, "Great story, man," and then sat down across from me, fidgeting, sniffling, pulling on her earrings and sending smiles my way.

Kadish came in ten minutes late. He dropped his books, papers, and keys on the table with a thud, then moved his glasses to the top of his forehead and stared around the room for a couple of seconds, as if looking to see if he was in the right place. "Well, I think we can all agree that this is a highly accomplished story. Mr. Shapiro is a real writer."

After Kadish pronounced his judgment, most of my class-mates praised the story too; some felt bound to offer criticisms, perhaps out of envy, perhaps in an attempt to generate some discussion over the remaining sixty minutes. One student said the word "obdurate" at the end seemed out of place. Someone said that he didn't think a tallis could actually be rolled up into a tight little ball. Another student said that ending the story with the two characters walking away together seemed like a trite way of exiting the story. Then one student wondered if it would provide more of a twist at the end if the boy changed his mind and decided to stay with his mother. A number of other students became animated by this idea, agreeing that it might provide more of a psychological and dramatic reversal if the boy changed his mind. Of course I had planned on ending the story that way, but when I reached the final scene, I didn't believe that my character would actually go through with it. The scene that created the most problems for me was the fistfight at the bar mitzvah: It was the one detail in the story that felt like a real betrayal of Rachel.

Finally, Cat raised her hand. Throughout the term, it had been her habit to sit quietly through most of each class and then dis-agree with the drift of the discussion. Kadish called on her.

"I disagree with what everyone has been saying. If the boy changed his mind and stayed with his mother, the story would be less emotionally complex, less surprising, because that's the ending we want. He does have a stronger bond with his mother, but he doesn't understand how much he loves her. That's why the ending is so beautiful and sad."

I smiled at her and she winked back at me.

When Kadish gave me back his copy of the manuscript, I turned to the back for the comments. *See me about submitting this story for the Chandler Prize and publication in the Chicago Quarterly. A.* The Chandler Prize was awarded for the best work of fiction by an undergraduate student. Kadish was the editor of the *Chicago Quarterly*, a literary magazine published by the University of Chicago Press. I went to Kadish's office after class, knocked on the door, and waited for close to a minute before he opened it and stared at me.

"Yes, Mr. Shapiro?"

"You told me to see you about the Chandler Prize and the *Chicago Quarterly*?"

"Oh, right. Hold on a minute."

Kadish went back into his office and closed the door. After another minute, he came back out and stood in the doorway.

"Here's the form you need to submit your story for the contest. The deadline is tomorrow. You ought to be notified of the results in about a week."

I asked him who the judges were.

"Just me."

"You also said something about publication in the *Chicago Quarterly*."

"Yes. I'd like to publish the story if it's all right with you."

"Yes. Thank you very much."

Kadish nodded his head and then went back into his office.

I waltzed and whizzed my way down the four flights, holding the copy of my story with Kadish's comments as if it were a prize-winning lottery ticket. Bursting out of Cobb Hall, I heard my name. I turned around and saw the girl from class who called herself Cat.

"Hi, what's up?" I said.

"Which way are you going?"

I pointed down Sixtieth Street.

"Me too."

"You know, I don't even know your real name," I said to her.

"Not many people do."

"So, will you tell me?"

She stopped. "Well, only because you wrote such a great story." Then she put her warm, pillowy lips against my ear and whispered, "Bella."

"Bella," I repeated. "Bella Katz." Her vowels were flattened by a midwestern accent. "Highland Park?" I asked.

"Close. Shaker Heights." She paused. "So, look, would you like to go get a drink?"

"Well, I sort of have a girlfriend."

"You 'sort of' do or you really do?"

"I really do," I replied.

Her eyes became slits. "You know, I really wish you had let me know that before I told you my real name."

I looked at the ground and apologized. She burst out laughing. "Oh, man, I'm just yanking your chain. Thanks for not being a dog."

"You're welcome."

She lit a cigarette and said she was going back to the quad.

"You're not really going this way?"

She laughed again. "Too bad you have a girlfriend. I could have a lot of fun with you."

I met Rachel just outside the entrance to the dining hall. She kissed me on the lips and asked me how the class had gone.

"Pretty well," I said. "I'll tell you when we sit down." Before the class, I had planned to simply lie to Rachel: I would tell her that everyone in the class had hated my story and that I didn't want to show it to her. But I was so excited about Kadish's praise, so sure the story itself would redeem me, that I knew I couldn't pull off the lie I had invented for just this moment. Nothing I had ever done in my life had felt so right, so true, as writing that story, and Kadish's judgment had left me swelling with virtue.

We went through the line with our trays and found our usual small table.

"So Kadish loved my story," I said. "He wants me to submit it for the Chandler Prize." I decided to wait for her reaction before I told her about the *Chicago Quarterly*.

"Seth, that's wonderful! Especially because you didn't think the story was very good. I'm so proud of you. So . . . can I read it now?"

I reached in my knapsack and pulled out a copy for her.

"'A Stranger on the Planet,'" she read. "I like that title." But when she began reading the opening lines, her face became contorted with pain. Then she started turning the pages rapidly, scanning each one for just a couple of seconds. She slowed down when she was nearly at the end. I knew she was reading the scene in which the mother and stepmother get into a fistfight. I wanted her to speed through those pages too, but she studied them with a stunned look, the way someone reads and rereads a letter containing shocking news.

Finally, she looked up at me. "I cannot believe you did this. You promised me, Seth!"

"I just used some details you told me. The story is about me, not you."

"Do you know how violated I feel?"

"Rachel, no one who reads this story is going to connect it with you. I think you'll understand if you just read the whole thing."

"I've read enough," she said, and banged the story down on

the table. Plates clattered, and people turned to look at us. Then she leaned across the table and said in a low but furious voice, "You fucking liar."

"Liar? What did I lie about? I'm not hiding the story from you."

"When you kept telling me it was bad. You were so happy and giddy during the eight weeks you were writing this story, you had to know it was good. You lying, scheming asshole!"

She stood up to leave, slipping on her coat and hoisting onto her shoulder her knapsack in one deft motion.

"But I changed the ending," I said, as if that might exonerate me.

"Fuck you," she said, and left me sitting alone.

THAT NIGHT I SLEPT BY MYSELF for the first time since Rachel and I had gone to the blues bar back in February. During the week, Rachel wasn't in any of our usual places: our table in the dining hall or the section on the third floor of Regenstein where we studied together. She didn't return any of the telephone messages I left for her. The image of the battered look on her face as she read the story kept me awake at night—I don't think I had ever caused another person so much pain—but I would end up arguing with her in my head. She was a brilliant student of literature; how could she not understand the process of how an author transforms life into art? Kadish had been right about "Two by Two": The germ of the plot might have come from an incident out of my childhood, but I had directly appropriated Bellow's way of telling a Jewish story. But "A Stranger on the Planet" was *my* story. If Kadish had reported me to the admissions office after reading "Two by Two" and the university had decided to expel me, I would have more easily understood that punishment than Rachel's reaction. She was treating me as if I were as egotistical and as boorish as Tolstoy. Compared to the way Tolstoy treated Sonya, I was a saint.

A goddamned saint! Still, I sent her a letter of apology, saying no story was worth the sacrifice of our relationship. She didn't reply; perhaps she knew I was lying: I didn't regret writing the story.

A week later, I received a letter notifying me that "A Stranger on the Planet" had won the Chandler Prize for undergraduate fiction. Along with the letter was a check for one hundred dollars and an announcement of all the winners of the English Department's undergraduate writing prizes. Rachel had won for best literary criticism. She would have received the same announcement. I left another message for Rachel congratulating her, but she didn't call me back.

I was graduating in a month. I had harbored hopes that Rachel and I might maintain a long-distance relationship, but now I wondered if she would even be speaking to me at commencement. Recalling Kadish's pronouncement about me in class—*Mr. Shapiro is a real writer*—pumped me up with more self-righteousness and defiance, and I decided to call Bella Katz. She answered on the first ring.

"Bella?"

"Come again?"

"Cat?"

"Seth, what's up?"

"How did you know it was me?"

"I told you. Not many people know my real name."

"I was wondering if you'd like to get a drink."

"Don't you have a girlfriend anymore?"

I spent about five minutes explaining, in an aggrieved and self-righteous fashion, everything that had happened between Rachel and me. I expected her to be appalled at Rachel's crude reaction to my art and to sympathize with my principled positions, but she said she would only go out with me on one condition.

"What's that?"

"I don't want to hear any stories about how your girlfriend doesn't understand you."

"Sure, fine," I replied.

Bella's standard attire was patched blue jeans and oversized peasant blouses, so I was surprised at how beautiful she looked without her clothes on. Everything about her was full and round: her eyes and lips, hips and breasts, the swell of her thighs. Nude, she had a glow and grace about her that I had never noticed when she was so indifferently clothed. I tried not to compare her with Rachel, tried not to think about how boring our love life had always been, but when Bella lay on top of me, kissing my lips, softly, lusciously, I remembered what sex was supposed to feel like, remembered how my legs had quivered when Zelda had put her hand on my penis ten years before.

Later, lying next to me, she said, "So is your girlfriend a lesbian?"

"What? No, of course not! Why would you say that?"

"You really know how to use your tongue. Someone had to teach you those moves."

I might have told her that I had developed those moves because I had read *The Bell Jar* in high school and become phobic about having sex with a virgin, but I recognized an opening and pounced. "You're jealous, aren't you?"

Her eyes welled up for a moment. "Look, man, I think we both know why you called me."

"Really? Why?"

"Because you wanted some babe who appreciated your story to fuck you."

"That's not fair," I protested.

"So? It's true, isn't it?"

"Then why did you go out with me?"

95

"Because I like you and I wanted to fuck you too. But it's all right if you don't call again. I know you still want to get back together with your girlfriend."

My face probably fell by a couple of inches.

"Look, it's a human thing, Seth. You knew I liked your story, and you knew that I was hot for you, so you called me up. You don't have to feel bad about being human."

"I guess."

"You're nice, Seth, but you're not as nice as you want everyone to think you are. I mean, you are being a little bit of a dog."

"So do you want me to leave?"

"Remember that story Kadish read on the first day of class? 'My First Fee.'"

"Yes."

"Remember when the narrator said he wasn't planning on writing down any of his stories until he was as great as Tolstoy?"

"Yes, so? Your point is . . .?"

"My point is that we just had some really amazing sex, but it never would have happened if you believed you had to be a saint every minute of the day."

I gave her a puzzled look. She laughed and said, "Oh, Seth, if I had expected this was going to be more than a one-night stand, I wouldn't have let you see how smart I am."

I wanted to protest that Rachel was one of the smartest people in the world, but before I could say anything, Bella laid her head on my chest and said, "Stay the night?"

"All right."

"I love sex in the morning. Don't you?"

I HAD NOT HEARD FROM MY FATHER since my freshman year, but I still made sure the registrar sent him a copy of my grades every term so he could see how well I was doing. My sadness over

Rachel reminded me of how much I missed him, reminded me that I was always disappointing the people I most wanted to love me. I decided to invite him to my graduation. In the letter I wrote to him, I expressed my hope that we could use this happy day as an occasion to mend our relationship. I told him that I was graduating magna cum laude and had won the Chandler Prize. I recalled how my father had written "EXTRAORDINARY" in response to "Two By Two," and, after a moment of internal debate, I decided to include a copy of "A Stranger on the Planet."

A week later, I received my father's reply:

Dear Seth,

Congratulations on your fine academic achievements. I would like very much to attend your graduation, but your letter did not include an invitation for my wife. Moreover, you still have not apologized for your vulgar outburst to her three years ago. I hope you will honestly examine the untenable situation you have created for me. Hortense and I are not interested in a relationship without a baseline of common courtesy.

Sincerely,

Dad

P.S. In the future, please address all your correspondence to both Hortense and me.

Sarah was graduating from Rutgers in a week. I phoned her and asked if our father was attending.

"Dad, Horty, Francois. The whole happy family."

"Francois too? How old is he now? Thirteen or something?"

"I'm sure he'll be happy to see you. He's always looked up to you."

A year earlier, I had shown Sarah a copy of a letter Francois had written to me. *Dear Seth, How goes it in collage land, where men are men, women are women, and collage professors tend to be gay.* He had included a poem that he had written and asked for my opinion of it. *I showed it to Dad, but he told me it sucked out-loud. Love (not the gay kind), Francois.*

"Well, Dad's not coming to my graduation," I said.

"Don't tell me you're surprised."

"Thanks for the sympathy."

"Seth," she said, the tone in her voice softer, more empathetic, "he's never going to change. I know it's difficult for you, but you have to stop hoping that he's going to love you someday."

"I know. I know. . . . So how did Mom react when you told her that Hortense is going to be there?"

"I haven't told her yet."

"You haven't? She's going to have a fit."

"I know. So I don't see any point in telling her until the very last moment."

"Did you consider not inviting Hortense for Mom's sake?"

"Dad owes me five thousand dollars upon graduation. I'm not going to jeopardize that money by antagonizing him."

"What if he wanted you to invite Joseph Goebbels? Would you do that for five thousand dollars?"

"I love you too, Seth," she replied, and hung up.

I had a box in which I kept all my father's letters. When I went to store away his most recent one, I found one he had written to me ten years earlier in response to a letter I had sent him after Eddie had broken my nose.

Dear Seth,

Hortense and I discussed your problem and we both believe that it would be impractical for you to live with us. Both of us work all day and you would be without adult supervision for too many hours. We both agree that you need to get away from your present situation and we think the best solution is for you to attend a boarding school. The tuition is really beyond our means (our vacation on the Cape last summer was our first in four years!), but we believe that the financial sacrifices on our part would be well worth it. Choate or Andover would be excellent choices. Let us know what you think. By the way, your mother called me three times last week to insist that Eddie did not punch you in the nose. She modified her story, explaining that you and Eddie were playing and that he accidentally fell on you. I have no comment except to say that the whole situation is bizarre.

Love,

Dad and Hortense

Eddie hadn't actually punched me. One Sunday near the end of August 1969, Eddie and I had been sitting next to each other on the couch watching baseball. He had been in his bathrobe all day, hadn't shaved, and was in his usual posture, bent forward, one hand on the channel dial, changing back and forth between the Yankee and Mets games. I told him to quit it, that I had already missed hundreds of pitches. He replied that this was his house and that he could do whatever he wanted. I told him that this wasn't his house. He was living here for free.

"You little snot-nosed brat," he said, putting his face right in front of mine. "You're one word away from a serious bruising."

"Word," I said.

Suddenly he was on me, placing me in a headlock. I tried to bolt, but he fell on top of me with all his weight. I landed on my nose and blood spurted everywhere. I flailed violently under him, calling him a "goddamn gorilla." My mother came out from her bedroom. "Oh stop this," she cried. "The two of you, just stop this!" Eddie let me up, and I put my hand to my nose. At the sight of my blood I became enraged and punched him in the mouth, bloodying his lip. I could see in his eyes that he was frightened of me, and I became wilder, punching him two more times in the face before fleeing down the steps and out the door. I walked the streets for about an hour. My nose felt like it was wadded up with cotton, and an intense pain pinched me between the eyes. My cheeks were scraped red where his beard had scoured against me.

The next day I woke up with two black eyes and my nose still hurt. My mother took me to the emergency room of the hospital. She told the doctor on duty that I had tripped and fallen. A week later, I had surgery to repair my broken nose. I left the hospital looking like a raccoon—a white cast over my nose and two black eyes. When the kids in the neighborhood and at the town pool asked me what had happened, I told them I'd had brain surgery.

I had gone along with the lie my mother had told the doctor in the emergency room, but after my surgery I realized my broken nose was my ticket out. I wrote my father a letter telling him that Eddie had punched me and broken my nose. I added that my mother and Eddie fought constantly with each other and I was afraid Eddie would get violent with me again. I said I wanted to come live with him, reminding him that the school year began in a week and it would be great if I could start the term in Cambridge.

Returning the ten-year-old letter to the box, I knew that Sarah was right about our father: He would never change. He was going to her graduation because all she expected from him was the five thousand dollars he owed her for going to Rutgers. He wasn't coming to my graduation because I expected him to love me unconditionally.

MY MOTHER WAS WAITING for me at Newark Airport. The moment I caught sight of her—inhaling deeply on a cigarette, a distraught look in her eyes—I knew that Sarah had told her about Hortense.

I bent down to kiss her, but she didn't bother to say hello.

"God give me strength to get through this weekend," she sighed.

In the car, she lit another cigarette.

"Mom, we'll be home in thirty minutes. Can't you wait until then to light up?"

"Look, Seth, I'm going through a very traumatic time right now. You don't know how upsetting it is to me that that woman is going to be at my daughter's graduation."

She began to cry, and I decided I would rather deal with the cigarette fumes than my mother's hysteria.

The next morning we drove to New Brunswick. Seamus sat in the front. I was lying down in the backseat, trying to nap, but in my mind I kept repeating to myself, *How often have I lain beneath rain on a strange roof, thinking of home.* I had been up until five in the morning writing an English paper for my brother on *As I Lay Dying.* Seamus was an excellent student—he had been admitted to Brandeis—but his strengths were science and math. He was diligent and bright enough to do well in his English courses, but he was thoroughly stymied by *As I Lay Dying.* The night before, I had tried to discuss it with him.

"Doesn't the family in the book remind you a little of us?" I had asked him.

"Us? You don't really think we're as strange as the family in this book."

"Think of your name. Seamus Shapiro. That's as strange as any of the names in the book. Jewel. Vardaman. Darl."

"You always exaggerate things."

"I know, but that's what helps me understand the book."

"Maybe I'm too literal to understand literature."

"See? We're like the family in the novel. All the siblings are different. Cash is literal and responsible, just like you. I'm a combination of Jewel and Darl. Angry, romantic, overly vulnerable."

I could see that Seamus was processing this information.

"Does that help?" I said.

"Actually, it does."

"So, we're also like the Bundren family because we can't communicate our deepest feelings to each other."

"I don't agree with that."

"All right. Think about this. Dad is like Addie. He's not present, but he's still a powerful force in our lives. We still define ourselves in relation to him."

"I don't agree with that either. Dad is more like the father in the novel. Self-centered. Not very honorable. I don't think of Dad as our family anyway. You, Sarah, me, and Mom. That's our family unit."

I told Seamus that maybe it would be easier if I just wrote down some of my ideas and then he could use them however he wanted. At nine o'clock, I sat down at the same desk I had avoided all through high school when I had homework. By five in the morning, I had written twenty pages about siblings and parents, language and loneliness. When I finally did go to bed, my mind was so revved up that I couldn't fall asleep. Lines from the book kept pulsing through my head, viscerally as a beating heart. I realized this was the way I read, and I forgave myself a little for "Two by Two."

In the morning, I showed Seamus what I had written. For the first time that I could recall, my younger brother expressed admiration for me.

"I'm amazed at how well you understand this book," Seamus said. "It was incomprehensible to me."

I found myself feeling amazed too, amazed that Seamus and I had grown up in the same apartment, experienced the same two parents, but had turned into such completely different people. He had directly told our father all the things I had always wanted to say myself, but Seamus had been more adult about it than I could ever have been. I had expressed years of pent-up hurt by telling Hortense to go fuck herself.

Seamus asked me if I thought it was ethical to use what I had written for him.

"It's fine," I replied, "as long as you just use the ideas and don't copy any of the sentences."

"Are you sure?"

"I was writing it for you, Seamus, not for a class. I was thinking of you when I wrote it; I was thinking of our family, so the ideas are just as much yours as mine."

RUTH CHAIN-SMOKED THROUGHOUT the long drive to New Brunswick. She had her window down, but the wind just blew the smoke into the backseat. I thought: *My mother is a fish. My mother smokes like a fish.*

The commencement exercises at Rutgers were huge, and I wondered if we would even see my father. Sarah had told Ruth where to meet her after the ceremony; perhaps, thinking strategically, she had told our father to meet her at another location. Afterward, as we walked to the spot Sarah had designated for our meeting, I could see that my father, Hortense, and Francois were already there, standing with Sarah. Ruth spotted them a second later. "Oh, Jesus Christ Almighty," she sighed.

As we approached, I could tell that my mother was trying to summon tears. She held out her arms and embraced Sarah for a long time. When she pulled back, her eyes were indeed damp and her mascara a little smudged. "I can't believe my baby girl is a college graduate!" Then everyone stood around doing their best to avoid eye contact. Hortense and Francois were standing a couple of feet behind my father. I noticed that Hortense had written *Merde!* all over the commencement program. Francois was wearing blue-jean overalls with a tie-dyed T-shirt underneath. His golden waves of Pre-Raphaelite hair fell to his shoulders. He was ignoring all of us, reading a paperback book—Dostoevsky's *Notes from Underground.*

Finally my mother turned to my father and extended her hand. "Hello, Elliot. How are you?"

"Very well, Ruth. Thank you. Would you like to say hello to Hortense?"

"I'm standing right here if she'd like to say hello to me."

Elliot stepped to the side. "Hallo," Hortense said. "Congratulations."

"Thank you," Ruth replied. "I have much to be proud of." Then she said to our father, "Aren't you going to say hello to your sons?"

He gave Seamus and me a tight-lipped smile. "Hello, boys."

"Hello, Horty. How are you?" I said to Hortense. Sarah glared at me, but Francois's lips had curled into a smile.

"I see you brought some light reading for the commencement," I said to him.

"This whole commencement thing is so *pseudo*," Francois declared.

"You mean like your pseudo farmer's clothing?" I asked.

Our father erupted into laughter; we had the same high-pitched, obnoxious laugh. Francois gave him a malevolent look and then banged his copy of *Notes from Underground* down on our father's Leica.

"Watch it!" our father said angrily.

"Oh, no! Did I harm the Holy Orifice?" Francois replied.

Hortense began speaking to her husband in very fierce French.

I noticed tears sliding down her cheeks from beneath her enormous sunglasses.

"All right, Sarah, we're leaving now," our father announced.

"You mean we're not all going out to lunch together?" I said.

"Why? So you can write a *story* about it?" my father answered.

"What story?" Ruth asked. "Seth, did you write a story?"

"No, I didn't write a story," I said.

"Then what did your father mean?"

"Nothing. He didn't mean anything."

"All right, Sarah," our father repeated impatiently, "we're going." He handed her an envelope. "Congratulations."

Then he turned around and walked away with his wife and son. Sarah looked at me. "You two are just like each other."

"Who?" Ruth asked. "Who is just like each other?"

"Nobody," Sarah replied.

"Seth is nothing like your father, if that's what you mean," Ruth said.

I resisted reminding my mother of all the times she had taunted me by saying, "Elliot Shapiro! Elliot Shapiro! You're just like him."

"I feel so sorry for their child," Ruth said. "I tell you, I must have done something right with the three of you."

Sarah said she was famished and wanted to go get some lunch.

"Oh, before I forget," Ruth said, searching around in her purse, "I have something for you from the Zelmans." She handed Sarah two envelopes. When Sarah opened the second, she spent about a minute reading the letter inside it, then her eyes welled up and brimmed over with tears.

"It's from Aaron," Ruth whispered to me.

Later that afternoon, as we were returning to the car after lunch, Sarah held me back for a moment and asked me if I could spend the night. Her roommate, Carrie, had moved out, she explained, and she didn't want to spend the night alone in her room in a half-empty dorm.

Ruth looked upset when we reached the car and I told her I was staying with Sarah.

"How are you going to get home?" she said.

"The bus."

"When did you plan this?" she asked us.

"About a minute ago," Sarah answered.

"Nobody tells me anything," Ruth sighed.

That night, after we had turned out the lights to go to sleep, I asked Sarah what Aaron had said in his letter. I knew she wanted me to stay so we could discuss it.

"He said that he hasn't been able to stop thinking about me for the last two years and he hopes we can get together."

"Do you still think about him?"

"All the time."

"So why don't you give him a chance?"

"I can't get past the way his father sexually manipulated Mom."

"So? That doesn't mean he's like his father."

"He loves his father."

"I love Dad, but that doesn't mean I'm like him."

"Maybe so," she said.

"Did Dad give you the five thousand dollars?"

"Yes. It was in the envelope he handed to me."

"Go to Italy and invite Aaron to join you."

"That sounds too nice."

"I have a graduation present for you."

"Oh?"

"Yes, I hereby give you permission to be happier than Mom without feeling guilty about it."

She was silent for a few seconds. Then I heard her quietly crying.

"Thank you," she finally said. "That's a very nice present."

"Do you really think I'm like Dad?"

"No, but you try to be. It's very strange. Why would you want to be like him?"

She was right. My sister had created a self by becoming the inverse of our mother: She was pragmatic and kept her feelings to herself. I hadn't created an identity so much as I had mastered an impersonation of my father—the sound of his voice, his speech rhythms, his mordant sense of humor, his discipline. But that's all it was—an impersonation of someone I could never really become. I might have been conscious of being under Bellow's spell when I wrote "Two by Two," but I hadn't realized the extent to which I had also been creating a character of whom my father would approve. If Isaac, my protagonist, wasn't very likeable, it wasn't because I had been trying to create a complex character; it was because I was trying to invent a version of myself—scientific, studious, emotionally detached—that my father would love.

In a strange room you must empty yourself for sleep. And before you are emptied for sleep, what are you. And when you are emptied for sleep, you are not. And when you are filled with sleep, you never were. I don't know what I am.

TWO DAYS LATER, back in Chicago, I found Rachel sitting alone at our regular table in the dining hall. I took it as an encouraging sign and approached the table with my tray.

"Can I join you?"

"If you want."

I sat down and Rachel asked me about Sarah's graduation.

"Stranger than you could imagine."

She gave me a small smile; I decided to test the temperature between us.

"Francois banged my father's Leica with his copy of *Notes from Underground*."

Rachel was laughing now.

"I've missed you," I said, and extended my hand across the table. "Do you forgive me?"

"No." Then she took my hand and said, "But I've missed you too."

"Friends?"

"Yes. Friends."

That night we shared a bed again, and I read to her from *As I Lay Dying*. Before turning out the lights and going to sleep, I confessed that I had slept with another woman. Rachel thanked me for telling her.

"You're not upset?" I said.

"No. We had stopped seeing each other. You had every right to go out with another woman."

How could she feel so betrayed by my story but apparently feel nothing when I confessed that I had slept with Bella? I had told myself that I was confessing to Rachel because it was the right thing to do, that I didn't want us to have any secrets between us. But hearing her reaction, I admitted to myself that I had told her about Bella because I had wanted to see if she was capable of sexual jealousy.

Two weeks later, Rachel and I sat next to each other in Rockefeller Chapel for the commencement ceremony. As I paged through the program, I noticed that it listed all the prizes awarded to undergraduates, and I prayed that my mother wouldn't see that I had won the Chandler Prize. Rachel had told her father and stepmother to meet her at the corner of Blackstone and Fifty-ninth Street and her mother to meet her at Kenmore and Fifty-ninth. She would see her mother immediately after the ceremony and then go out to lunch with her father and stepmother. We would go out to dinner that night with our mothers and Sarah and Seamus.

When we came out of Rockefeller Chapel, Ruth, Sarah, and

Seamus were standing right out in front. Ruth was smiling, but she didn't look happy.

"You didn't tell me you won a fiction prize!" she exclaimed.

"It's not a big deal," I said.

"So am I going to get to read this story?" She sounded thoroughly aggrieved.

"Sure," I said, and then introduced Rachel to my family.

"Very nice to meet you," Ruth said.

Rachel told me she needed to go meet her mother. She kissed me on the lips and said she would see us later.

My mother stared at me.

"Is she your girlfriend?"

"It looks that way."

She turned to my brother and sister. "Did either of you know your brother had a girlfriend?"

Sarah admitted that she did; Seamus said it was news to him.

"How come I'm the last one around here to know anything?"

"Mom, I just graduated magna cum laude from the University of Chicago. Can you try to be happy?"

That night we all went out to dinner at the Berghoff. As I expected, Seamus was scrutinizing the menu as if he were in a Torah study group, looking for anything without a trace of *treyf*, and Ruth blanched when she saw the prices. Then I announced that Rachel and I were using our prize money to treat everyone to dinner. Ruth turned to Joan, Rachel's mother. "Do we have the most wonderful children in the world?"

"I would say so," Joan replied. "Rachel and I are so close I tell everyone we're more like sisters."

"My son and daughter are best friends. That's one of my proudest achievements as a mother."

Sarah downed her wine and whispered to Rachel and me, "I'm going to need a lot of alcohol to get through the evening."

"Me too," Rachel murmured back, and swallowed her glass of wine.

Rachel and Sarah both laughed.

"What? What's so funny?" Ruth exclaimed.

"Nothing, Mom," I replied, and poured wine into her glass. Ruth drank it all in one gulp.

Then Joan asked me if I had ever been in therapy.

"Mom!" Rachel hissed.

I squeezed her hand under the table. "No, I haven't," I answered.

Ruth's eyes were shiny from the alcohol. "Oh, he'd probably just tell the psychiatrist what a bad mother I was," she commented.

Seamus, still puzzling over the menu, suddenly looked up and exclaimed, "Mom, I'm sure Seth would never do that! I'm sure Seth appreciates that you've tried your best to be a good mother."

Joan returned her attention to me. "I think you might find therapy extremely helpful to your writing. I have a number of clients who are writers, and our therapy has helped them to unlock their creativity. I've been doing regression therapy with one of them, and he's found it a very empowering experience."

"I'm afraid if I regress any more I'll turn into an embryo," I told her.

Both Rachel and Sarah burst out laughing, but our mothers looked perplexed. Then Ruth said, "Well, actually, Seth and Sarah experienced a very traumatic birth."

"Mom!" Sarah and I said simultaneously.

"Don't tell that story at the table," Sarah said.

But of course Ruth went ahead and told it. She recounted how after the obstetrician had untangled the cords, he had immediately put his mouth over mine and sucked out a plug of mucus. After Ruth related this detail, I turned to Rachel and said, "Now, aren't you glad you know that? By the way, how are you enjoying your schnitzel?"

Ruth continued the story. We were on respirators for ten days, she said, and it was touch and go, but a rabbi came to pray over us. When she came to the part in which Sarah and I were finally able to breathe on our own, she said, "I thanked the doctor, but the doctor said, 'Don't thank me.'"

Sarah and I interjected in unison: "Was anybody praying!"

My sister and I laughed, but Ruth looked distraught.

"Thanks a lot," she said to us. "Thanks for absolutely nothing!"

I poured more wine into her glass. "Drink up, Mom. Try to be happy."

Two DAYS LATER, I sent my mother a copy of "A Stranger on the Planet." On the way to the airport, she had reminded me three times to send her my story. She wrote back right away.

Dear Seth,

I cried when I read your story. I'm crying now, as I write this letter, just thinking about how beautiful it is. Your love for me comes through in the story, but it was still painful for me to see my faults so exposed. I cried the most when I came to the scene of you and me placing our fingertips on the balloon so that Nanny Esther would recognize the pressure from our fingers when the balloon reached heaven. Of course I remember the day we did that at Wollaston beach in Quincy, but you were only four years old. How could you possibly remember that? I know I wasn't a very good mother to you, and I felt great guilt after reading the story. Well, I suppose that's my cross to bear. I'm overwhelmed by your talent and memory.

Thank you for your love and honesty. May the next one hundred and twenty years be full of happiness for you.

Love,
Mom

Immediately after reading my mother's letter, I walked from my dorm room to campus and found Professor Kadish in his office.

"Yes, Mr. Shapiro, what can I do for you?"

"Is my story really going to be published in the *Chicago Quarterly*?"

"Yes. I didn't send an official letter of acceptance because I thought we had an understanding. Why? Do you want to try one of the national magazines? It's fine with me if you do."

"No, it's not that. I think my story has some problems."

"What kind of problems?"

"Some of it is too directly borrowed from *Henderson the Rain King*."

"How so? I didn't notice any similarities."

I brought out my copy of the book. "On page thirty, Henderson's Hungarian violin teacher says, 'Dear, take de bow like dis vun, not like dis vun, so.' In my story, the mother's Romanian patient says, 'No, darlink, you must do like dis one.'"

Kadish laughed. "That's nothing. Not a big deal."

I had never seen Kadish so warm and gracious.

"But I was very conscious of borrowing from *Henderson*."

"Everything is fine, Mr. Shapiro. You've earned your success."

Of course I really wasn't concerned about any similarities between my story and *Henderson the Rain King*. When I read my mother's letter, I thought of how she had sacrificed herself for me by fucking Abe Zelman. I thought of her lying beneath his huge brown belly for all those minutes because of the words I'd said and couldn't say.

"Professor Kadish, if it's all the same to you, I'd rather not publish the story."

Kadish stared at me for a moment. "Very well. If that's what you want." Then he returned his attention to the papers on his desk. I felt shattered; he wasn't even going to ask me why, or encourage me to reconsider.

"Some people might be very hurt if I publish the story."

"If you say so."

"Don't you see how that might be possible?"

Kadish looked up at me. "My daughter told me you were one of the nicest men she's ever met," he said.

He had discussed me with his daughter! He knew we were friends! For a moment I wanted to retract my retraction.

"Thank you," I said, but I knew he hadn't meant it as a compliment.

ON OUR LAST NIGHT TOGETHER, Rachel and I made love slowly and ardently. She was moving back to California the next day. I kissed every inch of her. Perhaps, despite all the kisses I had planted on her body over the past six months, I had missed a secret spot, like a hidden door, which, if kissed, would send her falling madly, hopelessly in love with me.

Afterward, she cried in my arms. "I don't understand why I don't love you more than I do," she said. "You're exactly the type of man I've always wanted to fall in love with. It doesn't make sense to me."

"Right city, wrong season," I said.

"What does that mean?" Rachel asked.

"Don't you remember that's what Professor Krzyzowski said about teaching Tolstoy during the winter term? I keep thinking that applies to us. We're in the right city, but something's wrong."

"We'll be friends for life. I know we will."

I didn't really believe her. I recognized myself as emotionally lazy, not the type of person to keep up a long-distance friendship. But then six months after she moved to California, Rachel called me up and told me she had a woman lover. She asked me if I was weirded out. I said no, not at all. I was relieved, actually. Her revelation explained everything. When we were boyfriend and girlfriend, we had never discussed sex, but that was all we talked about after Rachel realized she loved women. We had found our true topic, our theory of everything. In the years to come, we would go on vacations together, and we always shared the same bed. Camping out in the Sierras, or lying next to each other at night in a rental cottage on Wellfleet, enveloped by the scent of pine and sea air coming in through the bedroom window, she would tell me all about her lovers, tell me how one woman loves another woman. I felt as if I were hearing the deepest secrets a woman could tell a man, and I never wrote another story again.

THE GRAMMAR OF LOVE

• SEPTEMBER–DECEMBER 1984 •

Allbright, Moses. Allen, LaDonna. Bates, Jamal. I knew every name by heart, intoned each one to myself as I walked down the hall, but when I entered the room and told the class my name, no one wrote it down. A smile twitched my lips, and I repeated my name. No response. Was I really here? Would they notice if I turned around and walked out? I sat down and began calling out names. Beaton, Andre. Cummings, T. J. I paused to match faces with names, but no one looked me in the eye, and by the name Dalrymple, Daryl, I was in a panic that I would never teach these students anything. From the back of the room, I heard baby noises vibrating the air with longing and wonder. I looked up and met the baby's gaze. His bright black eyes were fastened on me. He strained forward in his mother's lap, one hand opening and closing like a summons. McDonald, Roland. Now the baby was responding to each name by clapping on the desk and letting out loud peals of delight. Washburn, Angela. Head bowed shyly, she spoke into the baby's ear, quieting him. I watched them for four or five seconds, catching myself in a bad habit of staring too long at intimate moments in public places. The baby reached for her ear and my heart swelled. I repeated the name: "Angela Washburn."

"Here," she whispered.

"Thank you," I replied.

I HAD LIVED IN HYDE PARK on Chicago's South Side for ten years, having arrived as an avid eighteen-year-old, certain that literary fame and an exalted life of the mind awaited me, but I had never been south of Sixty-second Street before I began teaching at Martin Luther King State, a primarily black commuter college at Ninety-fifth and King Drive. Now, three mornings a week, I assailed the safe borders of my life and drove deep into the dark heart of south Chicago, past boarded-up storefronts, abandoned movie houses, and gutted, skeletal apartment buildings, past dealers in door-ways and addicts swaying down the middle of the street in search of a morning fix; after fifteen blocks the desolation gradually gave way to supermarkets, hardware stores, used-car lots, small lawns, and bungalows. But in my nightmares my car stalled or ran out of gas before Seventy-fifth Street and a gang of black men closed in on me. "Let me go!" I shouted, holding my textbook, a bible of grammatical rules, high above my head. "I have important work to do! I'm teaching subject-verb agreement today!"

SIXTY-THIRD AND MARTIN LUTHER KING Drive. Sixty-fourth and King Drive. Sixty-fifth and King Drive.

"More education don't hurt anybody."

The second time I taught my class we went over exercises from the textbook. Each student read a faulty sentence out loud and then revised it. Their voices were wooden and uncertain, every face blank. Only the baby, reaching toward me like a castaway on a raft, seemed to truly recognize me.

"More education don't hurt nobody," said the student, Tanya Toney. She looked doubtful. "Man," she sighed, "that don't sound right neither."

I asked if anyone could revise the sentence correctly. A few hands went up.

"More education doesn't hurt anybody," said a woman in the front row.

"Yes," I said. "The faulty agreement is between the subject and verb, not between the verb and object. Does everyone understand?"

The baby's head tilted and tottered like a gyroscope.

Look, we're all in this together, I wanted to say. Can we *agree* on that? I'm probably unqualified for this job. I know very little about English grammar. I only memorized these rules last night. I've never been south of Sixty-second Street. So we'll learn all these rules together. Is that a fair agreement? We'll learn all about subjects and verbs, nouns and pronouns. We'll memorize every irregular verb. All two hundred of them! Then we can really begin to understand each other!

AT THE END OF THE SUMMER, I moved out of the graduate-student apartment building where I had lived for six years and into a small one-bedroom apartment nearby. My new next-door neighbor was a blind man named Raymond. For years I had seen him walking around the neighborhood, his head raised and his white cane pointing to the ground in front of him like a divining rod. I always marveled that he knew exactly where he was going.

Two weeks after I moved in, Raymond and I approached the building at the same time. "You're my new neighbor, aren't you?" he asked, as I held the door open for him. How did he know me? My footsteps? An odor? I raised my elbow and buried my nose in my armpit. I'd passed him a number of times but had never thought of introducing myself. What would I have said? *Excuse me, you don't know me, but I see you all the time.*

Raymond cheerfully invited me into his apartment for a beer. I had never imagined a blind person as being happy. Then I reminded myself that I had twenty-twenty vision and was miserable.

I told Raymond about my class.

"Did you study linguistics?" he asked.

"No, divinity."

"Are you religious?"

"Not especially."

He looked puzzled. "Did something happen?"

"Oh, no, nothing like that," I said and laughed. "Religious belief isn't a requirement for divinity school." That's the same explanation I had given my mother when I enrolled and she worried I was converting. The answer had never completely satisfied her. At my graduation, she had said, "So now what am I supposed to call you? Doctor? Father? Reverend?"

"What was your specialty?" Raymond said.

"Religion and literature." I explained that I had analyzed similar modes of address to lovers and to God in metaphysical poetry. Then I told him that I had sent out more than fifty job queries but hadn't landed a single interview. That's why I was teaching basic English, part-time, at Martin Luther King State.

"Do you believe in the soul?" he asked hopefully.

"Not that I'm aware of."

"Are you in love?"

"Yes. With a lesbian who lives two thousand miles away."

Raymond laughed. "You're in sad shape, brother."

Rachel had recently completed her dissertation too, but with a PhD from the Stanford English Department and a sexier topic than mine—*Colonizing Desire: Constructions of Sexuality in the Works of Caribbean Women Writers*—she had received multiple

job offers and had decided to accept a two-year postdoctoral position at Stanford because she had fallen in love with Lucinda, the
woman she hoped to spend her life with, but it was all very complicated. Not only was Rachel's lover married, but she also happened to be Rachel's thesis adviser. Lucinda was coming up for
tenure in the fall, and she didn't want to compromise her chances
by leaving her husband for a former student, so she and Rachel
were keeping their relationship secret for another year. I was the
only person who knew about them.

"What about you?" I replied. "What kind of shape are you in?"

"I'm religious. I believe in the soul. I'm not in love."

He appeared to be in his midtwenties.

"Have you ever been?"

He shook his head, and I felt a little bad. Maybe I wouldn't
have asked him something so personal if he could see me. (But
what I really wanted to know, the question I was dying to ask,
was how he walked around the neighborhood. Was it an extra-
sensory feat? In the black world behind his eyelids, did he see the
streets of the neighborhood like veins of light on a radar screen?)

Just before I left, Raymond said he thought we were going to
be great friends.

"Why do you think that?" I asked him

He smiled with his lips pressed together. "Because I don't think
you have any friends," he said. Then held his fist to his mouth,
trying to suppress a laugh.

"I'm glad to be such a source of amusement to you."

But he was right. After six years of graduate school, I had
formed no close attachments. Every woman I had slept with I had
met in Regenstein; after a time, the relationships had begun to feel
as transient and anonymous as prison dalliances. My emotional
lifelines were my weekly phone calls with Sarah and Rachel.

As I moved to leave, Raymond asked if he could see my face.

"What?" I asked dumbly, though I knew exactly what he meant.

"Like this." He placed his fingertips on my forehead, as if anointing me. With exquisite slowness, he drew his fingertips down my face, tracing eyebrows, nose, lips. My skin was burning, my muscles drawn tight. Our faces were inches apart. His mouth was half open, his eyeballs off target, like the eyes of someone looking through the dark side of a one-way window. I couldn't fathom the reverence in his face. "Relax," he whispered. I placed my hands over his. "I'm sorry," I said, "but I really have to go."

"CAN ANYBODY TELL ME WHICH verb ending is used with all singular nouns and third-person-singular pronouns?"

A man in the front row raised his hand. He was the shape and coppery brown color of a Bosc pear.

"Say your name," he demanded.

"Excuse me?"

"Your name. How you say it?"

"Shapiro."

"Spell that."

He was glowering, but when I wrote my name on the board, he smiled with recognition. He had no upper teeth, only a ridge of shiny brown gum.

"Hey, man, you *Eye*-talian?"

"Italian? Me? No."

He looked disappointed, as if he were sure he had had the right answer to a question.

"Damn if I didn't think you was *Eye*-talian. Where y'all from, then?"

"You mean my family?"

"Right. What country they from?"

"The Ukraine."

"Where's that at?"

"Beyond the Pale."

His name was Daryl Dalrymple. When his turn came, he read, "John and Mary asks a lot of questions." He puzzled over the sentence, rubbing his brow, pressing down on his thighs. Then he looked up at me and winked conspiratorially.

"Don't see nothing wrong with this sentence, Shapiro."

I asked him what the subject was in the sentence.

"John and Mary."

"The verb?"

"Asks."

"Is the subject singular or plural?"

"Plural."

"So how do you get the verb to agree with the subject?"

"Plural! John and Mary *asks* a lot of questions. Damn," he said with a laugh, "*you* asks a lot of questions."

I explained the rule.

"You saying, a singular subject got an 's' on the verb, but a plural subject ain't got no 's'?"

"Exactly."

"God*damn*," he sighed.

Finally it was Angela Washburn's turn to read. I looked in her direction and called her name. The baby cooed like a pigeon under the roof of an old house. She whispered in his ear for a few seconds before responding to me. I leaned forward, longing to hear her words.

"Tom like to read, but I loves to dance."

I said something to her about the first-person singular. The baby laid his head against her breast and closed his eyes, as if the secret frequency between us had gone dead.

THAT NIGHT IN BED I REPEATED TO MYSELF: "I loves to dance. . . . I love to dance." Only one letter separated us. *I love, you love, he loves, we love.* I marveled at the way the verb opened up like a daylily. How easily *I love* blossomed into *we love*! Conjugating the verb over and over, I experienced a sensation of movement, like a widening echo, a journey outward. But after a time the motion of the verb transported me to my nightmare world: Sixty-third and King Drive, Sixty-fourth and King Drive, Sixty-fifth and King Drive. I thought of the bombed-out buildings, the elevated tracks blocking the sun like a twenty-four-hour eclipse, and I realized that *I loves* won't flower overnight into *I love*. That "s" was as solidly planted as an old tree root.

ONE NIGHT RAYMOND CAME to my apartment and questioned me about love.

"A man and woman are secret lovers for forty years," he said. "They see each other only two times a month, when they spend the afternoon in a hotel room in a strange city. But they write to each other every day. Some of the letters are extremely erotic, but mainly they chronicle births, deaths, marriages, business deals, the sweetness and bitterness of longing. The man's view of life is especially black. He complains that everyone is after his money. He hates his wife and business partners, can't communicate with his children, mistrusts everyone except his lover. He tells her that she is the only person he has ever loved, the only thing that is decent, beautiful, and true in his life. The woman is also very unhappy, tied to a marriage that is emotionally and spiritually dead. Now here is the question: Why don't the two lovers ever get married?"

I said, "Maybe he's afraid she'll ask for lots of money and be like all the rest."

"No. In fact, in his letters he pleads with her to accept money. He tells her she is the only person he's ever wanted to share his money with."

"Well, perhaps she doesn't want to leave her husband and cause her family pain."

"Possibly—but what is a couple of years of pain in return for many more years of happiness?"

"I have no idea, Raymond."

"I think the two lovers liked things just the way they were. If they were married, they would have lost the element of imagination. They could have loved each other every night, but they'd have lost the chance to *imagine* loving each other every night."

"Where did you hear this story?"

"From my grandmother. We discovered her love letters after she died. I always thought her story would be a great movie, but who would be interested in a movie like that in this day and age?"

"You go to the movies?"

Raymond smiled cagily, as if this was the question he had been maneuvering me to all along. "Every day."

THE NEXT AFTERNOON I shadowed Raymond around the neighborhood. I knew he had never been in love, I knew he believed in the soul, but I didn't know how he got from the library to the liquor store to the supermarket. There had to be more to it than simply memorizing every street. He had to know their system—how the streets conjugated, the irregular forms of a route—as if the neighborhood were his secret language. Walking in his footsteps, I thought of the dull syntax of my own life, of the six years I walked the same route between my graduate-student apartment building and a library cell every day. I wouldn't see other streets in the neighborhood for weeks. I wouldn't go beyond the borders of the neighborhood itself for months. How could I have let that happen? At an intersection, waiting for the light to change, Raymond and I were brushed up against each other in the middle of a crowd of people. I knew he was going home, and I recited to myself, *Fifty-sixth and Stony Island . . . Fifty-sixth and Cornell . . . Cornell and Fifty-fifth . . . Cornell and Fifty-fourth. . . .* He turned and looked up at me. "Seth?" I held my breath and kept silent, as if I were hiding in a closet with someone else's love letters or diary. The light changed and I went my own way.

IN LATE SEPTEMBER, Rachel's mother was diagnosed with liver cancer and given approximately two months to live. Rachel moved back across the bay to her mother's house in Berkeley to care for her and help both of them come to some type of peace about their relationship. It was even more difficult for her and Lucinda to regularly call each other, so Rachel called me every night. Rachel had never come out to her mother, and she was in a quandary about whether to introduce her mother to Lucinda, as her lover, before her mother died.

"Why is it so difficult?" I asked her. "Your mother wouldn't be judgmental."

"I know she wouldn't, but she'd have all these theories about why I'm gay, and I know we'd just end up arguing."

"So maybe you're doing the right thing."

Her mother still thought we were a couple—she kept a photograph of Rachel and me at our college commencement on her bedroom bureau. For Rachel, it had been a convenient ruse, a way to keep her mother from trespassing too far into her emotional life.

"She keeps asking me to go to her lunatic therapist with her."

"The one who does regression therapy?"

"Yes. She thinks that if the therapist can regress us back to the time when I was an infant and she was a young mother, we'll be able to emotionally reconnect."

"Are you going to do it?"

"No. I told her it wouldn't help because I didn't believe in it." Rachel started crying. "Why am I such a bitch? She's dying. Why can't I do that for her? I mean, wouldn't you do something like that with your mother if she were dying?"

"Rachel, you're not a bitch. If my mother dies a prolonged death, I only hope I can be half as gracious and generous as you are to your mother."

She began crying again. "Oh, Seth, I miss you."

"I was thinking of coming out to visit for Thanksgiving. That might be a nice last Thanksgiving for your mother. Just the three of us. You, me, and her."

"Yes, I'd like that. I'd like that very much."

"'IF YOU PRACTICE THE PIANO REGULAR, you will soon be able to play real music.'"

Angela Washburn stared at her book. The baby stared at me. His blunt, fleshy arm moved back and forth like a wand. I imagined he was inviting me to enter their aura of intimacy. I beamed back a reply in stealth: *I love, you love, he loves, we love. . . .*

"If one practice the piano regular, one will soon be able to play real music."

She didn't even look up to see how I would respond to her answer. I explained that the sentence was wrong because of the adverb and not the pronoun. "Do you understand, Angela? 'Regular' is an adverb because it modifies 'practice.' So there should be an 'l-y' at the end of the word." I repeated this rule as ardently as if I were reciting Keats. The baby reached for me, but she pulled down his arm as if drawing a shade.

MOST DAYS RAYMOND AND I had lunch at Sol's, a neighborhood deli run assembly line fashion by ten or twelve Vietnamese. They labored at a furious pace, swabbing rolls with mustard and mayonnaise, slicing pickles and tomatoes, slapping meats and cheeses onto bread, shouting in loud bursts of Vietnamese.

Only Raymond slowed them down. When he came tapping through the door, they eyed one another as if he were the strangest sight they had seen in this strange land. Otherwise, their only connection to the world beyond the counter was through the items on Sol's menu. "You chop livah! You hot dog!" the workers shouted out as customers proceeded through the line. I always ordered juice, because the word allowed me a sense of connection with Sol's Vietnamese.

"You jew-is!" the juice worker would shout at me.

"Damn right!" I always shouted back. "And what about it?"

"Ya, ya," he'd reply, with a huge smile, "you jew-is!"

TWO OR THREE AFTERNOONS A WEEK I went to a movie with Raymond. I felt sinful, but weekday afternoons were the best time to go to the movies with a blind person. The theaters were nearly empty, so Raymond and I could talk without annoying people, although the first few times I succeeded in annoying Raymond. I described everything—reaction shots, scenery, camera angles. He sighed, fidgeted, then shouted, "I know Meryl Streep looks sad. I'm not deaf too, you know!" The three other people in the theater all turned to look at us as I slid down in my seat.

Eventually my technique improved. At a revival house, we went to see a Hitchcock double feature: *Shadow of a Doubt* and *Strangers on a Train*. With my lips an inch from his ear, I drew Raymond into the world of visual echoes, light and shadows, murderous hands. In *Shadow of a Doubt*, when young Charlie moved her hand down the banister to show Uncle Charlie she is wearing the ring that link him to his crimes, Raymond gripped my forearm as I described the exchange of looks between them. I had never known anyone to get so worked up at the movies.

At the end of *Strangers on a Train*, Raymond said, "I just love Bruno Anthony's voice. I could come here every day and listen to him seduce Guy Haines."

"Seduce him?"

"Of course. Couldn't you tell that Bruno is in love with him?"

"Raymond, Bruno is a psychopath! He murders an innocent woman for thrills."

"No," he declared happily, "he murders for love."

RACHEL'S MOTHER WANTED TO BE CREMATED, her ashes scattered in the Pacific Ocean. But Rachel couldn't bear the thought of her body going up in flames, and she had secretly bought a burial plot for her mother.

"I know it's a really bad thing to do," she said to me during one of our nightly calls. "I mean, it is her body, and I'm not honoring her beliefs, but I want to be able to visit her in a cemetery, to know she's in a physical place."

"It's a Jewish thing, and you're more Jewish than your mother."

"I kept thinking of your story 'Two by Two.' The impulse to be buried among family is so powerful, so *true*."

I had actually been thinking the same thing. A couple of months before, I had driven by a cemetery and was overcome with dread: What if I lived out my days in Chicago and was buried here, alone, far from my family? I tried to laugh it off, but after nearly ten years in Chicago I still didn't feel at home. I missed my family. I missed the East. My life had stalled out. Twisting the phone cord around my finger, I looked around my apartment. I had bought everything secondhand: my toast-colored sofa, the faux-wood desk, the industrial-looking metal bookshelves. I had described the decor of my apartment to Sarah as "graduate-student emeritus." Would I ever get out of here?

"Seth, I'm sorry I overreacted to that story you wrote back in college. That was a very confusing time for me, and the story made me feel so exposed."

"Who knew all that tension was really about sex?"

"I did," she replied. "But I just didn't know how to name it."

THE NEWSPAPER SAYS THAT *on the average person a college diploma is worth two hundred thousand dollars more than a person who has no college diploma. On the other hand, by the list of jobs, you are basing whether or not to go to college, is a incomplete list.*

I spent hours studying Angela Washburn's language, as if her blurred grammatical patterns and derailed subordinate and independent clauses were a map to her soul. On her paper I wrote lengthy comments about her faulty comparisons, with the weary heart of someone floating a message in a bottle. One day, though, she showed up at my office, her paper in her hand, her other arm holding the baby.

"This ain't so good, is it?"

Good or bad. Right or wrong. Black or white. Don't think this way, Angela, I wanted to say. I wanted to tell her I regarded these grammatical rules as a prism refracting her iridescent intelligence.

I asked her where her subjects were.

"My what?"

"Your subjects. Where are your subjects in this sentence?"

She stared at her paper, searching for her subjects; her baby stared at me, his head tilting and swaying, his eyes bright with wonder. Finally she answered, "They everywhere."

I laughed. "They sure are."

The baby bleated with delight and clapped his hands on my desk.

Angela, as if embarrassed by the excitement, looked down at

her paper and smiled shyly. She read another sentence: "The most problem and hurt is knowing and hoping the future one want do not exist after college."

I asked her what the main emotions were in this sentence.

She gave me a searching look, like someone hearing news she can't quite believe. "Hurt and hope."

"Yes! Excellent! Do you see what the problem is then?"

"My sister, she went to college, but she can't get no job."

Ask her what her sister does now, I told myself. Ask her about her hurts and hopes. Tell her you hurt yourself by walking the same insular route every day for six years, building your routine into a wall, and now you hope to learn a way out.

Instead, I asked her about her gerunds.

"My what?"

"'Knowing' and 'hoping' are your gerunds. The problem is that you attach them to the same complement and thereby cancel out your meaning."

She gave me a bruised look, then turned her eyes away.

ANGELA WAS NOT IN CLASS THE NEXT DAY.

Daryl Dalrymple, as always, was sitting in the middle of the front row. "What's your rap today, Shapiro?"

"Irregular verbs." He extended his hand so I could lay a little skin on him. "All *right*," he said.

I asked Daryl to read the first sentence of his composition. He faced the class and recited, "I was born and breaded in the South."

A number of students laughed.

"Damn right I was," he said. "In Meridian, Mississippi."

"After your mama breaded you, how she fit your big butt in the frying pan?"

Now everybody laughed.

"Y'all saying something 'bout my mama?" Daryl challenged the class.

"What's the infinitive form of the verb?" I interjected.

"Breed," someone answered.

"Right," I said, relieved. "To breed."

"Breed!" a woman repeated incredulously. Her name was Yvette Woolfolk. More moralist than grammarian, she said, "You know, I read in this Alex Haley book how they used to breed black folks like they was horses. That's how their birth records were kept. Like they was horses!"

"That's right, that's right," someone responded. Then there was a chorus of "yeahs" and "amens."

I wasn't aware of how red my face had become until one of the students said, "Hey, man, why you look so guilty?"

"You don't look beyond pale now, Shapiro," Daryl said.

RACHEL'S MOTHER DIED TWO days before Thanksgiving. I arrived the next day and we went to the funeral together. Rachel kept close to me, holding my hand during the service at the synagogue, leaning against me for support as the rabbi chanted Kaddish at the grave. Most of Rachel's relatives presumed I was her boyfriend. *How long had I known Rachel? Where was I staying? At Joan's house? How nice that Rachel doesn't have to be alone. How long was I planning on staying?*

Some of Rachel's childhood and graduate-school friends had come to the funeral. I knew that Lucinda was among the mourners and kept trying to figure out who she was. I was flabbergasted when Rachel finally did introduce me to her. She was slight and plain, scholarly looking, her eyes large behind a pair of wire-rimmed glasses. This was the woman Rachel wanted to spend her life with? The woman she pined for night after night?

After the services, everyone gathered at Joan's house. Rachel's

relatives had brought enough food to feed an army of Cossacks—
bagels, rye breads, and seeded rolls, mounds of lox and sturgeon,
platters layered with cold cuts, bowls of fruit salad, and plenty of
vodka and scotch. Throughout the afternoon and evening, I was
keenly aware of Rachel and Lucinda. Rachel didn't act any differently with her than with her other friends—no extralong glances,
no surreptitious hand squeezes—and I marveled at how well they
pulled off this difficult act. At one point I noticed Rachel going into
her bedroom; Lucinda followed a couple of minutes later. I kept
looking at my watch: five, ten, then twenty minutes. I occupied
myself by drinking scotch. I had seen Rachel kiss and hold hands
with some of her girlfriends, she had told me the most graphic
details of her sex life, and it never bothered me, but imagining
Rachel and Lucinda lying next to each other on the bed, holding
and comforting each other, was deeply unsettling. It shattered the
illusion I had maintained that I had become the most important
person in her life again.

After all the guests had left, Rachel and I collapsed into her
childhood bed together, our arms around each other. I asked her
if she had told her mom about Lucinda before she died. Rachel's
eyes welled up with tears.

"No, and now I regret that I didn't."

"You don't have anything to regret, sweetie," I said.

"I actually did go with her to see her dumb therapist."

Rachel told me how the therapist had tried to regress them
by instructing Rachel to lie down on Joan's lap as her mother
read her *The Runaway Bunny*. Rachel and I both laughed. Then
Rachel began crying again.

"The fucking thing was actually effective," she said. "I felt
loved and safe. I didn't want to get up."

I had never felt so close to her, not when we had read Tolstoy
to each other in bed every night as undergraduates, not when we

went on our yearly vacations, staying up all night and discussing sex. I held her tightly as she cried, feeling an electric intimacy. How could she not be feeling the same thing? She kissed me good night, told me she loved me, and turned over to go to sleep. Thirty minutes later we were still wide awake; we had probably changed positions about fifty times, as if we were trying to figure out a secret handshake.

"What are you thinking about?" Rachel finally asked.

"About everything."

"Are you thinking you want to make love?"

"Yes. Are you?"

She studied me in the dim light and kissed me.

"You know I'm in a relationship," she said.

"Is that a yes?"

We kissed again; I ran my finger over her nightshirt, lightly grazing her nipple. She shuddered and squeezed my ass, then she hiked her legs up and removed her panties. "Seth, baby," she said, "put your mouth on me." My tongue traced only two or three arabesques before she came, bucking convulsively. Oh, Lord, how different this was from our nights together in Chicago, when I would kiss her all over her body—and not just in the usual places but on the arch of her foot, the rim of her ear, the back of her knee— feeling as if I were trying every light switch in a darkened house, all to no avail. Perhaps Lucinda, or some other woman, had found the light in her body; perhaps her body was buzzing with booze, longing, death, and reunion. She lifted herself on top of me.

"Do you have any protection?" I asked.

"No," she said, and began to ride me.

We locked into a powerful rhythm, our bodies moving back and forth in unison. I spent myself explosively, copiously.

The next morning at ten we were awakened by one ring of the phone.

"That's Lucinda's signal," Rachel explained.

I ran my tongue up and down the nape of her neck, pressing close so she could feel my yearning.

"Wait fifteen or twenty minutes," I said.

"No, I have to call her right back. She'll wonder if I don't."

"Tell her you were in the shower."

"We don't lie to each other."

I watched Rachel rise from the bed, enjoyed a brief glimpse of her beautifully arched back and rounded bottom before she covered herself with a robe and went into the kitchen to call Lucinda. I felt the pang of loneliness that sometimes struck me when I woke alone in my own bed. I waited for thirty minutes before I gave up hope that she was coming back.

The day was busy with appointments with bankers, lawyers, realtors. In the evening we went through all of Joan's belongings—diaries, bundles of old letters, photographs, childhood dolls and drawings. We discussed everything except the fact that we had become lovers again. The night before, I had dreamed of flooded plains, of lakes and rivers breaching their banks. Could this be a sign that she was pregnant? I wanted to tell her about my dream, wanted to ask her if she too thought it was a sign, if she was trying to become pregnant, perhaps acting on some impulse to beat back death by creating life. I had so many questions for her: Was last night going to change anything between us, especially if she was pregnant? Was it about us, about how intensely close we had become over the last two months, speaking for hours on the phone every night? Or was she simply consummating with me all the pent-up ardor she felt for Lucinda? Now that we were lovers again, I had become thoroughly self-conscious, totally strategic, aware of everything I couldn't say.

When we went to bed that night, I cupped her breast. Rachel removed my hand and repositioned it on her belly. She said that she just wanted me to hold her.

"Did you tell Lucinda about us this morning?" I asked.

"Tell her what?"

"That we made love."

"No."

"Are you going to tell her?"

"I don't know."

I had an erection that wouldn't go down. I kept shifting positions. I wanted to keep holding her, but the blood in my penis wouldn't ebb. Finally, Rachel said, "Let me help." She sat up beside me, put her hand inside my underpants, and began pumping away. She didn't kiss me or lie next to me. Occasionally she smiled at me; once she yawned. This was an act of kindness, not love, something only someone like her could do for me—a close friend, a woman, a former lover. I suddenly felt isolated from her, isolated by muscles and blood, isolated by this reminder that our relationship had its limits. Cleaning myself off in the bathroom, I had to fight to keep from bursting into tears. When I returned to bed, Rachel leaned into me. I squeezed her hand, then rolled over to the far side of the bed.

The phone woke us at eight the next morning, ringing three times before Rachel answered it. From the sound of her voice—surprised, then soft and affectionate—I knew it was Lucinda on the other end. I went into the kitchen. For two hours I drank coffee and read the paper. Maybe Lucinda was ending the relationship. Maybe she was telling Rachel that she couldn't go on with the secrecy and adultery, not to mention the unprofessional nature of their relationship. Yes, Lucinda was ending the relationship, Rachel would be pregnant, and I would move from Chicago to California, and we would get married. I'd stay home with the baby, become a house husband. I was considering names for our child when Rachel finally came into the kitchen. I knew from one look at her face that none of this would come true. "What's going on?" I asked. Rachel said that Lucinda had told her husband about their affair.

"What's going to happen now?"

"They're going to separate."

"I suppose that's good news for you."

Rachel gave me a pained smile. "We'll still have to keep things secret until after Lucinda comes up for tenure," she said. "It's going to be difficult."

"So, did you tell her about us?"

"Why do you keep asking me that?" she snapped.

"I thought you didn't like lying to her," I replied.

I LEFT THE NEXT DAY. Looking out the window of the plane, I watched the topography of the country change like a time-lapse film of a flower blooming: The coastline and green hills became the Rockies, which leveled out to the Great Plains. My spirit gradually deflated as I gazed for hours at the patterned farmland of the Midwest and then at the tracts of suburbia. When my plane banged down on the runway in Chicago, it felt like a knock to my soul. Just as the shuttle van from the airport deposited me in front of my building, I saw Raymond coming out the door with his white cane.

"Raymond. Hi."

When he heard my voice he turned around. "Oh, hi, Seth. Did you go visit Rachel for Thanksgiving?"

"Well, her mother died. So I ended up going for a funeral."

"Oh, my condolences. But I'm sure Rachel was glad to have you with her."

"I don't know. Rachel and I slept with each other. Now I'm very mixed up."

"I thought she had a serious girlfriend."

"She did. She does."

"So now she's a lapsed lesbian?" Raymond laughed. He was the closest thing I had to a best friend in Chicago, but he always thought my problems were hilarious.

"The sex was amazing. Better than any sex we used to have when she was my girlfriend."

"You want me to feel bad for you about this?"

"No, but I mean how do you explain that?"

"Do you know what Tennessee Williams said when he was asked about his sexuality?"

"No. What?"

Raymond smiled naughtily, then said in his best Blanche DuBois voice, "I've always been rather *flexible*."

THE NEXT AFTERNOON RAYMOND KNOCKED on my door and asked me if I wanted to go to the revival house and see a John Wayne Western called *The Searchers*. I agreed to go when he said I wouldn't have to annotate the movie for him. "I've seen it dozens of times," he told me. "You'll love it."

Not long into the movie, John Wayne's brother and sister-in-law are massacred and their two young daughters kidnapped by Indians. John Wayne and some other cowboys go off to look for the girls. They find one of them raped and murdered and spend five years searching for the other one. Eventually they find her—she has grown up into Natalie Wood—during a raid on a Comanche camp. John Wayne raises his hand to kill her because she has become a wife of the Indian chief, but then he has a change of heart and rides home with her on his horse.

I thought the movie was fine, but I didn't love it, and I didn't share my opinion because I knew Raymond, who had spent the movie leaning forward in his seat and holding his fist to his mouth, was strongly moved. I wasn't in the mood to hear him explain everything I had failed to notice.

Afterward, we went next door for a beer.

"Isn't that a beautiful story?" Raymond said.

"Beautiful? Raymond, John Wayne spent five years on his horse looking for Natalie Wood, and then he almost scalped her because she was fucking an Indian."

"But at the last moment he was transformed by love."

"Oh, now you're going to tell me that John Wayne really wants to sleep with his teenaged niece?"

"No," he replied, with a lascivious laugh. "He wants to sleep with his sister-in-law."

I recalled a subtle exchange of looks between John Wayne and the sister-in-law, and I knew that Raymond was right. How many times did he have to see the movie to catch that?

"Seth," Raymond continued, "couldn't you see how ill at ease in the world John Wayne is? How he isolates himself from love and caring? But when he discovers Natalie Wood, he realizes his capacity for nurturing and love. She's his best half and he finally becomes a whole person. That's why it's a beautiful story."

"Raymond, sometimes I wonder if you and I see the same movies."

"We see the same movies, Seth, but sometimes I wonder if you have any imagination."

"I have imagination, but I also know something about real life."

Raymond smiled beatifically. "You're really threatened by me, aren't you?"

"What are you talking about?" I exploded.

"You always have to claim you know more about life just because you're sighted."

"Jesus, Raymond, who said anything about sight? I just think that sometimes you romanticize life. That story you told me about your grandmother, for instance. I think if you knew anything about the way people really love, you would know that your grandmother and her lover must have endured great pain. Two people who love each other don't keep apart just because they'd rather *imagine* being together. I'll tell you why your grandmother and her lover stayed together for so many years. Because the alternative was probably nothing—no romance, no intensity, nothing. And even if the price is extreme pain, most people would rather have pain than nothing."

"That's just your interpretation."

"No, that's my *experience*! Look, Raymond, I once had a relationship with a married woman. My lover was unhappy in her marriage, just like your grandmother. I pleaded with her to leave her husband for me, but she didn't want to think of herself as the type of woman who would leave her husband for another man. But you know something? The more painful things were between us, the more inflamed our loving became. I remember one afternoon toward the end. We had been making love for hours in the July heat. Our bodies were plastered together with sweat. At that point the pain was realer than the love. But looking at our feet, I felt oddly detached. I realized we could end the relationship right then and spare ourselves more agony, but I didn't. We couldn't. And do you know why? Because the alternative would have been nothing. All she would have had was her bad marriage. And what would I have had? Nothing."

Raymond drew back.

"Why did you tell me that story?"

"What do you mean? You told me a story about love, and I told you one. That's all."

Actually, the story was mostly made up. My affair with the married woman had lasted less than a week, but I had embellished it because I always felt so outmatched by Raymond in our discussions about love and movies.

"I'll tell you why. Because you're so insecure. So you have to tell me all about your sweaty sexual adventures. But let me tell you something. I really feel sorry for you if this is the view of love your experience has given you."

SIXTY-THIRD AND KING DRIVE. *Sixty-fourth and King Drive. Sixty-fifth and King Drive.*

For three blocks I frantically pressed down on the gas pedal, but my car only sputtered and wheezed until the life completely drained out of it at Sixty-fifth and King Drive. It was an arctic Chicago morning in December. Far down the deserted street, I could see the swaying lights of a bus. The windshield of my car was beginning to ice over. I bundled up in my coat and ran across the street to a coffee shop. The place was crowded and noisy; everyone stared furtively at the white boy wearing a necktie with cheeks the color of a Red Delicious apple. I called the emergency road service from the pay phone, then squeezed into the only free space at the counter. A man a few seats down from me tipped his cap and smiled as if I were an old, familiar friend. I stared straight ahead. On the wall facing me were portraits of a honey-haired, blue-eyed Jesus and an airbrushed Martin Luther King gazing out as if heaven were just beyond the horizon. Between the two pictures was a hand-printed sign warning the patrons not to curse when ladies were present.

The only lady present was a stout, freckled, cinnamon-colored woman working behind the counter. Her style was more Sunday-school teacher than waitress, and she wielded her coffeepot like a Bible.

"Who was it lived in the land of Uz?" she asked the men at the counter, the pot poised above their heads.

They all stared down into their plates.

"You, Brother Jackson!" she said. "Don't you know?"

Mr. Jackson looked warily at the raised pot.

"Noah?" he ventured.

"No, it wasn't no Noah," she said, thumping the pot on the counter. "It was Job, a man of blameless and upright life."

She worked her way down the counter, pouring coffee and posing questions.

"How many criminals was crucified alongside of Jesus?"

"Two," said one of the men. "One on his left, the other on his right."

"That's better," she said. "That's better."

"What kind of easy questions y'all asking this morning, Sister Broadnax?" another man said. "Ask him what was the names of them two criminals."

"What names?" she replied, her eyes narrowing.

"Don't tell me you don't know."

"Well, what was they?" she demanded impatiently.

"Leroy and Marvin."

The whole counter exploded in laughter. I smiled into my coffee, having become invisible, except to the man three seats away, who had been staring at me from the moment I sat down. When the seat beside me became free, he moved over and sat down on it. I was suddenly enveloped in an odor of oil and sweat. His face was sprinkled with white stubble, his down vest and overalls spotted with dark, shiny stains.

"Morning," he said.

"Morning."

"Your name is Seth, right?"

"Yes. . . ."

"You don't remember me. My daughter introduced us at the graduation last spring."

"Yes, now I remember. You're Naomi Freeman's father. I'm sorry. I didn't recognize you."

"Well, I'm not wearing my Sunday best today. I just got off

work. The cold's froze up everybody's boilers. I don't usually work nights, but folks has to have heat. Oh, Mrs. Broadnax," he said to the woman behind the counter, "this boy here went to the divinity school with my daughter."

"You a preacher?" she asked me.

"Well, not exactly. . . ."

"You don't have a church?"

"No."

"Don't worry, honey. You still young. You'll get yourself a church soon enough."

There were some scattered amens from the men at the counter.

"We all belong to the Zion Baptist Church," Mr. Freeman explained. "Mrs. Broadnax is a deacon. She keeps us honest every morning."

"So I've noticed."

She held the pot above my head. "More coffee, Reverend?"

RAYMOND AND I AGREED NOT TO go to the movies anymore. "We're both too emotional for it," he said. He was over at my apartment, and I volunteered to go down the block for some beer.

"Rachel called just after you left," Raymond said when I got back.

My heart jumped; I hadn't heard from her since I had left California, close to a month ago. "Do you mind if I call her back?"

"Of course not."

I went into the bedroom and called her.

"You never told me Raymond was gay," she said.

"Raymond? Gay? Are you sure?"

"Of course he is, Seth."

"Did he tell you he was?"

"No, but I can just tell."

"Are you sure?"

"Seth, sweetie, he may be blind, but you're deaf."

I told her I'd call her back later. I knew that she was right, had probably known it all along, but hadn't been able to assimilate the fact into my world. Perhaps Raymond was right: I didn't have any imagination, certainly not the type of imagination I needed to negotiate my way through life.

I returned to the living room. "Raymond," I said, laughing, "Rachel thinks you're gay."

"Well, she ought to know, shouldn't she?" He crossed his legs and smiled.

"How come you never told me?"

"I thought you knew."

"How was I supposed to know?" Then, in exasperation, I added, "How do you know? You've never had sex!"

Raymond laughed, tried to say something, but was overcome with more laughter.

"What's so amusing?" I asked.

"'How do I know?' What is that supposed to mean?"

"I've had sex. You haven't. I mean, Rachel didn't know she was a lesbian until she slept with me."

"Well, that explains it then," he replied, collapsing into another paroxysm of laughter.

"Raymond. Shut up. Stop laughing at me."

"Seth, how do you know that I've never had sex anyway?"

"Because you told me you've never been in love."

"So? Have you been in love with every person you've had sex with?"

"Well, have you had sex?"

"You know, this is beginning to feel like a cross-examination. I don't know why it even matters."

"Because you've been dishonest with me."

"When?"

"When you told me you've never been in love. You knew I was talking about women."

He posture suddenly turned rigid.

"No, Seth. You were talking about blind people. You couldn't imagine a blind person as sexual. I'm sorry if you think I was being dishonest. But I really don't think I'm responsible for your ignorance."

He swigged the last of his beer, then found his way to the door, leaving me alone.

I DIDN'T TALK WITH RAYMOND FOR WEEKS. He didn't knock on my door; I didn't knock on his. When we both approached the building at the same time, I held the door open for him and he went by without a word. One day I walked past Sol's and noticed him sitting at a table by the window. He was eating salami on rye. I stared at him until I was dizzy with hunger.

I placed my order and proceeded through the line. In front of me a schoolboy, barely able to see over the counter, was testing the vocabulary of Sol's Vietnamese.

"Jap," he said experimentally.

"You chili dog!"

"Jap! Jap!" he said more boldly.

"You grape pop!"

"Kung-fu!" he shouted, and leapt into a martial arts stance, drawing one hand behind his head and waving the other in front of him as if he were casting a spell.

I ordered a root beer, but the juice man was so happy to see me that he called out, "Ya, jew-is!"

Raymond, his chin stained with mustard, stood up abruptly, grabbed his cane, and angrily beat his way out, leaving a half-eaten sandwich. The Vietnamese watched him with open-mouthed amazement.

ANGELA WASHBURN WAS NOT THE ONLY mother in the class, and all the other mothers banded together when one of the men, Tazama Sun, declared in a paper that landlords had the right not to rent apartments to women with children. "If I owned a building," he said, "I wouldn't allow no childrens. They noisy. They destroy the property. A man have a right to protect his investment." Tazama Sun had slanted eyes, a pencil-line mustache, and was partial to leather jackets and gold chains. I guessed he was in his early forties.

"Do you have childrens?" one of the women asked.

"Hell, no. What do I want with babies?"

"I know about men like you," Yvette Woolfolk said, her arms crossed high on her chest. "You the type I warn my daughter about. Y'all go crazy if you suspect your lady even looking at another man, but when she's pregnant with your baby, you out the door, yes you are."

"That's right, that's right," some of the other mothers chimed in.

Another woman objected. "Don't say all mens is like that. I been married twenty years to the sweetest man before Jesus."

"I didn't say all of them," Yvette Woolfolk replied. "Just ones like *Tarzan*."

Tazama Sun smiled and rocked back in his chair, tracing the line of his mustache with a thumb and forefinger.

Then one of the women looked at me. "How about you? How you treat your wife?"

I said that I wasn't married.

"But you so polite!"

"He real quiet, though."

"I bet he has himself lots of lady friends."

"How about it, Shapiro," Daryl said. "How many lady friends you have?"

I could feel my face turning bright red. Angela Washburn embraced her baby tightly and buried her face in his neck. I wanted to move to the back of the room, sit in the empty chair next to them, and tell her that I was in pain too.

"He so quiet," Daryl said, "you can hear a rat piss on cotton. But some ladies like that. Yes, they do. They like that a real lot."

I WAS EATING LUNCH at Sol's when something outside excited all the Vietnamese. They raced out to the sidewalk for a better look. Through the window I saw Raymond jerking his head around like an angry and frightened marionette. I left my lunch and went outside. The Vietnamese were laughing uproariously. The laughter agitated Raymond even more. He was cursing and swinging his cane violently around his feet like an erratic compass needle. Pedestrians stepped around him. Realizing he had momentarily lost the language to find his way home, I walked over to him. "Raymond," I said. He twisted around, his face in a commotion of fright and relief. We were silent for some seconds, all the words we could say to each other standing like a wall between us. Then, in my most intimate voice, I said, "Fifty-sixth and Stony Island. Fifty-sixth and Cornell. Cornell and Fifty-fifth. Cornell and Fifty-fourth. . . ."

AFTER BEING ABSENT FOR A WEEK, Angela Washburn and her baby were waiting outside my office.

"My baby been sick," she said. She paused, then added, "Ain't no one else I can leave him with."

The baby was resting on her shoulder, his eyes rheumy. I resisted an impulse to reach out and stroke his cheek.

"Is he better now?"

She looked me in the eye. "He all right," she said softly.

In my office, she read from a new composition. "Last winter after my baby was born we almost froze is the reason we got us a new apartment." The baby reached out to me. His fingers, centimeters from my nose, plied the air as if he were practicing piano scales.

I was on the verge of asking if they were warmer this winter. Is there no one else to stay with? Are you all alone, Angela? Is it just you and the baby? My palms were moist, and I could feel the blood rising in my neck, heating up my face. "Your trouble is caused by a faulty predicate. The linking verb 'to be' forms a sort of equation."

The baby wailed like a siren, his eyes screwed tightly shut, his forehead wrinkled from the strain. Don't cry, don't cry, I wanted to say, but these were not my words. Angela bounced him lightly on her lap, whispering in his ear, "Be cool, sugar. Be cool." When he didn't quiet down, she searched around in her purse, coming up empty-handed.

"I left his bottle in the car."

"You can leave him here if you want to get it."

She gave me a frantic, flustered look.

"Really. I can watch him."

She sat the baby down in the chair and went out. His wails became even louder. I waved and smiled at him, but to no avail. His face was a miniature portrait of agony and grief. I couldn't resist any longer. I got down on my knees and brought my face close to his. His cries ebbed, like a balloon slowly expelling air. His back eyelashes were matted with tears. He stared at me with glistening, wondrous, slightly crossed eyes as the huge, complex landscape of my face loomed in front of him. He reached out and grabbed my nose, the sweet fingers of his other hand brushing over my features with a spidery grace, as he emitted breathy, satisfied sounds. I closed my eyes and the world changed tenses: I was keenly aware of living in the present, aware of every inch of my face, of every follicle and cell, of being defined, shaped, loved. I heard his mother's footsteps coming down the hall. I knew I should open my eyes and stand up. But I didn't move a muscle. Even when I knew she was standing in the doorway, watching her baby hold my face in his hands.

PART

TWO

ORPHANS

• 1987–1989 •

On November 22, 1963, I turned seven years old and discovered a major fault line in my character. At approximately 1:15 the school principal, Mrs. Miller, charged into my classroom, crying out that the president had been shot. After a moment of shocked silence, I burst into laughter. Everyone turned to look at me. Then Wendy Feingold began laughing too, and so did Sven Bjornsson, and then Nina London joined in, and soon, like a contagion, all my classmates were convulsed with laughter. I felt exalted and criminal, pyromaniacal. I was notorious for my laugh, loud and honking, truly obnoxious—indeed, I had been sent to Mrs. Miller's office three times that year because of it—but she and my teacher, Mrs. Carmichael, only looked stunned. School was let out for the afternoon. On the streets, adults were crying everywhere. Even the automobiles appeared dazed, moving at the slow-motion pace of a funeral procession. I saw an old black man in a fedora crying at the wheel of his Oldsmobile, and I wondered if I was still going to have my birthday party later that afternoon. We had invited ten boys in my class and ten of Sarah's friends over to our apartment, and for weeks I had been anticipating the mayhem and presents, but when I arrived home, my mother was already there, sitting on the steps of our apartment building, rocking back and forth, her eyes bloodshot, a cigarette burning between her fingers. Unable to bear her sadness, I said that maybe it wasn't really President Kennedy who had been shot. She looked at me quizzically. Maybe, I theorized, it was his twin brother, Tom.

TWENTY-FIVE YEARS LATER, I DID it again: I burst out laughing during a bout of emotional vertigo at the most inappropriate moment possible. Molly Quinn, the love of my life, was eight weeks pregnant, and we were meeting with a clergyperson about marrying us. Near the end of the interview, when the Unitarian minister asked me why I loved Molly, I became tongue-tied. Molly gave me an alarmed, disbelieving look, which froze me even more. Finally, unable to bear the silence any longer, I turned to Molly and said, "Excuse me, but can you tell me your name again?" and then exploded into peals of laughter.

WE HAD MET THE YEAR BEFORE, in August 1987. I was in my rent-controlled apartment in Cambridge, watching a Red Sox game, when a woman called me up, introduced herself as Molly Quinn, and told me how much she loved my act after seeing me perform at a local comedy club.

"Really?" I replied. I was a competent comic, not an inspired one. But in the 1980s, comedy clubs were all the rage, and even a mediocre comic like me could get regular bookings. When I was still living in Chicago, I had enrolled in stand-up comedy and improvisation classes at the Second City, mainly as a way to get out of Hyde Park and meet women. I began going to comedy clubs religiously, studying the more polished comics, and getting on stage at amateur nights. I spent three hours every day writing material for a comedy act. I liked how it was so immediately rewarding: I could figure out the structure of a joke or monologue and get a laugh on stage that same night, and it was so easy to reinvent myself this way. By February of 1986, I was earning more money doing stand-up on weekends than I received in my monthly paycheck from Martin Luther King State. In June of that year, Aaron Zelman, my soon-to-be brother-in-law, told me that a friend of his was vacating his rent-controlled apartment in Central Square in Cambridge and it was mine if I wanted it. *Yes! Yes! Yes!* I replied. My lifelong dream of living in Cambridge would finally come true.

"Do you get many calls like this?" Molly asked.

"Oh, sure, all the time. My phone never stops ringing. One of these days I'm going to get an unpublished number. I'll just keep it in the drawer with my unpublished novels."

"You write novels too?"

"No, no, it was just a line. Not a very good one, though, I'm afraid. But I am a writer."

"What do you write?" she asked.

"Checks. But all of them are fiction."

Molly laughed politely, then said: "Look, I usually don't do things like this, but I'd really love to buy you a drink."

I didn't say anything for several seconds, as if this were something I really needed to think about, as if I might be better off spending another night alone in my apartment.

"Well, I can understand if you're not comfortable with this," Molly said. "You really don't know anything about me."

"What do you do?" I asked brightly.

"I'm a lawyer for the state Ways and Means Committee."

"Ways and Means?"

"Taxes."

"Oh, right, taxes!" I exclaimed, as if everything were suddenly clear to me.

TWO NIGHTS LATER I MET MOLLY at a bar in Harvard Square. I showed up five minutes late by design, at 7:35, but I didn't see anyone I thought might be Molly, or anyone I wanted to be Molly. I ordered a beer, wondering what type of woman would be attracted to my hapless comedy persona, especially if she was bold enough to call up a complete stranger and ask him out. I opened my act by telling the audience that just the other day I was standing behind a beautiful woman in line at the bakery. I badly wanted to strike up a conversation with her and rehearsed in my mind all the charming lines I knew, but I just couldn't get the words out. When she was nearing the cash register, I finally piped up:"Excuse me, but do you mind if I ask for your number?" "Sure," she said, and handed me the ticket she was holding.

Eight o'clock. My bladder was the size of a Persian melon, but I was afraid to go to the bathroom. What if Molly just happened to show up while I was peeing? She'd think I had given up on her, and we would never meet. Just then I noticed a slightly built woman with a great mane of auburn hair that flared a rich red when it caught the light standing in the doorway. Molly! I was so stunned by her beauty that I could only stare dumbly at her. Seeing me, she crossed her hands over her heart and I waved. As she approached, I extended my hand, but she leaned forward and kissed me on the cheek.

"Oh, Seth, thank God you're still here. I had a meeting that went on and on and I was afraid you might have given up on me."

"Really, all this time I was afraid that you had given up on me. I'm so relieved that we have something in common."

She appeared a little perplexed, as if not sure whether I was trying to be funny or serious. I had to admit, I didn't always know myself.

After we sat down and ordered drinks, I excused myself to go to the bathroom. The bar adjoined a fancy Middle Eastern restaurant. Approaching the bathroom, I noticed my father and Hortense leaving their table and heading in my direction. I had not seen them in eight years, since Sarah's graduation from Rutgers. I fled into the bathroom and hid in a stall. Since moving to Cambridge, I never left my apartment without expecting to run into my father—perhaps at a movie theater or a bookstore or maybe just crossing the street in Harvard Square. I was always aware of him, like some tune dimly playing in my head. Sitting on the toilet seat, holding my head in my hands, I thought: The one time I leave the house without expecting to see my father and I run into him. This had to mean something, but I was too flummoxed to figure it out. I stayed in the stall for ten minutes, just to be safe.

When I returned to the table, Molly asked if I was all right.

"Oh, I'm fine," I said. "I just saw my father and stepmother, that's all."

"Your family lives close by? How nice."

"No, see, the thing is I haven't seen them in eight years, so I was hiding in the bathroom."

Her eyes widened with puzzlement, and I wondered why I simply hadn't told her a small lie. I wouldn't even have needed to lie; I could have just smiled and nodded my head.

"It's complicated," I explained.

"You didn't even want to say hello?"

"I've always loved my father, but his wife, Hortense, is another matter. She's the stepmother from hell," I said, adding an anxious laugh.

She sipped her beer, then looked around the bar, as if an impostor Seth had returned from the bathroom and she was looking for the real one, the Seth she had conjured in her mind when she called me.

"I could tell you one of my cruel stepmother stories, but I'm afraid you wouldn't believe me."

"Try me."

So I told her one of my best Hortense stories—about the time at Wellfleet when she refused to give me a clean plate at dinner until I ate all of my leftover jam from breakfast. I'd told this story so many times that it had a lacquered sheen to it, but as she listened, Molly's eyes had a depth of sympathy that caught me off guard.

"Oh, Seth, that is cruel."

"Do you know the meanest thing Hortense ever said to me?"

"What?"

"She told me I would never have children," I said, leaving out her theory that I was too much of a child to have my own children. "Can you believe that?"

"Why would she say something like that?"

"Who knows? We were having some dumb argument about money. I mean, I was only twenty years old. Who's thinking about children at that age?"

"I'm sure you'll have children," she said. "You'll be a wonderful father."

"Thank you," I said, feeling as if I had won an award I hadn't applied for. "What about you? Are you close to your parents?"

"I'm an orphan," she replied, holding open two empty palms, as if to show me that she had nothing to hide, had nothing at all.

"Oh, Molly, I don't know what to say."

"That's all right," she told me, reaching for my hand, as if I was the one who needed comforting. "We've just met. You don't need to say anything."

She told me that her mother had died when she was two and her father had died when she was twelve.

"I can't imagine how difficult that was."

She squeezed my hand, blinked away a tear, and said, "It still is." She went on to tell me that she was raised by her aunt and uncle, who lived in the same North Cambridge neighborhood her parents had, and that her aunt and uncle's household was large and loving. "All my cousins were like sisters to me. I've always wanted a big family myself," she confided. I confessed to her that as a child I'd had fantasies that my true parents—a sane, rich, and loving couple—would show up one day and rescue me.

"Seth, I have a small confession."

Our knees were pressed together under the table, and we were still holding hands.

"Oh," I said. It was either going to be a boyfriend or herpes, I thought. With my luck, probably both.

"It's not a big deal," she said. "I just wanted to tell you that I actually went to see your show three times before I could get up the courage to call you."

"Three times!" I cried, mortified. "I can't believe you heard my dumb lines three times."

"The third time I brought my cousin Nora with me. When you came on stage, I said, 'That's the man I'm going to marry some-day.' Nora said, 'Well, I suggest you call him and let him know.'"

I felt both exposed and absolved. "Is that a proposal?" I asked.

"No, I'm an old-fashioned girl. I expect the man to get down on his knees and propose."

"What did you think I would be like?"

"What you would be like?"

"After coming to my show three times. What did you think I would be like in real life?"

She looked down at the table for a moment, then gazed into my eyes. "I thought you would be very kind."

WE KISSED FOR A LONG TIME outside her apartment building. This was always the moment of a date I dreaded—to kiss or not to kiss. If you didn't kiss, if you looked at the other person knowing you felt absolutely nothing, well, then you went home feeling more unlovable than you did before you left the house. Sometimes I thought it was better just to kiss in order to inoculate yourself against such feelings, to maintain the illusion that, yes, you did have a very good time and maybe you would see each other again. But when Molly and I reached the door of her building, I knew that we would kiss. Oh, and what kisses! Long and lovely kisses.

After ten minutes, Molly had opened all but one button of my shirt and was pressing her lips against my collarbone.

"Maybe you should invite me in?" I said, a little breathlessly.

She looked at my exposed torso and laughed, as if she had just become aware that she was in the process of stripping me in the street. She put her hands inside my shirt and circled my waist with her arms.

"Oh, Jesus, Mary, and Joseph," she said in a low voice, "I didn't expect that I would be this attracted to you."

"I feel like I've just inhaled a canister of nitrous oxide."

She held me tighter and laid her head against my chest.

"Tell me," she said. "What did you think I would be like when I called you? Did you think I would be a lunatic or something?"

Was this a test? Give the right answer and I'd get to come in and live happily ever after with her? "I thought the woman I had been waiting for all my life had finally called me," I said.

She burst out laughing, a deep, soulful laugh enriched with affection, a laugh that could move a heart.

"You don't believe me?"

"No, but that's one of the sweetest lines I've heard in a long time."

"Oh," I said.

After opening my act with the story about standing in line behind the beautiful woman at the bakery, I would tell the audience that I had recently read a magazine article about highly functioning autistic adults. They hold down responsible jobs, appear normal in every way, but they never form any romantic attachments because they are dumbfounded by the subtleties and nuances of courtship. "Maybe that's my problem," I would say. "It's not me! It's a neurological disorder!"

"Don't look so concerned, Seth. I'm glad you said it."

"Does that mean I get to come in?"

She pulled down on the collar of my shirt and gave me an exasperated, what-am-I-going-to-do-with-you look. Then she closed her eyes and kissed me on the mouth, perhaps hoping I would turn into a prince.

"Yes," she said. "Come in, come in."

"I HAVEN'T DONE THIS IN A LONG TIME," she said.

We were lying next to each other on her bed.

"How long?" I asked.

"Two years. Maybe longer."

"Actually, it's been a long time for me too," I admitted.

"How long?"

"November 27, 1984." That was the night of Rachel's mother's funeral.

"You remember the date!"

"I'm strange in that way."

"I don't think that's strange. I think it's nice."

She turned out the light to remove her clothes. When I pulled back the sheet to look at her, she covered herself with her forearm and hand, like Botticelli's Venus, a gesture that stirred me deeply: She was as private as a night-blooming flower, and allowing me into her bed, into her life, I realized, was an act of faith.

Her breath was warm against my ear, and I felt as if every cell in my body had awoken after a long hibernation. As I traced the rim of her ear with my tongue her whole body shuddered. "Oy, oy, oy," she half sighed, half moaned.

"Oy, oy, oy?" I murmured in her ear. "What happened to Jesus, Mary, and Joseph? Are you converting already?"

"Keep kissing me like that," she said, "and you'll have me speaking in tongues."

"Where do you like to be kissed the most?"

"I don't think I can say it."

"Why not?"

"Twelve years of Catholic school."

"I see," I replied, not sure if I liked where the conversation was going. "Do you know I have a PhD in divinity from the University of Chicago?"

"Are you serious?"

"Totally."

"Oh," she said sullenly.

"You're not turned on? Women are usually so excited when I tell them that."

"Do you believe in God?" she asked me.

"I don't know. I don't know what I believe, to tell you the truth."

"I don't believe in God," she said.

"Any reason why?"

"Twelve years of Catholic school."

"Do you know how I learned to be such a great kisser?"

"How?"

"Twelve years of Catholic school."

"Shut up!" she replied, laughing.

"How about if I try to guess where you like to be kissed?"

"Good deal."

I kissed one breast, then the other, then kissed my way down the rungs of her rib cage and the white downy plain of her midriff.

"Am I getting close?"

"Yes. Very."

My tongue traveled lower. I eyed her face, but she had covered it with both hands, looking very much as if she were reciting the blessing over Sabbath candles.

"Oh, yes, good guess," she murmured. "Oh, yes! Good guess. Yes! Very good guess!"

We fell asleep that night in a damp embrace. When I woke in the morning, my hand was still cupping one of her small breasts, light and round as a Rome apple. I spent the next night in her bed too, and the one after that, and the one after that, and every morning we awoke so attached to each other's bodies, so in love, that I believed some vital ether must have passed between our pores all through the night, binding us together.

How suddenly a life can change! One night I was sitting alone and unloved in my apartment, the next night a woman cold-called me, and a month later I was living with her. We settled into a charmed routine: In the mornings I would write material for my act, but true inspiration usually struck later in the afternoon, when I went out and bought flowers, bread, wine, and ingredients for dinner at the pricey West Cambridge shops near Molly's apartment. Before we met, Molly had always worked late because she didn't like facing all those hours alone in her apartment, but now she left promptly at five, knowing that I was waiting for her with an abundance of kisses and kindness. At six o'clock, I would station myself by the bedroom window to catch sight of her coming down the street. She always appeared dazed and bereft, her gait slow, her steps small and timid, her arms crossed tightly across her chest. I thought of this as her orphan's stroll, and in that moment, repeated every day, I understood what had brought us together: we were two foundlings who had found each other; we had created a home that could keep an orphan safe in a world of death and loss.

SUNDAY NIGHTS WE HAD DINNER at her aunt and uncle's house in North Cambridge along with her cousins, Nora, Bridget, and Franny, and their families—a total of ten adults and seven children. I had never encountered a family more different from my own: Large, loving, close, voluble, immune to slights or arguments, they all joked and kidded without anyone getting offended. Throughout dinner, Molly would hold my hand under the table.

Her uncle John, a retired postal worker, sat at the head of the table, the object of his daughters' love and adoration. Behind him, on the dining-room wall, a holy triptych looked down on us: portraits of Pope John Paul II, John F. Kennedy, and Tip O'Neill, who had been Uncle John's childhood neighbor and friend. The first time I came to dinner, he told me a long story about how both their grandfathers had been brought over from Ireland in 1845 by the New England Brick Company. A local politician named Paddy Mullen had met their boat, brought them straight to City Hall, and registered them to vote. "On election day," John said, "he met them at the polls and handed them each a ballot. Since they couldn't read or write, he was kind enough to complete the ballot for them before they went in." No doubt his daughters had all heard this story a hundred times, but everyone in the family paid rapt and affectionate attention.

I wanted in on the storytelling too, wanted in on the adoration, wanted in on the Quinn clan, this family God had seemingly created in the opposite image of my own, but when I said to everyone in the room, "Do you know I turned seven years old on the day JFK was assassinated?" Molly stepped on my foot under the table. The Quinns all appeared a little puzzled, and Nora, who had seen my act and heard my Kennedy assassination story, shot me a look of concern. "That's why I'll always remember that day," I said, "November 22, 1963." Uncle John and Aunt Jean nodded solemnly.

In my act, I had changed the story so that I burst into tears upon hearing the news of Kennedy's death. No one in the class knows that I'm really crying because I'm sure my birthday party is going to be cancelled, and the principal and my teacher try to console me. Suddenly I know how it feels to be the most esteemed child in the class, and I let the tears rain down. My grief is contagious. All of my classmates start crying too, twenty-five first graders ululating over our dead president. "I loved President Kennedy," I cry out, and the other children cry that they loved President Kennedy too. My teacher and principal pat my back. I imagine the glowing report my parents are going to receive about my reaction, and I refuse to be consoled. "Seth, everything is going to be fine," my teacher says. "No, it's not!" I shout. "Who's going to help the Negroes and poor people now?" My classmates wail uncontrollably.

When I told Molly the actual story, she commented that she liked it better. "I think it's so sweet the way you tried to ease your mother's sadness. Actually, you're a lot nicer to your mother in the stories you tell about her than you are to her in real life." Molly was shocked the first time she heard me talk with my mother over the phone: My tone was impatient and irritable, my voice admonishing. Molly said I sounded like an angry parent.

ONE SATURDAY NIGHT THE QUINN CLAN came to see me perform— nine Quinns sat at a table, laughing more loudly and energetically than any other people in the audience. They all looked at each other when they laughed, as if they couldn't believe how funny I was, couldn't believe that they actually knew me. At Molly's suggestion, I edited out my riff on my childhood reaction to the Kennedy assassination. The day after they came to see me perform, all the Quinns repeated their favorite moments from my routine at Sunday dinner. They kidded Molly's Uncle John for not getting my PMS line. I had told the audience that I'd always had a problem merging into rotaries until I ordered new vanity license plates that said PMS. Now all the cars yielded to me.

"PMS?" John said bewildered.

"Premenstrual syndrome, Daddy," Nora explained.

"I still don't understand," he said.

"Daddy," Bridget said, "don't you remember how we all knew Franny was about to get her period because she had such bad temper tantrums? If anyone looked at her the wrong way, we'd have to retreat for cover under the dining-room table."

"Watch it, Bridget," Franny growled, holding her plate like a Frisbee, "or I'll PMS you!"

Everyone laughed and John's face turned red as he finally understood. Then he coughed out a laugh and said, "Good one, Seth," clapping me on the back.

The next Sunday when we arrived for dinner, John couldn't wait to show me something. He led me, Molly, and his three daughters outside and directed us to look at the back of his car. He had taped a piece of cardboard over his license plate and

written PMS on it in bright red Magic Marker. His three daughters and Molly all burst out laughing.

"Good one, Daddy!" Franny shouted.

"Let's test it out before it gets dark," John said.

The four women all piled into the backseat of his Buick; I had
no choice but to get in the front. He was seventy-three years old,
had had cataract surgery less than a year earlier, and his eyes
were magnified to the size of silver dollars behind his coke-bottle
lenses. Within two minutes we were on the Alewife Parkway,
headed for the rotary. Not bothering to slow down, John sped
through the rotary at thirty miles an hour. Car horns blasted us.
The women were all laughing in the back while I cried, "Jesus!"
and "Watch out!" John was tranquil as a Buddha.

"Aren't you worried about the police?" I asked.

"Daddy knows all the policemen in Cambridge, don't you
Daddy?" Nora said.

"That's right," he replied. "Every one of them."

His daughters thought this was hilarious too, and their peals of
laughter almost drowned out the car horns as he drove through
the next rotary at full speed. Molly put her hand on his shoulder.
"I think Seth is ready to go home, Uncle John."

"Seth," John said to me, "these letters work like a charm.
I'm calling my friend Tommy Cullen at the DMV tomorrow and
ordering new plates."

That night in bed Molly thanked me for being such a good sport.

"It wasn't some kind of test?" I asked.

"What type of test?"

"I don't know. To see how much of a Quinn I can be."

"Everyone adores you," she said. "They're all happy for me."

We twined our limbs together.

"How come no one says anything to your uncle about his
driving?"

"He's very proud. Besides, he's the dad. We don't question our fathers."

I asked her if she was ever tempted to call her aunt and uncle "Mom" and "Dad."

"Why do you ask?"

I told her that it struck me as a little sad when I heard her cousins call them "Mom" and "Daddy" while she had to call them something else. "It's like they have something that you don't."

"They do," she said.

I SPENT SATURDAY AFTERNOONS IN my own apartment. When Aaron had told me about it, I had agreed to rent it sight unseen, but I practically swooned the first time I saw it: a dazzle of gleaming pine floors, sunlight, and built-in bookshelves. It was small—a studio with an alcove study—but rent was stabilized at two hundred and fifty dollars a month. Of all the places I had lived—my claustrophobic, two-bedroom childhood apartment; my graduate-student hovel—this bright and airy Cambridge apartment, close to Harvard Square, minutes from the Charles River, was the first home that I had never wanted to leave.

When I went to my apartment, I told Molly I was polishing lines for my act and visiting Mara, my neighbor and best friend, but really I just wanted to be in my own place, to see my own books and my own prints on the wall, to have lunch by myself at one of the Indian restaurants down the street, then stroll down Massachusetts Avenue to Harvard Square and spend a couple of hours in the bookstores before walking back home along the Charles, past the roller skaters and scullers, past the slanting sailboats and the view of the golden-domed statehouse and the John Hancock Tower—a view that always provided a jolt of joy because it reminded me that I was no longer in the Midwest—and then napping for another couple of hours before I went to the clubs. I wanted some time to retreat into my routine, retreat into myself, to be reminded that my apartment, this home, was still waiting for me if I needed it.

I had met Mara a week after I had moved into my apartment in 1986. I was returning home from the Bread and Circus down the street when I saw a woman propping herself up against my door and vomiting.

"Are you all right?" I asked.

She didn't answer my question. "I'm Mara Pearl," she said. "I live on the fourth floor."

"Seth Shapiro," I said. "Do you always introduce yourself to your neighbors by puking in front of their doors?"

"No, usually I pee."

We both laughed, and I invited her in. She had wild, kinky hair, wire-rimmed glasses, and a gold wedding band on her finger.

I offered her tea or juice, but she said she was famished. I put together a plate of cheese, crackers, apple slices, and chopped liver. Despite being extremely thin and having just vomited, she practically inhaled the cheese and apples.

"This Bread and Circus chopped liver is excellent," I said, offering her some on a cracker.

She told me she was vegetarian. Then she asked what I did for a living.

"Stand-up comedy."

"No kidding! I do stand-up too!"

"For a living?"

"No, it's more of a hobby, a nostalgic thing. My family owned a small hotel in the Catskills and I always wanted to be a comic."

"Do you have a day job?"

"I'm a physicist. I teach at MIT."

"Oh, my," I said. "That's what I'd call a serious day job."

"Well, I probably won't be doing it for long. I'm coming up for tenure in a year, and my chances don't look good."

"Why not?"

"I'm orthodox. I don't work on Shabbat. I'm going up against colleagues who have barely left the lab in seven years. They've put in three hundred and sixty-four more days than I have. I'm a year behind all my competition."

I asked her what her research was on.

"Absolute time." She spent about five minutes explaining the theory to me, after which my brain felt like a shriveled frozen pea.

She had eaten all the cheese and apples and was eyeing the chopped liver. "Are you sure you don't want to try it?"

"Oh, why not?" she said, and slathered some on a cracker. "Oh, this is heavenly!"

I asked Mara what it was like growing up in the Catskills, and she became very animated, telling stories about some of the long-time guests at the hotel her parents owned, and then doing hilarious imitations of them. I complimented her on her great Yiddish accent. "Yes, just another of my many useful skills," she replied drily, but she was smiling, and I could see that the compliment pleased her. Then she said that she had lived in the town of Bethel, where the Woodstock concert was held.

"Wait a minute!" I said. "Did your mother let a girl named Zelda spend the night during Woodstock?"

Mara's eyes widened behind her glasses. "No!" she exclaimed. "You're that Seth?"

"You're that Mara?"

We both laughed and embraced each other, like long-lost relatives finally reunited.

"Oh, God, I gave that Zelda so much grief," Mara said. "I lectured her about how the counterculture was just an excuse for being hedonistic and self-centered. I told her all the true revolutionaries were the scientists at NASA. She kept telling me about this boy named Seth she had met on Cape Cod and how the two of us were exactly alike and that we had to meet. She actually gave me your address. Of course I never wrote to you. To think I might have had a real friend when I was a teenager."

"You wouldn't have wanted to know me when I was a teenager," I said. "Did you have any friends when you were a teenager?"

"Not a one!" she said, as if this were a point of pride for her. "But I'm so glad we finally met. Zelda told me that you and I were soul mates, and now you're here."

I squeezed her hand, and suddenly she began crying, leaning her forehead against the palm of her free hand.

"Mara, what's the matter?"

"I'm pregnant," she said. "I didn't know for sure until today."

"You don't want to be pregnant?"

"No. My husband spends every waking moment in his lab. He's going to want me to have an abortion because we don't have the time or money for a baby, but of course I'm not going to get an abortion, and that's going to strain an already bad marriage." She used her index finger to clean out the last of the chopped liver from the container.

"Why did you marry your husband?" I asked her.

"I'm very impressed by credentials."

I told her that I had a PhD from the University of Chicago.

"Are you coming on to me?" she asked.

"Not very seriously."

"Good," she said. "I need a friend."

"Me too," I told her.

MY FAMILY AND MOLLY'S decided to celebrate Thanksgiving together at Aunt Jean and Uncle John's house in Cambridge. My mother, Sarah, and Aaron drove up from New Jersey. Seamus declined to come. My mother said it was because he couldn't eat the food, but I didn't believe her and called him up.

"This is because Molly isn't Jewish," I said to him.

"I am uncomfortable with it, yes," he said.

"What if we get married? Are you going to refuse to come to the wedding?"

"Have you proposed to her?"

"No, but I might."

"I'll believe it when I see it."

"What is that supposed to mean?"

"You're not the most serious person, Seth. I really can't see you as a married man."

"You know why you became an Orthodox Jew, don't you, Seamus?"

"Tell me," he said.

"Because of your name. *Seamus Shapiro.* It deeply traumatized you, and your orthodoxy is just a way to normalize your identity."

He hung up.

As Molly and I drove to her aunt and uncle's, I asked, "Who are the Pilgrims, and who are the Indians?"

"Relax, Seth. Everything will be fine."

Molly was meeting my mother for the first time.

"Well, I guess we'll know a year from now when we see which family dies from smallpox."

Molly laughed. "That's bad," she said. "Really bad."

"What's bad? Me or the punch line?"

Despite my anxiety, everyone got along famously, especially my mother and Aunt Jean, who shared a love of cigarettes and books. The day felt very much like an official coming out for Molly and me, the bringing together of our two families. Since

Sarah's and my birthday was so close to Thanksgiving, we celebrated that occasion too, and I was deeply moved that everyone
in Molly's family had bought gifts—not just for me but for Sarah
too—and beautiful gifts at that: hardcover books, sweaters, earrings, pottery. It was far and away the best Thanksgiving I ever
had. What a bounty of food and love! My mother did pretty well
until the end of the meal when, relaxed by three glasses of wine
and the graciousness and good humor of the Quinns, she decided
to tell the story "Was Anybody Praying?" As soon as she began,
I kicked her hard under the table. "Ouch!" she cried. "Why did
you kick me?"

Then Sarah chimed in: "Mom, don't tell that story at the table."

Our mother took a swig of her fourth glass of wine and gave
Sarah a Bronx cheer.

"Sarah is right," I said. "Now is not the time." I knew that
Molly had told her cousins about the way I treated my mother,
but they all looked shocked.

"Oh, stop raining on my parade," my mother said, and
proceeded to tell everyone the story of how Sarah and I were
born premature, with our umbilical cords twisted around our
necks. All the Quinns smiled politely when my mother included
the detail about the doctor sucking a plug of mucus out of my
windpipe.

After dinner, we retreated to different areas of the house with
our coffee and drinks. My mother claimed Molly and went off in
a corner with her. Sarah and I were sitting at the opposite end of
the living room.

"God, what do you think Mom is saying to Molly?" I asked.

"Do you want me to see if I can read her lips?" Sarah replied.

"Sure. If you can."

Sarah studied our mother for a moment, then said, "She's telling Molly about your first well-formed bowel movement."

"Shut up," I said, punching her lightly on the shoulder.

"Don't worry about Mom. Molly glows around you."

"Do you think I should marry her?" I asked.

"Of course," Sarah said. "What are you waiting for?"

"Oh, I don't know. Everything is so great that I keep expecting something bad is going to happen."

"Like what?"

"Like I'll be discovered, found out."

"What do you think she's going to discover about you?"

"That I'm not worthy. That I'm too strange for anyone to love me."

"The feeling never goes away, Seth."

"You still feel that way? With Aaron?" Aaron was a prince, sane and stable, his whole life devoted to my sister.

"Every day," she answered.

I found this oddly comforting, a reminder that my sister and I shared more than a similar chromosomal profile.

Later that night, I resolved to propose. Molly and I were in bed, lying in each other's arms. I wasn't on my knees, but wasn't this even better—our bodies bound together in a golden postcoital glow? I was about to pop the question when Molly said, "Seth, your mother said something really strange to me."

"What?"

"She made me promise not to tell you, but it was so bizarre I have to say something."

"Yes?"

"She told me to get pregnant so you would have to marry me."

"What did you say to her?"

"I told her that's not how I prefer to do things."

"How did the subject come up?"

"She asked me if we were serious about each other, and I said yes."

"God, I don't believe that woman."

"Seth, promise me you won't tell her I told you. I promised her I wouldn't say anything to you."

"I won't say anything. Not a word."

A WEEK BEFORE CHRISTMAS, I was sitting up in bed on a Sunday morning, reading the paper, sipping coffee, when Molly stepped out of the shower, one small towel turbaned around her head, a larger towel wrapped around her body, and a damp, lemony scent wafting from her. She sat beside me and said, "Seth, honey, I'm late this month."

"Late?"

"My period."

I put my cup down on the night table. "Oh, right. Your period. Can you do a pregnancy test or something?"

"I'm doing one right now. I bought the test yesterday. We'll know in about two minutes." We exchanged anxious smiles and she went back into the bathroom.

Though I knew it was completely irrational, I immediately imagined that my mother had had something to do with it, as if she were a lonely old woman from a fairy tale who turned out to be a magical helper.

Molly returned from the bathroom. I moved to the end of the bed, and she sat on my lap, holding the test.

"Does this circle look blue to you?" she asked.

"Yes, very blue."

"It is blue, Seth! I'm sure I'm pregnant. I've been nauseous all week. I'm never late. This has to be blue!"

She began laughing and crying simultaneously.

"Does this mean you're happy about it?" I asked.

"Yes, yes. Very happy . . . and you?"

"Well, it's certainly a surprise," I said, but I realized that I really was happy, as if my deepest longings—for a family, for a life with Molly—had their own subterranean life and were suddenly erupting from the ground. "But, yes, I'm happy. Truly happy."

We embraced, her cheeks damp against my face.

With my lips against her ear, I said, "So, I guess this means we'll be getting married."

She pulled back. "Is that a proposal?"

"Yes."

"Can you do a little better?"

"Oh, yes, of course," I said, thankful for the prompt. I told Molly to stand up. As her towel fell away, I knelt down and seized her hand. Looking up at her body, white and coppery, positively luminous, I proposed: "Molly, I love you more than words can say. I want to spend my life with you. You are truly, in every way possible, the woman I've been waiting for all my life, and that's no line!"

THE BABY WAS DUE IN LATE SEPTEMBER, and we planned on a May wedding. Of course I was dreading the call to my mother, and of course she let out a cry of joy when I delivered the news that we were engaged. I knew I was going to have to tell her sooner or later that Molly was pregnant, so I decided on sooner.

"By the way, Mom, Molly is pregnant."

"When did that happen?" she exclaimed.

"When we were having sex."

"No, I mean when did you know she was pregnant?"

"Two days ago."

I sensed her doing the math.

"Did Molly say anything to you?"

"About what?"

"Nothing. Is she there? I'd like to congratulate her."

I put my hand over the receiver and called out to Molly to pick up in the other room.

"Hello?" she said.

"Oh, Molly, sweetheart, I'm so happy for you!"

"Thank you, Ruth. We couldn't be happier."

"Seth?"

"Yes, Mom."

"You can go now. I want to talk to my new daughter-in-law."

"Bye, Mom," I said. I put my hand over the mouthpiece and pressed down, then let go of the button.

"Molly?" my mother said conspiratorially.

"Hi, Ruth."

"You didn't tell Seth what I said to you at Thanksgiving, did you?"

"No."

"Well, see, I was right, wasn't I? He has to marry you because you're pregnant."

"I hope he's doing it because he wants to, not because he has to."

"Of course, of course. Oh, Molly, honey, I'm so happy I could crow! I want you to know that I consider you more than just a daughter-in-law. I want you to know that you can think of me as your mother."

Molly didn't say anything.

"Molly?"

"Yes?"

"Did I say something wrong?"

I could barely keep myself from interrupting and saying, *Yes, you said something wrong!*

"No, Ruth. Thank you very much."

"I mean it, darling. You can call me Mother."

"Ruth."

"Yes, doll?"

"Seth wants to speak to you."

Molly called out to me. I depressed the button on the phone and removed my hand from the mouthpiece.

"Hello?"

"Goodbye, Ruth," Molly said.

"Goodbye, doll. I love you."

Molly hung up.

"Seth?"

"Yes. I'm here."

"Molly said you wanted me."

"Oh, right. I just wanted to say good-bye."

"Good-bye, honey boy. I love you."

"Bye, Mom."

I went into the bedroom. Molly was lying under the covers, crying quietly.

"Molly, what's the matter?" I said. "What did she say to you?"

"Nothing. She didn't say anything."

It was the first time we hadn't been completely honest with each other, and it felt as if a small breach had opened up between us, a sudden coldness, like a draft from a window.

CHRISTMAS REJUVENATED US. The only time we had discussed our different religions was in reference to Christmas. Molly told me she didn't care about the religion of our children, but Christmas was important to her, and when we were married with children, she wanted to have a Christmas tree and exchange presents on Christmas morning. "Fine with me," I said. "The tree, the presents, the carols. We'll do the whole megillah." We bought a tree together at a local farm stand. I enjoyed the bracing nip in the air, the piney scents, the hot cider. All my life I had experienced Christmas as an outsider, and, I had to admit, it felt nice to be an insider, to be among the tree buying, present-shopping Christian hordes. At home, Molly brought out boxes of Christmas accoutrements: a tree stand, ornaments, stockings. We positioned the tree by the window. Molly put on a tape of Elvis singing Christmas songs, and poured us both mugs of hot cider, and we spent the evening decorating the tree. She told me that most of the ornaments had belonged to her mother; on the top of the tree we placed a wooden angel that had belonged to her mother's mother.

Christmas morning we exchanged presents. I was overwhelmed by all the presents she had bought for me: a beautiful pale green cashmere sweater ("to match your eyes," she said), books, Celtics tickets, and my very first compact disc: Marvin Gaye's *Midnight Love*. "What am I going to play this on?" I asked, and she handed me another present. Of course I knew it would be a CD player. "Molly, this is too much!" I protested, though in fact I was thrilled at being the recipient of so much generosity.

"Well, it's really for both of us," she explained. I handed her my present—a small square box—and said, "This is just for you."

Immediately her eyes welled up with tears. I hadn't given her a ring yet, and I knew she had been wondering if I would get around to it. She opened the box and removed a thin gold band with a pear-shaped, many-faceted diamond set in it. Tears coursed down her cheeks. "Seth, this probably cost you a fortune. How could you afford this?"

"I paid for it with my bar mitzvah money," I replied.

She gave me one of those bemused looks that meant she wasn't sure whether I was being funny or serious.

"I'm completely serious," I said. "I haven't touched that bank account in nearly eighteen years and it was worth more than five thousand dollars."

Molly plugged in the CD player and put in the disc. Marvin

Gaye's sexy, silky falsetto sang "Sexual Healing." She pulled me close, leaned forward on her tiptoes, and began tracing the rim of my ear with her tongue. At that moment, my happiness was so divine that I believed I could feel my soul bursting free of my body.

NOT LONG AFTER THE NEW YEAR, Molly had a proposal for me: She wanted me to quit comedy.

"Why would I want to do that?"

"To have a job with more normal hours once the baby comes. You're out late every night. I'd rather not be home alone when I'm getting up all night with a new baby."

"I see," I said. "I see."

"Seth, we can't do anything on weekends because you're always performing. I'd like to be able to go to a movie on a Saturday night or go away to Vermont for a weekend. I just want our relationship to be more normal."

Normal? I thought. *What are you doing with me if you wanted normal?* But wasn't that what I wanted too? Wasn't that what I envied about Sarah and Aaron? Wasn't that the reason Seamus turned Orthodox? Wasn't that why I had resolved to propose to Molly on Thanksgiving?

"So if I quit comedy, our life will feel more normal to you?"

"Yes."

"Well, I'm not exactly blazing my way to greatness."

Molly nodded her head.

"Come on!" I protested. "Didn't they teach you to tell little lies in Catholic school?"

"We don't believe in little lies. A lie is a lie."

"I see," I said again, as if this might be a potential problem for us. "You don't like the fact that I'm a comic, do you?"

"Seth, I fell in love with you when I saw you onstage."

"Remember," I said, "no little lies. A side of you disapproves of my comedy."

She looked at me thoughtfully, carefully considering her words.

"You have a PhD from the University of Chicago. I think you can do something more meaningful with your life."

She had the moral authority to say this, since she could have used her extensive knowledge of the tax code to earn big bucks in the service of a private law firm rather than in the service of the Commonwealth of Massachusetts.

"So what do you have in mind for me?" I asked. "Become a house husband?"

"No, this." She showed me a brochure for a private school called Back Bay Academy. She told me that her friend Amy taught at the school and that one of the English teachers there had fallen ill (with AIDS, she added sadly) and the school needed an immediate replacement.

"You want me to teach high school?"

"Look in the back," she said. "Virtually all the teachers have PhD's. Amy tells me it's not much different from teaching at a small liberal arts college."

I looked at the faculty profiles: Not only did they all have PhD's, but most of them were from Harvard and Yale. I told Molly that I might be underqualified to teach at this high school.

"You might actually like it," Molly said. "You have a wonderful capacity for nurturing, Seth. It's what I love most about you."

"You mean like John Wayne after he discovers Natalie Wood in *The Searchers*?"

"Exactly!"

We had recently purchased a VCR, and one of the first movies I rented was *The Searchers*. I plagiarized all of Raymond's best lines. *John Wayne discovers his capacity for nurturing and love. He becomes a whole person.* If Raymond supplied the content,

I supplied the context. I told Molly that was the story of our relationship: I was like John Wayne—surly, lonely, unloved, and unlovable—and then I found her and discovered my capacity for nurturing and love. She completed me, helped me become a whole person. Molly had told me that was the most beautiful thing anyone had ever said to her.

"Sure, why not?" I said.

"Here's the application."

The school required a recent writing sample. Since the only things I had written recently were one-liners for my act, I looked through the box where I kept all my old graduate-school and undergraduate papers. I tried rereading my PhD thesis, but it was about as enjoyable to me as eating from a box of cornstarch. I read through some of my graduate-school papers, but got bored after a page or two of each one. Near the bottom of the box, I found a copy of "A Stranger on the Planet." I was immediately drawn in by the story, feeling as if I were reading the transcript of a dream about my mother and me. After I read the last sentence, I felt a curdling in my heart: This story was the most meaningful thing I had accomplished in my life, and I had kept it closed up in a box for nearly ten years. I had turned my life into a joke. Literally.

Two days after I sent in my application, I received a phone call from the headmaster of Back Bay Academy, Dr. Archibald Merritt. He told me that I was ideal for the position and that it was indeed splendid serendipity that I could begin right away. In my application letter, I had whited out my last two years as a stand-up comic and said that I had been subsisting on a small inheritance in order to write full-time, but that I would need to look for employment in the next month.

"We all thoroughly loved your story," Dr. Merritt said. "Do you plan on sending it out?"

In the application, I had said that "A Stranger on the Planet" was my most recent story, which, of course, was technically true. "Yes."

"Where to? The *New Yorker*? The *Atlantic*?"

"Yes," I replied. "The *New Yorker* and the *Atlantic*."

The next day I showed up for my interview. The school occupied two brownstones of prime real estate in the Back Bay. As I would later learn, everything was made possible by Dr. Merritt's family fortune, which he had used to found the school in the 1950s. The school didn't require a uniform, but the students all looked the same anyway: They favored an androgynous look, as if they were trying to efface both their sexuality and their privilege, perhaps attempting to trample on the Brahmin spirits that had once trod up and down the same marble staircases in this beautiful building. During my tour of the school, Dr. Merritt took me to visit a class. The students were all brilliant, all business, eight of them sitting around an oval seminar table discussing the "Box Hill" chapter of *Emma*. Outside the windows, I could see sailboats moored in their slips along the Charles River. I knew that Dr. Merritt would offer me a job, and as I gazed at the view, my heart exhaled with relief: I would never step on a stage again.

I LOVED TEACHING AT BACK BAY ACADEMY. Molly had been right: The work was far more rewarding than stand-up comedy, and our lives felt blissfully normal and rich. I loved waking up at the same time as Molly every morning, loved sharing the shower with her, loved hearing her purr as I massaged shampoo into her scalp and slowly soaped her body, loved having breakfast together, loved putting on a tie and coat and leaving the house with a briefcase in my hand. I especially loved my commute. I drove my car to the Alewife T stop, where I parked it, and rode the Red Line to Charles Street. Riding the train, I always envisioned myself through my father's eyes, imagining him, twenty years before, watching a movie about my adult life. He would see me wake up next to Molly, my beautiful wife, would see us leaving the house together in a neighborhood recognizable as West Cambridge. He would see me get on the subway in my coat and tie, a briefcase at my side, blending in with all the other commuters—the professors, administrators, secretaries, and students who would be getting off at Harvard. Would I be getting off at Harvard too? No. I keep riding the train, which, past MIT, becomes crowded with doctors, residents, interns, nurses, and patients getting off at Charles Street. I get off at this stop too and move with the crowd in the direction of Massachusetts General Hospital. Could it be possible? Could I be a doctor? But I head off in a different direction, down Charles Street, then hike up one of the side streets and stroll past the beautiful nineteenth-century homes in Louisburg Square. I enter a brownstone on Commonwealth Avenue, a place that's clearly recognizable as an exclusive school, and he sees me go into a small classroom with wood-paneled walls and a baroque chandelier. I sit at a seminar table and lead a masterful discussion of *The Scarlet Letter* with ten very bright and animated students. In the classroom, I am always my best self—smart, amusing, skillful, patient, vibrant, and kind. I'm not a Harvard professor and I'm not a doctor, but he sees, with surprise and pride, that I have an honorable and dependable job, that, despite everything, I have arrived safely at a normal adulthood.

WE SET OUR WEDDING DATE FOR MAY 15 and planned to hold it at the Fruitlands Museum in the town of Harvard, a rural suburb west of Boston. The museum was on the ridge of a hill surrounded by apple orchards. Molly forecast that the white blossoms on the trees would be in full bloom in the middle of May. In March we began shopping around for a clergyperson to marry us. I called some rabbis, but the only ones willing to marry an interfaith couple charged a small fortune. Then a friend told us about a Unitarian minister in Cambridge who would marry just about anybody, and we scheduled an appointment with her.

A day before our appointment I was in my usual position at the bedroom window, waiting for Molly to come home. When I caught sight of her walking down the street, she appeared more bewildered than usual. At one point, about one hundred steps from the house, she stopped completely and let her heavy purse and briefcase fall to the sidewalk. She looked around, disoriented. Then a car pulled to a stop next to her. The driver rolled down his window and said something. Molly smiled and pointed to our building. The car drove away and I raced outside and down the block.

"Molly, sweetie, are you all right?"

Her face was drawn. "I'm all right. Just a little light-headed."

"Let me help you," I said, lifting her purse and putting my arm around her waist. "Thank God I just happened to be looking out the window."

Molly was not feeling well enough to eat dinner and lay down in the bedroom. I pulled some books on pregnancy off the shelf— I think Molly had bought out the entire women's health section. At the kitchen table, eating the Cajun meatloaf I had prepared, I looked up miscarriage in the index. *One-third of all pregnancies end in miscarriages. Eighty-five percent of all miscarriages occur during the first trimester, usually due to a random error in the genetic code.* I brought Molly a cup of herbal tea and sat next to her on the side of the bed.

"Do you have any lower back pain?" I asked.

"A little."

"Any bleeding?"

"Some."

"Molly, we need to call the doctor."

"Her office is closed. I don't want to go to the emergency room."

"Maybe we ought to cancel our appointment with the minister tomorrow. I think it might be better for you to see your doctor."

"I don't want to cancel, Seth."

"We can always reschedule."

"I told you I don't want to cancel. Do you?"

"No," I relented. "I can't wait to go."

THE UNITARIAN MINISTER'S NAME was Lydia Cartwright-Preston. Somewhat zaftig, deeply tanned, with a set of dazzling white teeth, she was attired in stiff blue jeans, an old pair of Earth shoes, a plain red turtleneck, and a gaudy vest of Central American design. The rug on the floor was emblazoned with Navajo motifs, and the bookshelves were crowded with various small totems—an African mask with exaggerated mouth and lips, a carving of a woman with Incan features and a great round belly, and a herd of five or six miniature elephants. Except for a framed print advertising a display of quilts by Mennonite women, I didn't see any evidence of Christianity, which relaxed me somewhat, but not much.

Lydia Cartwright-Preston offered us coffee, tea, and scones. Molly declined; I accepted a cup of coffee, suppressing an urge to say, *What, no cider and blueberry bagels? I thought that was traditional Unitarian fare.*

"Congratulations, you two!" Lydia said. "Parenthood is a beautiful journey, but an exhausting one too. I hope you're both feeling centered."

"Centered?" I queried her.

"We're both very happy. Thank you," Molly said.

Lydia then asked us to tell her a little about ourselves. She turned to me with her blinding, high-voltage smile. I told her I taught English at a private school. Molly told Lydia she was a lawyer.

"A *tax* lawyer," I added.

Both women gave me puzzled looks.

"I just thought it was important for you to know how little we have in common."

Lydia laughed politely; Molly looked straight ahead, as if steeling herself for the dentist's drill.

"Well, I know you two do come from different faith traditions. I'm comfortable with that, but I do require that you can attest to some belief in a higher power, that you can offer some expression of spirituality." She turned to me. "Seth?"

"Yes, definitely," I answered.

"You consider yourself a spiritual person?" she said, trying to get me to refine my answer.

"Deeply spiritual." I smiled beatifically. I wanted this interview to be over so Molly could call her doctor.

Molly told Lydia that I had a PhD from the University of Chicago Divinity School.

"No way!" Lydia exclaimed.

"See, I told you," I said to Molly. "A total turn-on."

"Excuse me?" Lydia asked.

"Nothing," I replied.

"Molly, can you tell me about your relationship with God?" Lydia asked.

Molly blanched. "Well, in all honesty, I don't believe in God."

"Yes, I see," Lydia said, looking thoughtfully concerned, as if Molly had just informed her that she suffered from a chronic and painful ailment.

"But I do have a commitment to social justice," Molly added.

"That counts, doesn't it?" I interjected.

"Where does your commitment to social justice come from?" Lydia asked.

"From twelve years of Catholic school," Molly answered.

I tried to catch Molly's eye, but she didn't look my way.

"So you did have a religious upbringing," Lydia said.

"Yes, I believed very ardently when I was a child."

Keep going, I messaged Molly telepathically. Tell her about the time you swallowed a relic, a splinter of bone supposedly from a saint, because you thought it would endow you with holiness. Tell her how you went door to door in Cambridge soliciting money for pagan babies in China and Africa. Tell her about the time you climbed Croagh Patrick, a mountain in the west of Ireland climbed by hordes of barefoot pilgrims every July. Tell her you climbed it the summer after your father died, and that your relatives kept their shoes on but that you insisted on climbing it barefoot like a true pilgrim. By the time you came down, your feet were bloodied and blistered.

"What happened to your faith?" Lydia asked, leaning forward.

"Well, for one thing my mother died when I was two. Then my father died when I was twelve. It was difficult for me to believe in God after that."

"Oh, my, I'm sure that was very difficult for you," Lydia said.

"It still is," I interjected.

"Yes, for many people the mourning process is a lifelong journey," Lydia commented.

"I think," Molly continued, "the real turning point came for me one day when I was thirteen. I was showing my new fountain pen to the girl next to me in class. Our teacher, Sister Priscilla, asked me if I was bored. I told her, yes, I was. Some of the other children laughed. Sister turned beet red. She demanded I apologize, but I didn't think I had anything to apologize for. I was only telling the truth. We were taught it was a sin to lie, and I would have been lying if I had said I wasn't bored. Of course I couldn't explain any of this, so I just refused to apologize. Sister Priscilla became enraged. She berated me for being insolent and incorrigible. She said that surely my parents had done a poor job of raising me. This went on for about five minutes, until I was crying uncontrollably. Then Sister Pricilla asked me if I was ready to apologize. I told her no. 'Then why are you crying?' she asked. 'Because you're being unfair to me,' I said. She asked the class if anyone thought she was treating me unfairly. For a couple of seconds no one said anything. Then Billy Costello stood up. Poor Billy Costello! He had eight brothers and sisters and his father was the school janitor. Sister was always giving him grief for coming to school with holes in his clothing. 'Molly's right, Sister,' Billy said. 'You were being unfair. Very unfair.'"

Molly's eyes welled up.

"To this day," she said, "I think that was one of the kindest and bravest acts I've ever witnessed."

Molly shut her eyes tightly, holding back a flood of tears.

"Well, I'm sure your own act of resistance was very empowering for you," Lydia said.

"Does that mean we pass?" I asked.

"Yes, I would like to work with the two of you."

"Great!"

"In the time we have left," Lydia said, "I'd like to hear what you both love and esteem about the other."

Neither of us said anything. I was imagining Molly as a thirteen-year-old schoolgirl, an orphan in a plaid skirt and kneesocks, lips trembling, cheeks shiny with tears, holding true to her beliefs, refusing to bend or bow, and my heart seized with an inchoate love for her. I wanted to save her, wanted to be as brave and true as young Billy Costello, but I was paralyzed with doubt. I was the strange boy who laughed out loud when the president was shot. I was the anti-Billy Costello! Oh, Lord, I *was* unworthy! Molly was crying quietly, crying, I'm sure, for her mother and father, for Billy Costello, for our baby, for us. What could I possibly say to her at such a moment?

"Seth?" Lydia prompted.

"Love and esteem?" I asked.

"Yes, why do you love Molly?"

ON THE BRIEF RIDE HOME FROM THE CHURCH, I was by turns obnoxious and repentant.

"Did you get a look at that office? What do you think? Was she going for a Cambridge meets Santa Fe style? If you ask me, it looked more like a multicultural theme park than an office."

Molly gazed out the window. When I pulled up to the building, I turned off the engine and said, "Look, Molly, I apologize. I mean, it was a dating-game question. You know I love you. I love you more than anything. I love you more than words can say." She kept looking out the window, using a trembling hand to shield the side of her face exposed to me.

Molly stayed in bed the remainder of the day, the bedroom door shut. I told myself it was best to leave her alone. In the early evening, I tried to numb myself by drinking scotch and watching the Home Shopping Channel. I was wondering whether to spend the night on the couch when I heard Molly call out to me from the bathroom. She was standing by the toilet, her head tilted against the wall. She stared at me, Ophelia like—eyes vacant, hair wild, her ghost white nightgown bloody.

"Oh, Molly, my love, are you all right?"

"I can't clean it up," she said.

"I can do that," I said brightly. "I can do that."

I put my arm around her and guided her back to the bedroom.

Then I returned to the bathroom and studied the gore in the toilet bowl until I saw it—a heart-shaped clot of plum-colored tissue. It even had a silky white tail. I didn't know how to dispose of it—I couldn't just flush it down the toilet—so I dipped my hand in the water, pinched it out, bound it in toilet paper, and placed it on top of the tank. Then, on my hands and knees, I scoured the toilet bowl until it gleamed. I cleaned like a madman, like a penitent. I would have cleaned every latrine in Calcutta if offered the chance.

Then I cradled the weightless thing in the palm of my hand and went out to our mattress-sized backyard. The moon, white as ice, cast a pale glow. On my knees again, I shoveled away two or three inches of earth with my free hand. Each breath I drew was painful, as if I had a needle in my heart. I laid the pulpy tissue in its shroud of toilet paper in the small trough and stared at it. I felt more ceremony was in order and attempted to say Kaddish—*yisgadal veyiskadash*—but I stopped, paralyzed with self-consciousness. The words sounded out of place, too remote from anything I was thinking or feeling. Did I believe in anything? Did I have any words that issued straight and true from my heart? I looked up and caught sight of Molly staring down at me from the bedroom window. We watched each other for four or five seconds; her face was unreadable, sphinxlike. I moved the earth back over the mouse-sized corpse and spent a long time patting the mound flat.

Molly was waiting on the couch when I came in. I sat down next to her. My body was oily with perspiration, and I was coated with black soil.

"Thank you," she finally said, her voice expressionless, a dead weight.

"I tried to say a prayer," I confessed, my voice splintering. "I tried . . . but I couldn't. I didn't know how."

I began crying and Molly reached for my hand.

"Seth, I know you watch me from the bedroom window. Did you realize that?"

I said I didn't and apologized if it bothered her.

"I can't say it bothers me. I just find it strange, like you're watching yourself have a relationship with me. I've had that feeling since the very beginning of our relationship. You're here, but you're not really here. I need more than that, Seth. I know you love me, but I need someone who is fully present, someone who is *in* the relationship and not just watching it."

"I'll do better," I said. "I promise."

Molly and I were married on May 15, 1988. As she had hoped, the apple trees were blooming with white petals; the day was so clear that we could see the arrowhead summit of Mount Monadnock in New Hampshire on the horizon. We didn't hire Lydia Cartwright-Preston to officiate, not wanting any reminders of that dreadful day. I had discovered that just about anybody can get licensed to perform weddings in Massachusetts, and so we were married by Mara. She had been right about her tenure— any chance she had disappeared once she was pregnant and gave birth. She was still married to her husband, Jonah, though not very happily, and was spending her days at home caring for her son, Eli, and attending rabbinical classes part-time at Hebrew College in Newton. Mara draped a tallis over her shoulders, bobby-pinned a yarmulke to the top of her head, and, under a purple velvet chuppah embroidered with doves and held up by Molly's cousins, she performed a service she had written for us. She read some scripture and poetry, told stories about Molly and me that were both hilarious and moving, and then pronounced her final benediction on us: "There is no such thing as absolute time. Our lives on earth go by in a blink of the eye. But what is time when you share your life with the person you love? May the next fifty years for Molly and Seth be an eternity of love and joy."

Molly and I spent our wedding night at the Charles Hotel. The next day we were going to Ireland for three weeks. We hadn't had sex since her miscarriage. In the days immediately afterward, Molly had fallen into a depression so deep and paralyzing that she couldn't get out of bed for many days. Her cousins came over to help attend to her, staying around the clock, sleeping on the couches and the floor of the living room. Her aunt and uncle visited every day. I felt displaced, reminded that all these Quinns were her real family. Molly and I were alone only at night. She lay in a fetal position on her side of the bed, books, magazines, boxes of Kleenex between us. She shuddered if I tried to touch her.

By March I had resumed holding her in my arms every night. I wanted to believe that sleeping next to each other for as many hours as possible would heal us. I wanted to believe that the invisible ether that passed between our pores during the night would restore our love. One night in early April I put my hand on her breast and pressed into her backside. She didn't say no, but she didn't respond.

"It's been a long time," I said.

"I know," she replied, "and you've been very patient with me. You've been very kind, Seth."

"It's all I know how to do."

She squeezed my hand.

"So, is that a no?"

"Yes."

"Yes, it's a no?"

"I just can't, Seth. I'm not ready."

"That's fine," I said. "That's fine."

"I know it's strange, but I want to wait until our wedding night," she said.

"No, I understand," I said. "Like a new beginning. Like doing things in the right order this time."

"Yes," she replied. "Something like that."

"We can pretend we're virgins," I said.

ON OUR WEDDING NIGHT, WE kissed and fondled awkwardly. When I was stiff, Molly lowered herself on top of me. She could see in my eyes that I was wondering about contraception; her own eyes filled with tears. "I want to try again," she said. "I want to get pregnant tonight." She rode me with a feral energy, her eyes squeezed tightly shut, her face contorted with pain and rapture, as if trying to outrace the ebbing of blood in my penis, or outrace death. I kept my eyes wide open, feeling mystified and oddly moved, as if I were watching her act out a feverish dream.

Over the next three weeks, we fucked in bed and breakfasts across Ireland, from Dingle to Dublin. We fucked on hillsides, the ground spongy beneath us, and inside ruined abbeys. But her period still came on schedule. I heard her crying behind the bathroom door a couple of days after we had returned. When she came out, her eyes were red. I put my arms around her and said, "I guess we'll just have to keep having sex." She smiled wanly, as if that was the last thing she wanted to do.

All throughout the summer we made love every night, and each month I would know her period had come when I heard her crying in the bathroom. For twenty years, except for those three months when she was pregnant, her period had come as regularly as the sunrise, a reminder that she was capable of bearing children. But now, no matter how many times we made love, we couldn't stop the bleeding.

BY NOVEMBER, WE HAD STOPPED going to bed at the same time. Sex had become joyless, a chore. It numbed our hearts, turned our bodies against each other. Molly had started staying late at the office again, usually not coming home until long after I had eaten and was in my study grading papers and preparing for class. She would help herself to leftovers and read the newspaper at the table. Lying awake and alone at night, I would calculate the number of times we'd had intercourse since our marriage in May. Approximately twenty-seven times a month for six months: one hundred and sixty-two times. I recalled facts from the pregnancy books I had read: A man typically ejaculates three hundred million sperm during intercourse, but the sperm's four-inch trip up the fallopian tubes is so perilous that only a handful survive. One book I read had compared the odds to those of a person attempting to swim across the Pacific. In a period of six months, I had sent more than forty-eight billion of my sperm jetting blindly through Molly's reproductive tract, but not one had survived the journey.

FOR CHRISTMAS, WE DECORATED A TREE together, as we had the year before, but Christmas morning we drove to her aunt and uncle's house to exchange presents there, hiding from each other in the capacious embrace of her extended family. Molly went to midnight Mass with her relatives, and every Sunday after Christmas she continued going to church.

"Does this mean you believe in God now?" I asked her one day as we were driving to her aunt and uncle's for Sunday dinner. Molly no longer held my hand under the table.

"I don't know," she said, looking out the window at the ugly winter landscape, the snowdrifts blackened by car exhaust.

"About God . . . or about us?"

It was the first time either of us had brought up the state of our marriage.

"Both," she replied after a pause.

"Molly, what's happened to us?"

"I don't think you really wanted to get married. The only reason you proposed was because you knocked me up."

"Molly! That's not fair!"

"Seth, watch out!" she exclaimed as I nearly plowed into the car in front of me going through the rotary.

"Actually," I said, "I had planned to propose on Thanksgiving night last year. I was all set to pop the question, and then you told me about how my mother said you should get pregnant so I would have to marry you. It ruined the moment."

"You had plenty of time to propose after Thanksgiving. You can't go through life blaming everything on your mother."

"I was ready! I wanted to marry you before you were pregnant. I was less than five seconds away from proposing to you before you told me about your conversation with my mother!"

"So what are you saying? That things would be different if you had beat me to the punch that night and proposed?"

"Maybe."

"Seth, you couldn't even tell me why you loved me in that minister's office."

"How about the time we watched *The Searchers* and I told you that you completed me, that you turned me into a whole person? You said that was the most beautiful thing anyone had ever said to you."

"You planned to say that in advance; I could tell."

"So? I still meant it."

Molly started crying. "I'm sorry," she said, "but every time my period comes I feel the loss of our baby all over again."

We had arrived at John and Jean's house. I turned the motor off, but we remained in the car, our breath gradually fogging over the windows.

"I know," I finally said. "I know. I feel like we've had to begin our marriage with a death in the family." But it wasn't just the death of our baby; I felt her dead parents in bed with us too, as if all that fucking was an attempt to resurrect them.

Molly's gloved hand reached for my gloved hand. "Yes, that's how I feel too."

"Maybe we ought to put the idea of a baby on hold," I said.

"I'm thirty-five, Seth. I don't have time to put a baby on hold, especially if I've already had one miscarriage."

"But look what it's doing to us!"

She began crying again.

The day after her miscarriage, we had gone to her doctor, who had told us that Molly's age, thirty-five, was probably a factor. Chromosomal abnormalities become more common with age, she had explained. "Yes, we both know that, but does this mean we keep trying?" I had asked. "That's your decision," the doctor had replied.

"I just mean," I continued, "that we became pregnant when we weren't trying. Maybe if we stop hoping you'll get pregnant, it might just happen." But hearing my own words, I knew how impossible that was.

She glared at me. "Are you saying I just need to relax?"

"No—I don't know . . . I don't know what I'm saying."

DURING THE SUNDAY HOURS WHEN Molly was at church, I visited Mara. My name was still on the mailbox by the front door, since I was illegally subletting my rent-controlled apartment.

As Mara let me in the weekend after my argument with Molly, she held a crying, bucking toddler. I sat at her kitchen table, which was covered with open notebooks containing the hieroglyphics of her profession. Despite the fact that she had been denied tenure and was studying to become a rabbi, she still spent hours a day writing out complex and beautiful formulas about time and space.

"Go ahead. I'm paying attention," she said, as she set her son,

Eli, still crying, down in a playpen and studied her notebooks. She knew I wanted to talk about Molly.

"Mara, I think Molly is returning to the church," I said.

"How do you know?"

"Because she goes to church every Sunday."

"Well, then, I would say you're right."

"It feels like a rejection of me."

"I don't think it's necessarily a bad thing. She's going through a difficult time, and she's looking for solace, for something to believe in."

"But I'm not much of a believer."

"So? Neither is Jonah."

"Yes, and look at how wonderful your marriage is."

Mara's eyes widened with hurt.

"Oh, Mara, I'm sorry. I really am."

"Well, it's not exactly a state secret."

"Do you know if anyone in his lab is working on a cure for foot-in-mouth disease?"

She laughed a little.

"This morning I found this on Molly's night table," I said and showed her a card with an image of Jesus on one side. On the other side was written:

> *May the Sacred Heart of Jesus be Adored, Glorified, Loved, & Preserved throughout the world, now & forever. Sacred Heart of Jesus, please pray for me. Saint Jude, Worker of Miracles, please pray for me. Saint Jude, Helper of the Hopeless, please pray for me. Amen.*

"It's a novena," Mara said.

"A what?"

"A novena. A prayer of petition."

"I wonder if I'm one of the Hopeless she's praying for."

"Seth, Molly's going through a hard time. You need to have faith in your marriage."

"Did you know that a man ejaculates an average of three hundred million sperm into a woman's reproductive tract? But the sperm's four-inch journey up the fallopian tubes is so hazardous that the chances at survival are similar to the odds of someone attempting to swim across the Pacific."

"No, I didn't know any of that. But it's very interesting. Thanks for telling me."

"Faith isn't one of my strong points. I feel that Molly and I are facing similar odds."

"But women become pregnant all the time despite the odds. Life is random and mysterious, Seth. It's not about playing the odds."

"I guess not."

"Think of it this way," she said. "Imagine a bucket in the middle of a huge, empty swimming pool. The pool begins to fill with water, but the bucket remains empty. You keep wondering when the bucket is going to become full, because it's taking forever for the water to rise. But you just need to remind yourself that at some point it's going to happen; you just don't know when. That's what faith is like. Someday your bucket is going to be full. You just have to have faith and patience."

I looked down at the table so that she wouldn't see how moved I was.

"You know," I said, "I think you're going to be very successful in the rabbi business."

The next night, I waited until Molly came home so that we could have dinner together. Afterward, I told her that I had something for her and handed her an envelope. Inside was a postcard of Croagh Patrick.

"Thank you," she said.

"Turn it over," I urged. On the back I had written out a novena:

Hail, Holy Queen, Mother of Mercy, our life, our sweetness, and our hope! To thee do we cry, poor banished children of Eve; to thee do we send up our sighs, mourning and weeping in this valley of tears. Turn then, most gracious advocate, thine eyes of mercy toward us! O sweet Virgin Mary. Amen.

"Oh, Seth, thank you. This is beautiful."

"It's a Novena for Impossible Requests," I explained.

"I know."

She appeared both touched and embarrassed, and in her expression—and in my gesture—I recognized how distant we had become, how I would have said anything, attestested to any belief, to become close to her again.

"What's your impossible request?" she asked.

"That we can be as happy as we were before we wanted a baby and still have a baby."

"That's pretty impossible."

"Molly, I know I'm not a religious person, but I've been thinking a lot about faith. I think it's like looking at a bucket in the middle of a huge, empty swimming pool. The pool begins to fill with water but the bucket remains empty. You keep wondering when the bucket is going to become full, but you just need to remind yourself that it's going to happen."

Her eyes welled up.

"Someday our bucket is going to be full again, Molly. I know it is."

She held me tightly. "Oh, Seth, sweetie, I hope so too."

That night we went to bed at the same time. We held and kissed each other cautiously. I moved her nightgown up and kissed her belly, then her panties. She arched her hips so I could remove them and I felt the coarse spring of her pubic hair against my lips. Tracing my tongue over her complex inner terrain, I imagined that I was sending her a message in Braille, my own prayer of petition: *Stay with me. Stay with me.* I looked up to see if she had placed her hands over her face in a posture of prayer, but she put them along the side of my head, pulling me up. "Love me, Seth. Love me," she said.

The next month her period came again.

ON THE MORNING of our first wedding anniversary, Molly and I were sitting at the kitchen table, drinking coffee, reading the paper, when I turned to the obituary page and let out a cry.

"Oh, my God! I don't believe this."

Molly came out from behind the business page. "What? What is it, Seth?"

"Hortense died."

"Who?"

"Hortense. My cruel stepmother."

"No!"

"Yes!" I replied, and showed her the obituary of the woman who had been married to my father for more than twenty-five years. I had always hoped Hortense would die before my father, but I had never really expected it to happen. At that point in my life, I was shocked when anything I hoped for actually came true.

Molly retreated back behind the business page.

"It says she died after a long illness," I said. "Do you think that means cancer?"

"Probably. . . . Why is her obituary in *The New York Times* anyway?"

"She was a coauthor on most of my father's papers."

"Seth, why do you read the obituary page so carefully every morning?"

"Excuse me?"

"You heard me. Most people read the sports page first, or the op-ed page, but you immediately turn to the obituaries."

"Are you saying I'm gay?"

She snorted with disgust and returned to the paper.

"Do you think I ought to send my father a note of condolence?"

She looked up and regarded me with a modicum of sympathy. "What do you hope to get out of it?" she asked.

"Nothing. I just think it might be a nice thing to do."

"Seth, you always have a motive."

"That's not fair."

She turned back to the paper, as if I was not worth her time unless I could be completely honest.

"All right, fine," I confessed. "I'm hoping that he'll call me right up and tell me he's always loved me and wants to be close in the years he has left."

"I wouldn't count on that happening."

"Why not?"

"Because people don't change that much."

"I disagree. People change all the time."

"Whatever you say," she replied.

I studied Hortense's obituary like a tract of the Talmud. It had appeared in the paper exactly a year to the day after Molly and I were married. Surely this had to mean something!

"You know what really gets me? She died without knowing I had children." I was unexpectedly flooded with emotion and heard my voice catch.

Molly put down the paper and cast me an angry look. "You don't have any children, Seth. Remember?"

"Oh, right! I'll try to remember that."

She glared at me, then began to tidy up various sections of the paper. I wanted to remind her of the time Hortense had told me I would never have children. I wasn't trying to be funny; I was recalling the cruelest thing Hortense had ever said to me.

"Well, you know what they could have said about her?" I said. "She's the woman who put the bitch in obituary!"

I nearly fell off my chair laughing as Molly pushed away from the table.

Then the phone rang, jolting my heart. Could it be my father calling to tell me about Hortense? No. It was my mother, calling to wish me happy anniversary. She asked to speak to Molly, but I lied and told her that she had just missed her.

"Do you have plans for tonight?" she asked.

I lied again, telling her we were going to the Rialto in the Charles Hotel.

"All right, doll. I love you both."

"Thanks," I said.

Five minutes later, right after Molly left for the statehouse, I called Sarah. I hadn't tried to imitate our father for years, but when she answered the phone, I said, "Hello, Sarah," in a dead-on Elliot Shapiro voice.

"Dad?" she replied.

"Can you tell me what two plus two is?"

"Jesus, Seth. You asshole."

"Look at the obituary page in this morning's *Times*."

"I was just reading it when you called. That's why you caught me off guard. For a moment I thought it was Dad calling to tell me about Hortense."

"Are you going to send him a note?"

"I don't know. Probably not. The obituary says she died after a long illness. If he wanted our sympathy, he could have contacted us."

"Do you know what the paper could have said about Hortense?"

"What?"

"She's the woman who put the bitch in obituary."

"You're bad," she said, laughing.

"I know."

"I bet you're going to repeat that line about ten more times before the end of the day."

"Probably," I replied. "But what can I do? I'm just so very bad."

I drove to the Alewife T stop as usual. I knew my father was probably at home, grieving, mourning. On the ten-minute ride between Alewife and Harvard, I wondered if I ought to get off the train at Harvard and go to his house. I could try to console him, tell him that I was in bad shape myself. We were father and son, after all, both of us bereft and mourning in our ways. But when the train pulled in to the Harvard stop, I kept my seat as the car disgorged passengers and then loaded up with new ones. As the train approached Charles Street, I found myself sitting across from a man about my age, but his skeletal face was splotched with lesions and he shivered occasionally, though he was wearing an overcoat that fit him like a king-sized blanket. I kept reminding myself not to stare, but I couldn't stop myself, couldn't keep from imagining that he was the teacher I had replaced. He eventually caught my eye and smiled wanly at me.

Usually the classroom was my refuge, but that day it was a place where my sadness only seemed to ripen. We were discussing Chekhov's "Lady with the Pet Dog," and I prayed that I would be able to hold it together. The students began by discussing why we sympathize with Gurov even though he is an adulterer, a woman-izer, a liar.

"Because Anna loves him, and she's so pure," said one of the students, Skylar Raab. Her long hair was twisted into a braid that reached the middle of her back; she wore an oversized button-down shirt (unironed, of course), jeans, and a hemp choker.

"But is she really so pure?" I replied. "After all, she's committing adultery too. She lies to her husband so she can meet Gurov."

"Well, it's more like she's innocent," said Jason LaForge. He had bangs that fell over his granny glasses, sheepdog style, and he was wearing a T-shirt with a whale on it that said "Save the Humans."

"Good," I said. "I think innocent is a better word, but, still, how can she be innocent considering she's committing adultery with Gurov?"

"Well, she's innocent because her *love* for him is so pure," Skylar said. "She loves him despite all his faults."

"Yes," I said. "Very good."

Sonal Mukerjhee put her hand up. "But why? I really don't understand what she sees in him. He's like twenty years older than her. He lies about everything. He's a serial adulterer." Sonal was also dressed casually, in a rugby jersey, khaki slacks, and red high-top sneakers, but she permitted herself the vanity—or was it an ethnic statement?—of highlighting her beautiful hazel eyes with kohl.

Many of the students nodded in agreement.

"Well, maybe that's the point of the story," I said, my voice overly urgent, almost desperate. "They love each other despite who they are. They're not pure, but their love is!"

Some nodded, but some looked at me strangely, puzzled by the burst of feeling I had let out.

"I think we need to go to the text," I said, and directed them to the last page. Then I read:

"Anna Sergeyevna and he loved each other like people very close and intimate, like husband and wife, like tender friends; it seemed to them that fate itself had meant them for one another, and they could not understand why he had a wife and she a husband; and it was as though they were a pair of birds of passage, caught and forced to live in different cages. They forgave each other for what they were ashamed of in their past, they forgave everything in the present, and felt that this love of theirs had changed them both."

I contorted my face to keep from crying, but the tears poured down anyway. The students all stared at me, curious and compassionate.

WHEN I ARRIVED HOME FROM SCHOOL, I sat down at the table and wrote my father a note:

Dear Dad,
 I was very sorry to read about your loss. I'm married to a wonderful woman and we're expecting a baby. I'm sorry too that we've never been able to reconcile our differences, but I want you to know that I've always loved you.

Love,
Seth

I placed it in an envelope and went out to mail it. Then I shopped for dinner in the stores along Huron Avenue. I bought two Rock Cornish hens, a baguette, haricots verts, an expensive bottle of wine, and flowers. *They forgave each other for what they were ashamed of in their past, they forgave everything in the present, and felt that this love of theirs had changed them both.* All afternoon, I repeated those words in my head, until I almost believed I was Gurov and Molly was Anna and we'd forgive everything in our past and forgive everything in our present.

I didn't know if Molly would return home at dinnertime, and my heart sped up when I heard her come in at six. She looked over the mail and played the messages on the machine before coming into the kitchen. Then she stared at the table I had set: the two golden hens, flowers in the center, an open bottle of wine, the loaf of crusty bread.

"What's all this about?" she said.

"It's our anniversary—and my way of apologizing for this morning."

She sat down with her coat still on. I sat too. She poured herself a glass of wine and gulped down most of it, and I knew that we were still Seth and Molly, not Anna and Gurov.

"Can you explain this?" she asked, and placed on the table a letter from the real estate management company for my apartment. It had come the day before, but I hadn't bothered to open it yet. I read the letter: The company was terminating my lease because I had been illegally subletting my rent-controlled apartment.

"I was subletting my old apartment," I said, understanding why she had been so angry with me that morning.

"I can't believe you would do something like that!"

"It's rent controlled," I explained.

"Seth," she cried in exasperation, "when people get married, they don't hold on to their old apartments."

"All right. I can see why you're upset, but you're acting like I betrayed you."

"You *have* betrayed me. That's exactly what this feels like, a betrayal! *Someday our bucket is going to be full again, Molly.* If you really believed that, if you really had faith in us, if you really wanted to be with me, you wouldn't have kept your old apartment."

We stared at each other. Of all my transgressions—laughing out loud when the president was shot, not proposing until Molly

was pregnant, becoming tongue-tied in the minister's office—
this, I realized, was the most serious. I had always been too cau-
tious to embrace what I most wanted; I had always played the
odds in life.

"Why did you open my mail?" I asked. My question was more
forensic than accusatory.

"I wondered why you were getting a letter from a real estate
company. It was bothering me, so I opened it."

"I see," I said. "I see."

"Seth, I can't do this anymore."

"This?"

"This!" she exclaimed. "You! Me! Hoping I'm going to have a
baby! Hoping we might be happy again! Everything!"

I looked at the beautiful table I had prepared.

"We can be happy again," I replied, but I could hear how empty
my words sounded.

"Seth, stop telling me things you don't believe."

"So? Now what?"

"I need to live by myself."

"Here?"

She nodded.

"You want me to move out?"

"Yes . . . do you think you could stay with Mara?"

"Probably. . . . Molly, I'm sorry I behaved so badly."

She backhanded her tears away. "Seth, don't blame yourself.
It's nobody's fault."

"Why do couples always say that?"

"Say what?" she asked, her eyes damp.

"'It's nobody's fault.' Of course this is my fault."

She stared at me, red eyed, then reached for my hand.

"I mean," I continued, "maybe that's the attraction of conspiracy
theories. They provide sensible explanations for random things.

Think about the Kennedy assassination. We watch the same film over and over, see Kennedy's scalp sheared off by Oswald's bullet for the hundredth time, but we don't want to believe that everyone's life suddenly changed because of something so senseless and random. So we invent theories and fictions to explain the unexplainable."

She smiled sadly, sympathetically. "That sounds like something you would say to one of your classes."

"It is," I confessed. "Word for word."

ON NOVEMBER 22, 1989, I was walking through Harvard Yard when I saw my father approaching from the opposite direction. I stopped when he was about ten feet away. He kept coming, head down. I didn't know if he was trying to ignore me or if he simply didn't recognize me. "Dad," I said. He stopped. For several seconds we just stared at each other, as if we were both encountering a warped image of ourselves. All of my childhood hopes immediately welled up: We were both alone, and he was finally free to love me.

"How are you?" I asked.

"Fine," he said, the word slicing like a blade. I waited for him to ask me how I was, but he didn't say anything more.

"Do you know what today is?" I asked him.

"No."

"The twenty-sixth anniversary of the Kennedy assassination."

"Happy anniversary."

"My baby died and my wife left me," I said.

He pressed his lips together and nodded his head vaguely. He might have been signaling, *Yes, I know. It happens to us all.*

"I'm sorry to hear that," he said.

"Did you get my letter about Hortense?" He had never written back.

"A letter? You wrote two sentences. I thought you wanted to be a writer. That was the best you could do? Two sentences?"

"Actually, I think it was three sentences."

"Two, three. It's all the same."

"But I wrote to you," I replied. "Doesn't that mean anything?"

"Two sentences," he repeated, as if this were the most damning evidence against my character. "Two sentences."

"What more did you want me to say? Recall the many wonderful experiences we shared?"

He bent his head and closed his eyes, as if receiving bad news. "Do you know what your problem is?" he said. "You remember everything that's unimportant."

"You know, you're right. You're absolutely right!"

He gave me a small, appreciative laugh, and I could see his small, tobacco-stained teeth.

"*I remember everything that's unimportant,*" I said. "That is *so* true. So many years of therapy, and you've had the answer all this time!"

He broke into peals of high-pitched laughter. I took it as a sign of affection, if not approval.

"Twenty-six years ago today I was in Mrs. Carmichael's first-grade class at the Stillman Elementary School. I burst out laughing when Mrs. Miller, the principal, told us that the president had been shot. I remember the morning you left us. We were all sitting at the table, and my mother was hitting you with a box of Raisin Bran, crying and pleading with you not to go. You were fending her off with one arm as you continued to eat. You were in your undershirt. I remember that you always waited to put on your shirt and tie until just before you left the house. You use Dunhill aftershave. You used to keep Johnny Cash tapes in your car because you loved his music but Hortense wouldn't let you play it in the house."

His eyes widened with emotion behind his glasses, and he put a hand against my cheek. Then he continued on his way.

ON APRIL 25, 2004, I was strolling up Concord Avenue with Grace, my four-year-old goddaughter, riding high on my shoulders, when I recognized Molly at about thirty yards. We hadn't seen each other since 1989, but her gait—timid and dazed—was immediately familiar to me. I waved to her but she didn't respond; she probably thought I was waving to someone behind her.

"Molly, hello. It's me. Seth."

"Oh, my God. Seth. I didn't recognize you."

We didn't embrace, though we were close enough to touch. Besides, my hands were holding on to Grace's ankles, and Molly's slender finger was banded with a gold ring.

"Is this your daughter?" Molly asked.

"No, my goddaughter." Then, to clarify my answer even more, I added, "She's the love of my life."

Grace was the daughter of my close friends and neighbors, Bea and Ken Simon. After I had moved out of Molly's house, I spent a month sleeping on Mara's futon before I found a place to rent—the four-room attic apartment of Bea and Ken's Victorian house in Porter Square. Bea and Ken, recently married, were rehabing the house themselves. He was an architect, she a photographer, and they had designed their dream home. After a month of hearing banging and laughter in the evenings and on weekends, hearing the sounds of two people joyfully building a life together rising up to my attic apartment, I volunteered to help out. Surprised, they offered to lower my rent, but I refused, explaining that they would be saving me thousands of dollars in therapy bills. Bea and Ken laughed, but they knew I was going through a divorce and was in bad shape emotionally. "Think of it as occupational therapy for me," I said. For more than a year, I helped them reconstruct their house, knocking down walls, stripping linoleum, installing Sheet-rock, and sanding floors. During the months when their bath-room and kitchen were gutted, they showered in my apartment and shared meals with me at my table. By the time the project was completed, Bea and Ken had become like a second family to me.

"I'm happy for you, Seth. You look just like each other."

"Thank you," I said proudly, not bothering to correct her mis-understanding about my relationship to Grace. "Gracie, my love, can you say hello to my friend Molly?" I said.

Grace bent down with her arms crossed angrily and said, "I'm not Grace!" To punctuate the point, she straightened the rounded brim of her yellow hat.

"Oh, excuse me. *Madeline.*"

"Madeline?" Molly asked.

"You know, Madeline. 'In an old house in Paris that was covered in vines lived twelve little girls in two straight lines. The smallest one was Madeline.'"

"Oh, yes, of course I know about Madeline. Well, it's nice to meet you, Madeline."

"Are you Madeline's Mommy?" Grace asked, staring at Molly's hair.

Molly paled, as if Grace had said something shockingly adult.

"Your hair," I explained. "Madeline has red hair."

"Oh, my hair, yes," Molly said, relieved. Then she asked Grace if she would like to touch it. Grace smiled shyly and nodded. Molly leaned toward us, and I could see how extensively her rich auburn hair was threaded with gray. Her skin was more porous and tex-tured than the last time I had seen her; deep lines ran between her nose and her mouth.

"I can see you're married," I said.

"Yes. Eight years. . . . And you?"

"No. Not married. . . . Any children?" I asked, though I was sure I knew the answer, had known it the moment I recognized her orphan's stroll from so far away.

"No."

"Uncle Seth. I'm bored!" Grace shouted. "You said we were going to buy my present."

"We are, we are," I assured her. "Tomorrow is Grace's—I mean, Madeline's—birthday. We're going to Henry Bear's Park so she can show me what she wants me to buy her."

"Well, happy birthday, Madeline," Molly said.

"Thank you," Grace replied.

"Molly's birthday is coming up soon too. May 2," I said.

Molly stepped back, placing her hand over her heart. "Seth, I cannot believe you remember my birthday!"

"Well . . . I was married to you," I stammered, suddenly self-conscious that my words had registered so powerfully. "I ought to remember your birthday."

"Hold on," Grace said. "You two were married?"

"Yes," I answered.

"Did you get divorced?" Grace asked, continuing to cross-examine me.

"Yes."

Then she asked Molly if she had any kids. Molly told her she didn't.

"It's against the law to get divorced if you have children," Grace declared.

"That's right," I told her.

Molly smiled at me, perhaps understanding a child's need to invent a world in which parents don't fall out of love or die.

"We're adopting," she said. "From China."

"I'm adopting!" Grace exclaimed.

"You're adopted," I corrected.

"I know that," she replied.

"Well, I didn't," Molly said, casting me a reproachful look through her smile.

Bea and Ken had adopted Grace four years ago. I knew so many couples with adopted children that I had come to think of Cambridge as a refuge for foundlings.

"Would you like to see a picture of my baby?" Molly asked me.

"Yes, of course!" I said.

"I have to prepare you, Seth. She's extremely beautiful."

"Of course she is."

"No, I really mean it. Shockingly beautiful."

When she showed me the photo, I nearly let out a cry. Molly hadn't been exaggerating. The baby had a high, round moonscape of a forehead. Her eyes, a pair of shiny black pearls, stared directly back into the camera, directly into the soul of anyone who held the photograph. I had friends who had daughters adopted from China, and I knew that all the children had been abandoned. Looking at the photograph, I wondered how this baby's mother could have gazed into those eyes one last time and then left her at a bus stop or a police station, or wherever she had abandoned her. How could anyone bear such a loss? I thought of the eight years Molly had probably spent trying to get pregnant, recalling the emotional and physical trial it had been for Bea and Ken when they were trying to conceive. I wondered how many more miscarriages she had suffered. How had she endured it?

"Oh, Molly, she is beautiful. Congratulations."

I gave her a kiss on the cheek.

"You're divorced!" a voice admonished me from above. "That's against the law!"

Molly and I both laughed, but we didn't stop staring at the photograph. Perhaps my kiss had awoken a long-dormant feeling between us: our arms were pressed against each other, our heads tilted together, our whole beings, it seemed, enveloped in a numinous aura, as if we were gazing at a photograph of the child we had always wanted, as if we had finally completed each other. Then Molly looked up at me with an enigmatic smile. Was she seeing the Seth that she remembered? Or the person she was hoping I might be when she called a complete stranger one night more than fifteen years earlier?

BOTH ENDS

F or her sixtieth birthday, Ruth planned a surprise party for
herself. The guests were told to come at eight thirty, but by
three in the afternoon Ruth had decided that eight thirty was all
wrong. I had just arrived from the airport and was pressing my
ear against the door. Sarah was attempting to provide Ruth with
plausible excuses for staying away from home until eight thirty,
but my mother complained that all her ideas sounded too phony.
She told Sarah they wouldn't be having this problem if Sarah
had planned the party for seven thirty like she had told her to.
I changed the position of my ear and closed my eyes, hoping to
divine other voices, other secrets, but all I heard, of course, was
my mother's plaintive voice and my sister's sober one.

I rang the bell and the voices stopped. Ruth opened the door,
her face so drawn that it looked six inches longer than usual. Even
the capillaries running across her eyeballs appeared agitated. For
a second I wondered if she actually recognized me, but then I
realized she was staring at the tiny scar over my right eye where

she had struck me with a heavy enamel cup more than twenty-five years before. Blood had splashed into my eye, and Ruth had shrieked and draped herself over me, as if someone else had pitched the cup across the table and she was protecting me from further harm. The scar was hardly visible anymore—a pale pink apostrophe in the middle of my eyebrow—but Ruth sometimes would brood over it as if it were some hieroglyph, recording all the sins and slights of my childhood.

"You couldn't have come last night?" she said.

"Happy birthday," I said, briefly kissing her.

I embraced Sarah lightly, careful not to press too hard against her belly. She was six months pregnant with her second child. She had a five-year-old daughter named Vanessa; Seamus, four years younger than me, already had two children: four-year-old Zipporah and one-year-old Avi. Seamus still lived in the same town we had grown up in, and all the children were spending the day and evening at his house. Sarah, Aaron, and Vanessa lived an hour away from our mother's apartment.

Both women appeared dazed, as if I had just interrupted them in an act of violence or intimacy.

"Is there a problem here?" I asked.

"We're just trying to come up with a believable reason for Mom to be out of the house until eight thirty," Sarah explained.

I turned to Ruth. "Is that all? I don't think anyone really cares, Mom."

"I care!" she declared.

"Mom," Sarah said, "I really think Seth is right about this one. Just say anything. Say you were at the dentist's or the doctor's."

"Sarah, no one comes home from the dentist's at eight thirty on a Saturday night. Oh, this whole thing is going to look staged!"

"Mom," I exclaimed, "this whole thing is staged."

She shot me an annoyed look.

"Look, Sarah planned this whole event because you wanted her to, and now you're acting like she's trying to ruin your birthday."

Sarah glared at me.

"Is that true, Sarah?" Ruth asked. "You're doing this only because *I* want you to? Well, then you can forget it. Tell the guests anything you want, because all I know is that I wouldn't show up now for all the tea in China!"

"Mom, Mom," Sarah pleaded. "Seth meant we're doing this because we love you. Right, Seth?"

Both women turned to me. "I have a great idea," I replied. "At seven thirty we'll put my overnight bag in the car, and Mom and I can go somewhere for an hour. Then we can walk in together at eight thirty, like Mom has just brought me back from the airport."

A triumphant look transformed Ruth's face. "Oh, yes!" she cried. "Oh, Seth, darling, I know I can always count on you to save the day!"

RUTH LEFT FOR AN APPOINTMENT at the beauty parlor not long after I arrived; Sarah and I went for a walk with Benny, our mother's beagle. Benny pulled Sarah along in the wake of his frenzied interest in every frozen turd along the curb. I ran after them every now and then to catch up. The houses on our street were uniformly small and drab, the patchy yards scattered with overturned tricycles, clotheslines, doghouses, outdoor furniture left to rust.

But after about ten minutes, we were in a completely different neighborhood of stately old Tudors and stylish ranch houses. Benny slowed down in front of a house with a grand, sweeping lawn. He circled a figure of a little black jockey statue holding a lantern that had been there for as long as I could remember.

"Go here, Benny. Go here," I urged from behind a telephone pole. He stopped circling and gave me a sorrowful look.

"Go wherever you want, sweetheart," Sarah said to him.

He lifted his leg and peed against the jockey's ankle. Then he looked up at Sarah.

"Yes, darling, that was wonderful," Sarah said.

This was our aunt Rhoda and uncle Barry's house. I caught up to Sarah and Benny.

"Are you angry at me?" I asked.

"Not too angry."

"I'm sorry if I caused you any grief back at the apartment."

"Don't worry," she said, with a dismissive laugh. "I've been getting grief all weekend. This morning she wanted me to call all the guests again and remind them to be on time. She also can't decide which outfit to wear, and for some reason that's my fault too. Plus she's upset that Marcy is spending more time with Vanessa than she is today."

Abe Zelman had died two years before. Since his death, Ruth and Marcy had been engaged in a mighty battle for the affections of little Vanessa, a battle in which my mother was heavily outspent. Marcy's latest salvos were the entire American Girl doll collection with all the accessories and a life-sized Steiff teddy bear from FAO Schwarz.

"She's also hoping Jimmy Conroy is going to show up tonight, and she's anxious about that too," Sarah said.

Jimmy Conroy, the principal of the school where Ruth had taught second grade for the past thirty years and where my siblings and I had all gone, had been her on-and-off-again lover for most of that time. The state of their affair had always depended on the vagaries of Mr. Conroy's relationship with his wife, his six children, and his church.

"Do you think he's going to show?"

"He'll try. I called him this morning. His wife knows about the party, and she's giving him a difficult time."

"You called him and he told you that?"

"Sure."

I realized that I wouldn't even recognize Jimmy Conroy if I saw him on the street.

"Seth, could you also try to get along with Seamus tonight for Mom's sake?"

"I'll try," I said, without enthusiasm. Seamus and I had not spoken in five years.

"You know it goes both ways, Seth."

"How does it go both ways?" I said angrily.

"I mean you could have called him or sent him a note after his children were born."

"Well, he could have called me after Molly left me. He must have known what bad shape I was in. A call from my brother would have been nice. But of course he couldn't call me because he didn't recognize my relationship with Molly. I mean, he wouldn't even come to my fucking wedding."

"Look, Seth, just try for Mom's sake. You don't know how painful it is for her that the two of you don't speak."

"All right, I'll try."

We walked a couple more seconds in silence, and then I cried out, "You know, I lost a baby! Don't you think he ought to have acknowledged that?"

"Of course I do," she said.

"By the time he's my age he's probably going to have six children. A whole household of little Tovahs and Zalmans and Yaels."

Sarah said, "Seth, Mom's also upset because you forgot her birthday again."

"Forgot her birthday? Where am I now? I'm here for her birthday."

"Today is Saturday. Her birthday was yesterday. She's upset because you didn't call her."

"Because I knew I was coming home today."

"Come on, Seth, you forgot to call her."

"Fine, fine. I'll apologize."

She didn't respond, and I put my arm through hers.

"Sarah, I'm sorry, but I never know the right thing to say to her."

"Tell her you love her," she implored me. "She just wants to hear you say it."

"All right, all right."

Sarah was silent for couple of seconds, then said, "You're going to have to say it at some point."

"I know," I replied.

Two weeks before, Ruth had been diagnosed with Stage III lung cancer. Inoperable, but treatable with chemotherapy. The five-year survival rate was five percent. None of us knew how many months Ruth had ignored the symptoms—bronchitis that wouldn't go away, wheezing, shortness of breath. Her doctor had wanted her to begin chemotherapy immediately, but she insisted on waiting until after her party.

"She claims that the last time you told her you loved her was the night of our bar and bat mitzvah," Sarah said.

"She remembers that?"

"Apparently. Do you?"

"Me? I'm the boy who remembers everything."

"Except for your mother's birthday."

THE TELEVISION WAS NO LONGER in the living room; Ruth had moved it into her bedroom years ago. When we returned from the dog walk, I went into her room to watch a baseball game. Lying down on her bed, I was enveloped by her stale, sad odors—the bitter residue of tobacco and the gamey scent of the dog. Then

I looked at the lace canopy above me, at the beautiful fretwork spiraling down the four posts, and I was reminded that this bed was the closest thing we had to a family heirloom. It was the bed where my mother had been born and conceived her children, the bed she and my father had slept in for the eighteen hundred and thirty-one nights of their marriage, and the bed she had often shared with me, Sarah, and Seamus in the months after he left. On those nights, she hummed lullabies in our ears and, in place of a prayer, always recited the same poem:

> Ample make this Bed—
> Make this Bed with Awe—
> In it wait till Judgment break
> Excellent and Fair

SOMETIMES IN THE MIDDLE OF the night she would rearrange us, shifting around the sheets, toys, and small bodies, saying softly, "Come on, kiddos, ample make this bed."

When I had last told her I loved her, on the night of my bar mitzvah, I was lying next to her in this bed. Eddie had fled just three weeks before. As I chanted from my portion of the Torah that morning, with the sun shining through the stained-glass windows of the synagogue, I had watched rainbows of light skate across the sacred parchment and felt as if the beams were refracted through my joyful heart. Eddie was gone, and Zelda was safely ensconced at an all-girls boarding school until I was old enough to come for her. I chanted my haftarah like a songbird released from the ark.

After the services, we had a party at the VFW hall down the street from our apartment. A man in a pink ruffled shirt and a black vest played an electric guitar and sang popular songs. All of the girls, most of them Sarah's friends, felt compelled to slow dance with me. I still had slight, iridescent bruising under my eyes from the surgery to repair my broken nose, the result of my fight with Eddie. Dancing with Cheryl Edelstein to "Little Green Apples," I held her tightly and breathed in the scent of her hair. With my hands between her lower back and her ass, I began to stiffen up. Embarrassed, I moved a step back. Cheryl and I stared at each other, our faces hot and red. Then she pulled me back into a bear hug, twirled a lock of my hair around her finger, and whispered in my ear, "I'm only letting you do this because you had brain surgery."

My mother was not having a very good time. The invitations had gone out with the names Mr. and Mrs. Edward Lipper, and, apparently, her father and sister had not bothered to tell any of the other relatives that the marriage was over. It was as if they had decided that this would be my mother's public humiliation for the shame of marrying Eddie, despite the fact that Rhoda had set them up by giving Eddie my mother's phone number. Every time I looked in Ruth's direction, she was holding a cigarette in one hand, a drink in the other, her face fixed in a pained, anxious-to-please expression as she explained about Eddie to another cousin, uncle, or aunt. Once I was standing close enough to her to hear her say, "I'm usually such a good judge of character. That's what bothers me the most. I've always had such excellent judgment."

That night Sarah was sleeping over at Cheryl's house. When I went to bed, Seamus was already asleep. In bed I read Zelda's letter for probably the hundredth time. I knew it as well as my haftarah. I began to touch myself, calling up visions of Zelda putting me in her mouth, but then I heard my mother crying in her bedroom. I waited a couple of minutes for her cries to subside, but they kept on, not loudly, but mournfully, incessantly, as if she had fallen to the bottom of a deep, black well. My mother had always warned me that I would cause her to have a nervous breakdown. Of all her dramatic declarations (*May God strike me dead if I'm wrong! I'm sending you to reform school!*), her threat of a nervous breakdown felt the most true, and I always wondered how I would know if she was actually having one. Hearing her cries that night, I understood that it was finally happening. I tried to think through the consequences. Would I have to call an ambulance? If I did, and she was hospitalized, where would my sister, brother, and I stay? My father wouldn't have all of us, and neither would Rhoda for more than a day or two. We would surely be separated.

I went to my mother's bedroom and stood in the doorway.

"Mom, are you all right?"

She shook her head back and forth on the pillow.

I went to her bed and lay down next to her. Finally, I said, "Are you thinking about Eddie?" She shook her head. Then I asked her if she felt bad that her life wasn't more like Rhoda's. She nodded. I told her that she was a much more accomplished person than her sister. She was brighter, better educated, more independent. Who cared if she didn't have a big house and a husband? She squeezed my hand, but she was still crying.

"What is it, Mom?"

"Your father. I'm still in love with him."

"I know."

"He's such a bastard."

"I know."

"He drives me out of my mind."

"Me too," I admitted, and we both laughed a little.

These were the truest words we had ever spoken to each other. I put my arms around her, and we lay together, bound by the knowledge that we were both in love with a man who would never love us back. I held her for a long time. When I finally asked her if she was feeling better, she nodded her head, then said, "Seth. Thank you." She would get through the night; we would all stay together and continue with our lives. She pressed the back of her hand against my cheek. I kissed her on the forehead and then briefly on the lips. I told her I loved her and went back to my own bed.

Now I NOTICED FOUR OR FIVE little black-rimmed holes in the comforter, and I imagined my mother lying on her side in the dark, the end of her cigarette glowing dimmer and brighter throughout the night. On my last visit home, I was sleeping in the other bedroom when the scent of a burning cigarette woke me up. I looked across the hall into Ruth's room. Benny was sleeping in the bed too. The television was on, as always, but Ruth was staring up at the ceiling, holding a cigarette to her lips. I watched the tip of my mother's cigarette brighten and exclaimed, "I don't believe this!"

"What? What?" she asked, as disoriented as if she had been in a deep sleep.

"You're smoking in bed! In the dark! That's what." Benny leapt up and began barking at me. "Benny, shut up," I shouted. Warbling nervously, he stepped backward over Ruth and, safely ensconced behind her, resumed barking at me.

"God almighty!" Ruth cried out in a highly irritated voice. "The television was on."

"You weren't watching it," I replied. "You were half asleep."

"I was wide awake," she said. "I was thinking."

"Mom, don't you know you were endangering our lives? Do you have any idea how dangerous this is?"

Later that night I looked in on my mother again. She and Benny were snoring fitfully. The light from the television blanched her face white as a death mask.

Now I heard her tired, heavy steps approaching, and I turned on the television.

"I won't disturb you," she said. "I just need to get some things."

She removed a blue silk skirt and a black cashmere sweater from her closet and, standing before the full-length mirror, held the outfit in front of her. Her gaze was enigmatic and sad, as if she were seeing her entire life in the mirror.

She noticed me watching her and asked how I liked the outfit.

"Great, fine," I said, and immediately hoped she hadn't noticed how angry I sounded.

She turned and faced me. "Is something wrong?"

"No, nothing," I said. "You'll look great."

"Well, I'm sixty years old," she said to the mirror.

"You might have a lot of years left," I said, "if you don't set this bed on fire." I pointed to the holes in the comforter. "You promised me you weren't going to smoke in bed anymore."

"That's from a long time ago," she said, lighting a cigarette and returning the clothes to the closet. "Oh, I can't decide."

"Is that your one cigarette for the day?"

"Yes," she replied, and brought out a white silk blouse and black skirt, held them in front of her, then regarded herself in profile. "Oh, I can't decide!" she exclaimed.

I told her I liked the other outfit.

She retrieved the first one again and studied it closely, brushing the skirt with the back of her hand.

"So I hear Mr. Conroy might be coming tonight," I said, thinking that this was also the bed in which the two of them had spent thousands of afternoons.

"Well, who knows?" she said. "If he comes, he comes—that's my attitude."

In the weeks since her diagnosis, she had been surprisingly calm, as if she had faced down or dodged the thing she had been afraid of all her life. I recalled, with shame, how, years before, Sarah and I had hoped her death would be sudden. We had both agreed it would be a nightmare if we had to attend to her while she died a slow, painful death. We had imagined the overwrought deathbed scenes. *"Just tell me I was a good mother!"* I would exclaim, imitating a refrain my sister and I had heard throughout our childhood. *"That's all I want to hear!"* I'd continue, dramatically crossing my hands over my heart and sending Sarah into a fit of laughter.

"Well, I think that's the right attitude to have," I replied. She always referred very obliquely to her relationship with Jimmy Conroy, even though it had been common knowledge among her friends and colleagues for many years. I knew for sure that they were lovers when I was fifteen. I had heard them come in one evening and kiss for a long time, and when I heard Ruth sing out, "Oh, Jimmy, Jimmy, I love you too," it was as if I had learned some fact about the world that I had already known in my heart. I knew because some mornings the scent of Mr. Conroy's Vitalis blended richly in our car with my mother's heavy perfume; I knew because when I was in elementary school, Mr. Conroy always inquired about my day with extra kindness.

Ruth stood before the bureau, one hand on her hip, meditatively twisting out her cigarette. Then she came over and sat in a chair by the bed, looking at me. I braced myself, expecting the familiar questions about whether or not she was a bad mother and was that why I didn't call her on her birthday or come to visit more often.

"Sweetheart, did you happen to go through a box of old things in my closet?" she asked.

"A box of old things?" I repeated, though I knew exactly what box she was referring to. It was labeled "Memories," and inside it were old diaries, photographs, birth and death certificates,

hundreds of letters, the nearly fifteen-year-old manuscript o.
Stranger on the Planet." I'd found the box on my last visit hom.
I hadn't been sure what I was looking for—I already knew so
much about my mother's life—but being alone in the apartment I
had felt a strong impulse to trespass and ruminate. When I found
the box, I'd read through everything in it, as if the contents of my
mother's life formed a novel I couldn't put down. Her story was
familiar enough to me, but each page offered a small surprise—
her thrill at discovering a rare pink lady's slipper in the woods,
or the electric shiver she felt in college when some boy simply
touched her wrist.

"You know," she said, "letters, photographs, personal things."

I had removed one page from an old journal. Could she have
noticed it was missing?

"No, Mom. I didn't go through any box."

I knew she wouldn't be angry if I confessed; in fact, she'd
probably be happy to know I was interested enough in her to go
through her personal belongings. But I wouldn't know how to
explain myself—either the violation or the interest.

"I'm sorry I didn't phone you on your birthday, Mom," I said.

"Did Sarah say something to you?"

"Who?" I replied.

Ruth required a couple of seconds to register the joke. Then she
laughed timorously, kissed me on the forehead, and went out.

About thirty minutes later, I went into the dining room. Sarah
had put up multicolored balloons and banners. The two women
were sitting at the kitchen table, where Sarah was doing Ruth's
makeup. Seamus was sitting at the table too, reading the newspaper. I hadn't seen him in over five years. He had a neatly trimmed
beard and kept his head covered with a stylish fedora. I gazed at
the tableau of my family. My mother was staring straight ahead
as Sarah, inches from her face, delicately combed her eyelashes.

Ruth appeared serene, deeply calmed by Sarah's hands. For a moment I felt myself transfixed by the mystery and beauty of Sarah's ministrations.

Then they all noticed me at the same time.

"Reb Seamus," I said. "Long time no see."

"Don't call me that," he replied and looked back down at the newspaper.

Ruth appeared distraught.

"All right, Mom," I said. "I think it's time to go get me at the airport."

IN THE CAR I SUGGESTED TO RUTH that we stop somewhere for a cup of coffee. She said that she was concerned one of the guests might see us.

"You don't want to go anywhere? You just want to drive for an hour?"

"Why not? I like driving."

Ruth drove onto the highway, heading east, as if she were actually going to the airport. We were silent for many minutes; Ruth kept glancing at the side and rearview mirrors, as if we were being followed. Then she asked if Molly and I kept in contact. She hadn't brought up Molly's name in a long time. I told her no, that I had not seen or heard from Molly in years.

"Well, maybe it's better that way. Just to move on with your life. God knows I would have been better off if I had done that with your father."

I didn't tell her that for months after we split up, I would call Molly in the evening, telling her that I loved her, until, finally, Molly said it would be better for both us if I didn't call her anymore. I didn't tell my mother that I still occasionally walked down Huron Avenue, hoping I would run into Molly.

"What about you and Rachel?"

"What about us?"

"Do you keep in touch with her?"

"We're still friends. We write and call occasionally."

"Do you think you'll ever be more than friends again?"

"Mom, I have to tell you something about Rachel."

"Yes?"

"She's a lesbian."

My mother looked out the window. "Why?" she asked quizzically.

"Because that's the way God made her."

"Didn't you sexually satisfy her?"

"Probably not, considering she's a lesbian."

"Well, that doesn't change anything. I still love her like a daughter. Would you tell her I said that?"

"Yes," I said, even though I knew I wouldn't.

"I don't judge anyone. I've made my share of mistakes."

"I don't think Rachel would view her being lesbian as a mistake."

"Oh, gee, Seth, give me a little credit. You know that's not what I meant. I'm a very open-minded person."

"I know you are, Mom."

We were on the turnpike, but she was driving very slowly in the right lane.

"Mom, why are you driving so slowly?" I asked.

"I'm just thinking."

She drove another minute in silence, past the exit for Secaucus, where the industrial odors—something like burning tires—were always strongest. My mother once told me that Secaucus used to be a place where pigs were slaughtered and that we were probably catching a whiff of the old pig industry. I knew that couldn't be true, but a part of me still believed it every time we drove this stretch of the turnpike.

"Did you know I had an abortion once?" Ruth said.

"You did? When?"

"Years ago. Do you remember that time when you were ten and Jimmy Conroy came to the house in the middle of the night to bring all you children to Rhoda and Barry's house?"

"Yes . . . that was because of an abortion?"

"I began to hemorrhage in my bed a couple of hours after the abortion and I phoned Jimmy. He called an ambulance, then brought you and your sister and brother to Rhoda's house."

"Oh, Mom, I'm so sorry."

"Well, the most difficult part was just trying to find someone. Abortions were illegal then. So I went to Uncle Barry's brother, Leslie. He was my internist, and I thought he might know someone I could go to. But he just started yelling at me, saying didn't I know that I was asking him to be an accessory to a crime? Then he said he was going to call Barry and let him know what I was doing."

"What an asshole!"

"What an asshole is right. He began dialing Barry's number right in front of me, so I pulled the telephone cord out of the wall."

"Good for you, Mom."

"Alice helped me find someone," she said, referring to her friend and colleague of three decades. "A cousin of hers. A black doctor in Patterson. I met him in his office and had to give him six hundred dollars up front. He said he didn't do the abortions in his office. I would have to go to his house the next night."

My mother always told the same two or three stories, cloying and overdramatic ones like "Was Anybody Praying?" Why had she told me this story, and on this night? Was it her way of letting me know that she was open-minded? Or perhaps she had always wanted to tell me, and my revelation about Rachel had provided her with an opening. Perhaps she wanted me to know that she still had secrets and mysteries, that I didn't know everything about her.

"Mom, I can't imagine how difficult that was for you," I said.

"The most difficult part was the week after, during Yom Kippur. I sat in the synagogue wondering if God was going to punish me for ending a life."

"You did what you needed to do, Mom, to keep us together."

"Seth, look," she said. "I want you to understand something about Jimmy and me. We knew each other for three years before we acted on our feelings."

"Mom, that's all right," I said uncertainly.

"I always wondered if you thought I was—well, you know, wanton or irresponsible, because of my relationship with him."

"Wanton? Of course not! Why would I think something like that?"

"You can be very disapproving sometimes."

"Only about cigarettes, not about sex."

"What?"

"It's a joke, Mom."

"Oh."

"Mom, I'm glad that Mr. Conroy's been in your life. I really am." I thought of the night when I was fifteen and had heard her sing out, "Oh, Jimmy, Jimmy, I love you too." I wanted to tell her that I had been secretly thrilled to hear her words that night, to know she had a life other than the one I saw every day, to know that someone loved her.

"Well, it hasn't been ideal."

"Was that why you married Eddie? Because of Mr. Conroy."

We hadn't mentioned Eddie's name since just after they had divorced, treating him like a nightmare that had come and gone.

"Oh, who knows? Mainly it was my own stupidity, but I suppose that was one reason. Rhoda and Barry gave me such grief about Jimmy. I thought if I got married, they'd finally approve of me."

"Well, it couldn't have been easy to find a husband with three young children."

"I suppose."

Ruth turned off the highway and negotiated a maze of arteries and ramps to reverse our direction. The landscape was complexly ugly, a netherworld of refineries, power stations, swamps, bridges, and low, toxic hills over which seagulls slowly circled. I had spent my entire life bracing myself against the tide of florid emotions that always seemed about to burst forth from my mother, but now I felt myself engulfed. I looked out the window so that she couldn't see the tears that had welled up in my eyes. I thought of my fifteen-year-old manuscript in a box in the back of her closet. She knew my stories and I knew hers, but we kept them stored away, in our hearts and in closets.

She reached across the seat for my hand. "God forgive me for saying this, but I think of you as the child of my heart. Of all my children, you're the one that's most like me."

CARS WERE LINED UP ALL ALONG OUR STREET. Ruth looked in the rearview mirror and said she was embarrassed to go in because her eyes were red from crying. I told her she looked fine, not to worry about it. Getting out of the car, we shut the doors loudly. All the lights went off inside the apartment.

We were showered with shouts and light and confetti. There were perhaps twenty people, old friends and colleagues of my mother's. Her eyes brimmed with fresh tears, as if the surprise were real.

"Oh, wow!" she cried. "Oh, wow! We just came back from the airport." I tried to stand behind her, but she put her arm around my waist and pressed her forehead against my shoulder.

"How do you like this son of mine?"

Rhoda and Barry came over to greet us. Both were fit and tanned, having just returned from their annual golf vacation in Hawaii.

"How's the birthday girl?" Barry said, regarding Ruth over the top of his spectacles.

"Say, you didn't really just come from the airport," Rhoda said to me.

I looked at Ruth, whose face had become alarmed and anxious.

"Certainly I did," I replied.

"I'm sure I saw you and Sarah pass by the house with the dog this afternoon."

I put my hand on Rhoda's forehead. "Rhoda, have you been feeling all right?"

Sarah draped an arm around me in a show of sisterly love, then, without anyone noticing, pinched me painfully.

"Sarah," Rhoda said to her, "please don't let the dog go to the bathroom on my statuary."

"Sorry, Aunt Rhoda," Sarah said.

Sarah excused herself to attend to things in the kitchen.

I wanted to hide out in the kitchen with Sarah, but on my way across the room I found myself belly to breast with Deborah, Seamus's wife. She was just under five feet tall and had a round, peachy-complexioned face. I didn't realize how long I had been staring down at her shiny blonde hair, wondering whether she was Orthodox enough to wear a wig, until she said, "It's real, Seth. Do you want to pull it just to be sure?"

"So, you know who I am."

"Don't be a clown. Of course I know who you are."

"Look, can I ask you a question?"

"Shoot."

"Did Seamus actually sit shivah for me when he heard I was marrying out of the faith?"

"Oy, Seth, you have to get over this. Really. Both of you are acting like children. You think this is a matter of principle, but it's just whacking off."

"Excuse me?"

"You heard me. All this righteous anger is just self-indulgent, no different from whacking off. It just leaves you lonelier."

"You know, Deborah, I think Seamus is very lucky to have found you."

"I know he is."

I located Sarah in the kitchen. She was rinsing glasses in the sink.

"What happened between you and Mom in the car?" she asked me.

"Nothing. Why?"

"She looked very drained when you came in."

"She always looks that way." I gulped a Dixie cup of champagne.

"Don't you think you ought to go a little easy on that?"

I looked into my empty cup, as if it contained an answer to her question.

Rhoda put her head inside the kitchen door. "So?" she said conspiratorially.

"So, what?" I replied.

She glanced back into the living room, as if spies might be shadowing her. Then she stepped into the kitchen, holding a plate weighted down with ribs and tortellini.

"So where's your mother's boyfriend?"

"You mean Mr. Conroy?" I asked.

"Right, right. Him."

"He said he'll come if he can," I told her.

"Well, I'm not holding my breath. I've tried to introduce your mother to some very nice men, but is she interested? Of course not!"

"Aunt Rhoda," I said, "the last man you introduced her to had one foot in the grave."

"Who? Mr. Pearlman? He's a wonderful man. He would have been very nice company for your mother."

"How old is he? Seventy-five?"

"Look, at her age your mother can't be too particular."

Then Rhoda asked me about Rachel. Rhoda had never met her, but no doubt my mother had been dreaming up a scenario for her sister about how I would finally marry the rabbi's daughter and live happily ever after. Normally, I would have been angry at my mother for putting me in this position, but instead I felt furious, finally, with Rhoda.

"How come you don't ask me about Molly?" I said.

"Because that's been over for five years."

"So? I haven't been with Rachel since college. It wouldn't have anything to do with the fact that Molly's Catholic?"

"Yes, I admit that I'd prefer you marry a rabbi's daughter. What's wrong with that?"

"Well, I'm not going to marry the rabbi's daughter."

"Why not? Is she married?"

"No. She's a lesbian."

Rhoda put her hand to the side of her face. "*Oy vey iz mir.* Do you know why? Was she molested as a child?"

"No. She had a beautiful childhood," I lied. "But I didn't sexually satisfy her." I felt Sarah give me another painful pinch.

"Look, I'm sorry to hear that," Rhoda replied. "But you know sex isn't everything in life."

"To some people it is," I said.

"Seth, doll, I have news for you. If you keep up that attitude, you'll never get married. You'll end up just like your mother."

"What's so bad about ending up like my mother?" I asked.

Rhoda appeared genuinely dumbfounded by this question. "Look, all these years she's been carrying on with a married man. Everyone in that living room knows about them. How she can live like that I'll never understand."

"Is that all you can say about our mother, Rhoda?" I asked.

"She raised three children. She's taught hundreds of other children to read. She's loving and generous. She has friends who value her. But all you and Barry ever do is treat her like her life is one big embarrassment."

"Say, look here. I only want what's best for your mother. You know that."

"Like hell you do," I said.

The lines of her mouth went rigid before she banged her way out the door.

Sarah turned to the sink, gripping the sides of it, her back shuddering.

"Sarah?" I said. I touched her shoulder and she turned to me, pressing her wet cheek against my neck and holding me more tightly than anyone had held me for a long time.

THE LIGHTS WENT DOWN, and a chorus of "Happy Birthday" rose up as Sarah and I came out of the kitchen bearing the candlelit cake, which looked like a small field of swaying fire. We put it down and stood off to one side, but Ruth brought her three children over, pulling Seamus and me close together. All four of us leaned into the heat and brightness of the flames. "One, two, three," Ruth counted, and we exhaled in unison, one capacious breath sending the fire sputtering and lurching. Ruth ran out of breath, and Seamus stepped back. Sarah and I raced to blow out the remaining candles. We were bent over, laughing, gasping, when the doorbell rang, freezing everyone for a moment. I reached for my drink and swilled it down.

Someone opened the door and accepted a delivery of thirty-six roses. People commented on their splendor and beauty as they were handed up to Ruth. She appeared a little embarrassed by so many flowers, by this extravagant gesture of love and regret.

She read the card that accompanied them, and I noticed a chain reaction of yearning passing from one guest to another, everyone joined together in a silent prayer for Ruth's happiness, everyone secretly encouraging her. She put the flowers down and smiled bravely.

Alice unfolded a T-shirt emblazoned with the word "SUPER-TEACHER" and signed by Ruth's twenty-eight second graders. She praised Ruth's diligence in teaching for thirty years. She estimated that that came to nearly one thousand students, "or about two thousand shoes that needed lacing at one time or another." Everyone applauded as Ruth dramatically kneaded her lower back.

More salutations and gifts were sent her way: Rhoda and Barry wowed everyone with a five-hundred-dollar gift certificate to Lord & Taylor. Sarah handed up her present. Ruth read the card and said, "Oh, honey, that's beautiful. Just beautiful. Can I read this out loud?"

Sarah nodded and Ruth read: "Dear Mom, I can't give you anything you don't already have. I can only return some of the gifts you have shared with me. I love you. Sarah." She opened Sarah's present, a leather-bound edition of Edna St. Vincent Millay's collected poems. She paged through the book until she found the poem she wanted, and then she read it aloud:

My candle burns at both ends;
It will not last the night;
But ah, my foes, and oh, my friends—
It gives a lovely light!

I silently accompanied her reading, for I remembered Ruth reciting this poem many nights to Sarah, Seamus, and me. My mother reached over some boxes and squeezed Sarah's hand. Behind me, I heard Rhoda whisper to Barry, "Is that the whole poem?"

Seamus gave her a menorah, then I stood up and handed her my present: an antique amethyst brooch. She opened the case and held the brooch up like a small trophy, and I realized that everyone was waiting for me to say something. I raised my cup and looked at my mother's expectant face. "To a wonderful mom. . . ." Then, in a rush, I added, "Thanks for all your lovely light!" I rapidly drained my champagne and put my arm around Ruth to let all the guests know that the speech was over.

Everyone applauded, but I felt dizzy and made my way down the hall. The bed in my old room was covered with coats, so I lay down on Ruth's bed. I put a pillow over my head, afraid that the room was going to begin revolving, the bed spinning faster and faster.

I felt a hand on my foot. Lifting the pillow, I saw Sarah standing by the bed with a cup of coffee. "I thought you might need this," she said.

I leaned back against the headboard, sipping. "I guess Mr. Conroy isn't coming," I said.

Ruth's laughter rose up over the din. "Doesn't sound as if she's very upset about it," Sarah replied.

"Actually, we were discussing him in the car. Mom was concerned I thought she was *wanton*."

"Wanton?" Sarah repeated, incredulous.

"That's the word she used. Can you believe it?" I set the cup down.

"The sad thing is she probably believes it. She's slept with three men in fifty years. God, I had slept with four boys by the time I was eighteen."

"Yeah, that's what I told her."

She laughed and conked me on the head with a pillow.

"She told me she felt a hundred times better after hearing that," I said, grabbing her wrist and placing her in a light headlock.

"Shut up! Shut up! Shut up!" She freed herself, still laughing. Then we both leaned against the headboard. Sarah tilted her head against my shoulder.

"Sarah?"

"Yes?"

"Do you remember that time Jimmy Conroy woke us up in the middle of the night and took us to Rhoda and Barry's house?"

"How old were we?"

"Ten or so."

"I try not to remember those years."

"That's probably a good idea."

I remembered him gently waking us up, telling us that our mother was in the hospital but that she would be fine and that he was taking us to our aunt and uncle's house. I remembered sitting with my brother and sister in the spacious backseat of Mr. Conroy's station wagon and Sarah—who usually never let a tear come to her eyes, even when I socked her in the back or yanked her ear—crying hysterically. Her tears had begun when we saw the bloodstained carpet outside our mother's bedroom and continued after Rhoda put us to bed in her guest room, in two single beds on opposite sides of a night table. Sarah was crying more quietly by then—an eerie, rhythmic moaning. Then I heard her choke out my name. I lay very still, my heart vibrating. She said my name again, keening it, pleading. I put my feet on the floor, which felt as strange as the surface of the moon, and climbed in next to her. She put her arm around me, and I could feel her body heaving with grief, as if she knew our mother would not recover.

"May I?" I said, my hand just above her belly.

"Of course."

I placed my hand on the small mound.

"Can you feel anything?" she asked.

"No. Am I supposed to?"

"Sometimes you can."

"I don't think I'll ever be a father," I said.

"You still have plenty of time. I mean, you are a man. You don't have the ticking clock problem."

"I wasn't thinking of the problem as biological."

"You'll find someone, Seth. I'm sure of it."

"I don't think so. Molly was my best chance. She loved me for all the right reasons, but I didn't love her well enough. I'm not sure if I'm capable of loving anyone very well."

"I don't think that's true," she said softly. "Don't think that way."

"All right. I won't. I promise."

Sarah told me she needed to get back to the party. It had become very lively. My mother's voice was especially loud and joyous. In three hours, after everyone was gone, my mother would be lying in this bed, her cigarette gleaming on and off through the night. But I imagined her standing in her bathrobe in the backyard of our old house in Massachusetts. On the page I'd taken from her old journal, she'd said it was the happiest morning of her life. The date was June 15, 1956, five months before she gave birth to Sarah and me, six years before her husband left her, years before she fell in love with Jimmy Conroy, before she struck me with a cup, before she combed the streets of Patterson in search of an abortionist and then almost bled to death in her bed. She and my father had moved into the house in January, and the winter had been brutal; old drifts of gray snow had remained on the ground through the end of April. But on the morning of June 15, the clear morning air vibrated with the trilling of birds. Ruth stood in the middle of the yard, overjoyed to feel the warmth of the sun on her face. She stepped out of her wet slippers and shuddered from a series of our convulsive kicks inside her. She squeezed the ground between her toes and cradled her belly. Her fingertips slowly navigated its entire surface. All was well: all wondrous and alive.

DANCING WITH ELIJAH

E ver since she was a young girl, my mother had been terrified of being pronounced dead on a Friday afternoon. Her fear came from an old family story. Her mother, Esther, had a younger brother, Samuel, who died at the age of twelve. The boy had been sick for a long time with a vague illness. He closed his eyes on a Wednesday night and still hadn't opened them by three o'clock on Friday afternoon. A group of men congregated around his bed, debating what to do. If the boy was dead, they were required to bury him within twenty-four hours, but they had to act immediately because they were prohibited from interring the body over the Sabbath. Samuel's father, Jacob, pulled back a curtain and studied the gray and gloomy sky. The December sun would set in less than two hours. He held a small pocket mirror under his son's nose. It remained clear, unclouded by any sign of life. The men exchanged somber glances, a rabbi nodded, and Jacob wrapped his son in a prayer shawl and buried him before the sun went down. For many years, Ruth had a recurring nightmare in which young Samuel opened his eyes inside the pitch black coffin, shouted for help, and pounded his fist against the lid, and all to no avail because the mourners had departed.

On the last Friday morning of her life, her mind in a slight morphine haze, Ruth reminded me not to let anyone bury her until after she had been dead for a full twenty-four hours. We were in a bright hospital room. Seamus was the only Orthodox Jew left in the family, and she knew very well that he would wait until after the Sabbath to bury her if she died by the end of the day. I held her hand and told her she didn't have anything to worry about. She still looked anxious, so I added that I would chain myself to her body if necessary. She laughed wheezily. Then she squeezed my hand and looked at me emotionally. "Seth, darling," she said, "I hope I was a good mother."

"Yes, of course you were." Tears slid slowly down across her temples. "Despite everything, I always felt loved," I added.

"Thank you, sweetheart," she said, and I finally felt that I had said the right thing, had reminded her of the one thing she did well—she had loved her children absolutely, unconditionally. Then I whispered in her ear that I loved her.

When she woke up Saturday morning, I was so relieved that I permitted a prayer of thanks to rise from my lips. She died later that afternoon.

RACHEL WAS COMING! We had not seen each other in twelve years, since her mother's funeral. When Sarah was married in 1986, I had sent her an invitation to the wedding, but she had called me up and asked if I expected her to pretend to be my girlfriend. I had replied that it would certainly make my mother happy if she did. Then she said that she wasn't comfortable pretending to be my girlfriend anymore. "Let me get this *straight*," I'd said. "Pun very much intended, by the way. You couldn't bring yourself to come out to your mother, but now you want me to out you to *my* mother?"

Rachel hung up on me.

We went two years without speaking or writing to each other. Then I sent her a long letter, apologizing for not dealing well with her relationship with Lucinda. I explained that for five years I had known I was the most important person in her life and it was difficult for me not to be connected to her in the same way anymore. I told her about my job, about Molly. When she wrote back, she reminded me that she had pledged to be my friend for life and she still meant it.

On Saturday night, I drove to Newark Airport to get her. She had made her reservation the day before when I told her I didn't think my mother would survive the night. At the airport, we embraced for a long time, then stepped back and studied each other.

"You look exactly the same," Rachel said.

"You look better," I replied.

"Liar," she said, laughing.

Actually, I was hoping she would say that *I* looked better. I wondered if she remembered our last night together in Chicago when, lying in each other's arms, she had stroked my face and told me I was going to look so handsome when I was older. The morning I turned forty, I faced myself in the mirror and thought that Rachel had been wrong about everything—my personal life, my career, my looks, especially my looks. I had pouches under my eyes, a deeply lined forehead, and the skin around my Adam's apple had become ringed with age. My nose, with each passing year, became more pocked and porous.

Driving out of the airport, I asked Rachel if she wanted to come back to my mother's apartment for a drink. With Ruth's death imminent, I had come down to New Jersey the week before, and I had been staying in my mother's apartment, the apartment

I grew up in, drinking my way through the dust-coated bottles of liquor Ruth kept under the kitchen sink. Rachel said that she was really exhausted and just wanted to go to her hotel and lie down. I was still disappointed that she was staying at a hotel. Before she came east for the funeral, I had told her she was welcome to stay with me. Rachel had replied that she didn't want to put me out. I had said that I wouldn't be put out. The apartment had two bedrooms, I reminded her. Of course I was really hoping that we would share the same bed. After all, who wants to sleep alone the night before he buries his mother? Rachel, no doubt aware of what I really wanted, had thanked me all the same and said she'd prefer to stay in a hotel.

After saying good night to Rachel at her hotel, I drove back to the apartment and immediately poured myself a drink. Sarah and I had already divided up our mother's belongings. Seamus had said he didn't want anything, shocking both Sarah and me. The two of us had easily split up everything. I just wanted Ruth's books and records. Sarah wanted our mother's bed, the china and the jewelry, which she offered to share with me because it was worth money. "No, no," I had said. "Those are things you can pass down to your children. Who knows if I'll ever have children?" Sarah had said I could always change my mind if I did have children someday.

Drink in hand, I went to the bookshelf, trying to decide which books I wanted to keep. Her collection was eclectic—e. e. cummings, Harold Robbins, Herman Wouk, Edna St. Vincent Millay, Thomas Wolfe, Shakespeare, Henry and Philip Roth, Theodore White, Abraham Joshua Heschel. I had read practically every book on the shelf by the time I had graduated from high school. I looked through one of the Harold Robbins novels, *A Stone for Danny Fisher*, recalled how avidly I had read it when I was fifteen, and decided I would simply keep every book. I put back the Harold Robbins and removed my mother's copy of *Pride and Prejudice* for the time being.

I had not been in contact with Molly for years, but after two stiff drinks, I was on the verge of calling her, certain that I still remembered her telephone number. I dialed it, deciding to leave things to chance: If it was the right number, then I would know I had done the right thing. A man answered and I put the phone back down. I called Rachel at her hotel.

"Rachel, can I come over and sleep with you?"

"Seth, no."

"I don't mean *sleep* sleep with you. I mean like sleep next to you." As I said this, I knew how fraudulent my words sounded. Of course I was hoping to score some sympathy sex.

"I don't think that would be a very good idea," Rachel told me.

"Come *on*. I slept with you the night before your mother's funeral!"

"Yes, and remember how badly that turned out?"

"I promise I won't tell Lucinda."

"Seth, I'm not saying no because I don't want to."

"Really?"

"Yes, and that's why it's a bad idea. Get some sleep, Seth. I love you."

"I love you too," I replied, and put the phone down.

I HAD TOLD SEAMUS THAT I wanted to deliver the eulogy for our mother; we had been in her hospital room just after she had died. "Absolutely not," he had said. "My rabbi's doing it." I had been angry, but I wasn't about to face Seamus down with our mother's body between us. I knew he didn't approve of the "Mom stories" Sarah and I loved to exchange. Perhaps Seamus was remembering the one time he and Ruth had come to see me do my comedy routine. I acted out my version of the deathbed dilemma over young Samuel, yukking up the Yiddish accents of the old men. In the twist I added to the story, Samuel suddenly awakens, but the old men are so caught up in their Talmudic tête-à-tête that they don't even notice him when he tries to get their attention. Finally, he rises from the bed and shouts out that he's alive. The old men stop their discussion and turn to look at him; then they tell him to shush and go back to debating whether or not he is dead.

My mother had laughed heartily, but Seamus, like Queen Victoria, was not amused.

The funeral was on Long Island, where all of Ruth's family was buried. I was surprised to see my ninety-six-year-old grandfather at the funeral home. His mind had been gradually splintering apart for the last ten years. He was on the arm of his other daughter, my aunt Rhoda, who cared for him day and night. Before senility set in, my grandfather had been cold and manipulative. He had expected his daughters to compete for his love, and Ruth had been no match for Rhoda.

I went over and kissed him on the cheek.

"Hello, Poppa," I said.

"Do I know you?" he replied.

I removed my glasses and brought my face close to his. "I'm Seth, Poppa. Your grandson. Ruth's son."

"Oh, Ruth. How is Ruth? I haven't seen her in so long."

Rhoda said, "Ruth is dead, Daddy. I told you this morning. She died yesterday."

"Ruth died? Does Esther know?"

"Daddy, Mother died thirty-five years ago."

My grandfather stared at the ground and placed a hand on top of his scaly, liver-spotted head. I imagined he could feel the brain cells whooshing out like steam from a kettle.

"What about Rose?" he asked, referring to his second wife.

"She died twenty years ago, Daddy."

Rhoda whispered to me, "I always tell him the truth, not that it matters to him in his condition. I could tell him that everyone is living happily on the Riviera and he wouldn't know the difference."

I wondered why Rhoda just didn't tell him everyone was wonderful, but she spent the most time with him and I figured she knew best. Then Rhoda said to me, "The woman who came with you. That's the rabbi's daughter, right?"

I told her she was.

"Is she still a lesbian?"

My grandfather looked up at Rhoda. "Who did you say was dead?"

"Ruth," I said, trying to be helpful. "She and Esther are together now, Poppa."

He gave me a perplexed look. "Do I know you?"

Rachel and I found our seats in the front row of the small chapel. I stared sullenly at my mother's coffin as the young rabbi of Seamus's congregation droned on about her life. He described her as a loving mother, a devoted grandmother, a woman who led "a good Jewish life." He kept repeating that phrase, and I knew he was running out of things to say.

Ruth's casket had already been lowered into the ground by the time we arrived at the cemetery. She was next to her mother, Esther (1912–1962); next to Esther was the plot reserved for my grandfather. Then came Rose (1915–1976), who was next to Esther's father, Jacob (1885–1955), who was next to his wife, Dvorah (1888–1933), who was next to her son, Samuel (1914–1926). Seamus, Sarah, and I stood together on the lip of the open grave and chanted the mourner's Kaddish: "*Yisgadal, ve yiskadash . . .*" Sarah and I tripped over the familiar Hebrew words, trying to keep up with our brother. I concluded with a resounding *amen* and then announced that I had something to add. Seamus looked at the ground and brought a hand to his brow. I reminded the other mourners that my mother had loved her biblical name, and then I recited Ruth's declaration of love to Naomi: "Your people shall be my people, and your God my God. Where you die, I will die, and there I will be buried. Nothing but death shall divide us." Sarah squeezed my hand and pressed her head into my arm. Seamus smiled at me, no doubt relieved. I wondered if he had any memory of our visits to the cemetery when we were children, and how our mother had fashioned those words into her own personal Kaddish. We had kept just far enough away that her words were a dim murmur as she recited them over her mother's grave; somehow we had known not to disturb her rare moment of privacy and grace. When she got down on her knees and plucked the grass along the borders of the grave (I always suspected she was just trying to get a little closer to her mother), I would go off in search of interesting headstones. I liked trying to conjure a complete life from the thin line of numbers engraved on a tablet. I was especially drawn to families who had all died on the same day (fire? disease? car accident?) and to children, like Samuel, who had died before their parents. (I closed my eyes and wondered what it felt like to lose your child.) On two or three occasions I had found husbands and wives who had died within days of each other. I always presumed one of them had died of sheer grief, and I had tried to imagine how two people could love each other that much.

The three of us each had a turn casting a spadeful of earth onto the casket, and then we stood around in the sunshine accepting more hugs and condolences. Some of the more remote relatives attempted to introduce themselves, but I surprised them by revealing that I knew everything about them.

"Oh, Cousin Sandy! Yes, of course I remember you," I said to a cousin of my mother's I probably hadn't seen since I was thirteen. "You're Mimi's brother. Do you still own that shoe store with her husband, Bill, in Hempstead?"

"Why, yes . . . ," he said, as if he had just learned these facts about his life.

I turned to Sandy's wife. "Selma, how are you?"

"Oh, I'm fine, doll, just fine," she replied, appearing moved by the illusion of familiarity I had created.

"How are your daughters, Susan and Mindy?"

Seamus scrolled his eyes up into his head.

"Is this your wife?" Selma asked, looking at Rachel. She and I were holding hands.

"Former wife," I explained. "But we've stayed very close friends."

Rachel cast me an incredulous look. Selma looked sad and perplexed.

"We were too young when we met," I continued. "We were just college students."

Just as Sandy was saying we had to get together soon, Selma pointed to a black woman accompanied by two black men.

"Who's that?" she whispered, even though they were a good twenty feet away. "Your mother's girl?"

She was referring to Alice, Ruth's closest friend and coworker for more than thirty years.

"Yes," I whispered back to Selma. "But Tara is lost."

Rachel burst out laughing.

"Now you know why we divorced," I said to my not-so-amused cousins. "She caused a scene every time we went to a funeral."

I excused myself and went over to Alice.

"I'm so sorry, Seth, honey," Alice whispered into my ear as we embraced. One of the men with Alice was Freddy, her husband. I didn't know who the other man was, but I was surprised to see that his eyes were red from crying. He wore a faded blue satin yarmulke.

"This is my cousin, Elijah," Alice said, introducing him to me.

"Oh, so you're Elijah," I said. It had never occurred to me that Elijah might be black. "My mother kept a postcard you sent her by the side of her bed when she was in the hospital," I explained. Ruth had kept a veritable shrine by her bedside—letters, photographs, a locket, an old menorah. On the front of the postcard was a picture of a woman standing barefoot in a field at sunset, holding a sickle. On the back, someone had written: "*If I keep you alive in my heart, not even death can divide us. May the Lord keep faith with you. Elijah.*" I had asked my mother who Elijah was and was disappointed when she said he had been our mailman years ago. I had been hoping she would tell me a story about Elijah being some secret lover.

Elijah nodded slightly.

"Thank you for thinking of her in such a beautiful way."

Whether it was remembering the words that Elijah had written to my mother or the long, difficult morning finally catching up with me, I was overcome at that moment; tears coursed down my hot, splotchy face. Elijah turned away to press a handkerchief against his eyes.

Everyone returned to their cars, but Seamus was still saying goodbye to Alice, Freddy, and Elijah. He briefly embraced each one of them, then tramped back to where his family was waiting. The plan was to meet up back in New Jersey at Manny's, a restaurant where Ruth and Alice had been regulars for over three decades.

As Rachel and I drove away from the cemetery, I said, "I apologize for last night."

"No need to," she replied.

"I was actually surprised you came out here for the funeral."

We were not nearly as close as we had once been, time and distance eroding our connection. Rachel didn't reply; I looked over and noticed she was crying.

"Rachel, what's the matter?"

"Oh, Seth, Lucinda and I are going through a hard time."

She told me that she and Lucinda wanted a family, and Rachel was the one trying to get pregnant because Lucinda was seven years older. On the morning she was scheduled for her third and last IUI procedure, Rachel and Lucinda had a brutal argument. Rachel wanted Lucinda to accompany her to the clinic but Lucinda refused to skip a department meeting. She didn't see any reason why Rachel needed her to come. Later, Rachel was lying on the examining table in the clinic and the technician, a young Filipino woman, was having trouble inserting the tube into Rachel's uterus. The pain was unbearable. "Fuck this," Rachel finally shouted. "Go get a fucking doctor to do it!" Eventually, the donor sperm was shot into her through the tube, and then Rachel was left alone in the room for thirty minutes, her legs and her life up in the air. Tears slanted down across her temples. She had never felt so alone, so angry. She wanted Lucinda to be in the room sitting next to her, holding her hand; she needed to know that Lucinda wanted a child as much as she did. She thought about how she had done all the sacrificing from the very beginning of their relationship. She had turned down an attractive offer from a prestigious East Coast university and accepted a position at a second-rate school in the Bay Area so Lucinda wouldn't have to leave her tenured job at Stanford. Lucinda had a lighter teaching load, a higher salary, and numerous leaves; Rachel's career, her scholarship, had stagnated while she taught four brain-numbing classes a term. She had sacrificed her career, and now she was sacrificing her body—powerful drugs were injected into it, blood was drawn out it, her belly was slit open for a laparoscopy—and Lucinda couldn't skip a fucking meeting!

"That's difficult," I said after Rachel had told me all of it. "Sometimes I wonder whether Molly and I might be married now if she hadn't miscarried. I mean, if not for some chromosomal abnormalities, my whole life might have turned out differently."

Rachel put her hand on my leg, and we rode in silence, two longtime friends and long-ago lovers, both of us motherless, both of us middle-aged, and wondering if we would ever be parents.

WHEN WE ARRIVED AT MANNY'S, I was happy to see Alice and Freddy were joining us. A line of people came over to offer condolences—Sammy, the waiter; Jules and Leon, the countermen; Rhea, the woman who worked behind the cash register; and many of the other regular patrons—Bob Robinson, Ruby Herzon, Ted Krell. Jules and Leon pulled together four tables to accommodate our large party. Everyone, except for Alice, who always ordered the same lunch, sought refuge behind their menus.

Seamus's two children, Zipporah and Avi, were sitting directly across from me, next to Sarah's children, Vanessa and Jason. I clowned around a little with Sarah's kids, who knew me because I always stayed with Sarah during my visits to New Jersey. But neither of Seamus's children would look in my direction, though seven-year-old Zipporah did lift her eyes for a microsecond, compelled, no doubt, by the same curiosity that did in Lot's wife. I wondered what they had been told about me. Seamus was not a rigid zealot. His orthodoxy was a suburban, contemporary variety: He kept his beard closely trimmed and covered his head with a handsome, wide-brimmed fedora.

The lunch crowd was enormous, and Sammy the only waiter, so we sat for an interminable amount of time after everyone had put their menus down.

Finally, Alice said, "I'm glad to see you two boys are getting along now. I know how much it meant to Ruth before she died."

"Amen," Freddy said quietly.

Seamus and I both pulsed arterial red. We weren't worthy of this pronouncement. The brotherly affection Ruth had witnessed during the last six months of her life was mainly an act for her

sake. I still wanted Seamus to apologize for not sending me condolences when he had learned that Molly had miscarried and then
when she left me, for placing orthodoxy before love and family,
but of course he wouldn't. Now that our mother was dead, I wondered what would keep us connected.

SAMMY FINALLY CAME TO THE TABLE to take our orders. His hands
had a chronic tremble and a heavy Star of David lay against his
sallow chest. When he got to Alice, he said, "The usual?"

"Sammy," she replied, "is that a Jewish thing?"

"Is what a Jewish thing?"

"Asking questions you already know the answers to."

I was surprised to see that Seamus was smiling; perhaps he had
caught this act before.

Sammy considered the question for a couple of seconds. "If
I do it," he concluded, "then it has to be a Jewish thing." And he
went back to work.

We all laughed, but my laughter suddenly turned into a high-
pitched honk. Everyone looked at me as if I were possessed. Zipporah stared the longest. Her eyes gleamed with tiny triangles of
light, which, to me, revealed a very avid nature. I winked at her
and she immediately looked down.

Sammy returned to the table, bringing complimentary bowls of
mushroom-barley soup for everyone.

"Thanks, Sammy," Alice said. "You're a good Jew."

He placed a bowl of soup in front of her, and replied, "I'd like
to know who told you there were any bad ones."

Before eating their soup, Alice and Freddy both bowed their
heads and prayed.

After lunch, I asked Seamus if he would come back to the
apartment with me.

"What for?" he asked.

"I want your advice about what to do with some of Mom's things."

"Seth, I thought we already did this."

"Seamus, just go," Deborah said.

"Oh, all right," Seamus replied, as if, as I suspected, he depended on Deborah to tell him the right things to do in life.

Everyone embraced and kissed good-bye until later that evening, when we would all reconvene at Seamus's house. Rachel told me that Sarah had offered to drive her back to her hotel and gave me an especially tight embrace. Then Seamus and I drove to the apartment.

"I remember Rachel from your college graduation," Seamus said. "She's a nice girl."

Apparently Seamus didn't know that she was a lesbian.

"Because she's Jewish?" I asked.

"Seth, don't start in with me."

"All right, Reb Seamus."

"Don't make fun of my name, either."

We drove the rest of the way in silence.

Seamus had avoided our old apartment since Ruth had gone into the hospital. I understood that it held memories that were just as bad for him as they were for me, but I also remembered bathing with Seamus in this apartment; I remembered the scar on his leg from a skin graft, the constellation of birthmarks across his back, the way his tush was pocked and puckered from injections our mother had given him for an early childhood illness. Recalling these details made me feel deeply intimate and connected with my brother, but I couldn't imagine communicating such feelings to him.

Inside, Seamus kept his coat on, apparently anxious to go as soon as possible. Despite his beard and hat, he looked exactly like Ruth, and seeing him standing in the living room I longed to hold my brother's face in my hands. Since I had no hope of doing that either, I asked him if he knew Elijah.

"Yes, we're friends," Seamus answered.

"You're friends? Really?"

"What's the matter, Seth? You don't think it's possible for me to have a black friend?"

"No, but—"

"But you think I'm closed-minded, don't you?"

"No, Seamus, I don't think Mom brought us up to be closed-minded."

"That's right," he said emphatically, as if this were the one thing we could agree on.

"Did Mom introduce you to Elijah?"

"No. He's a clerk at the post office. I see him every week when I mail my bills and buy my stamps."

"So he just introduced himself?"

Seamus reddened. "He told me that he and Mom were friends and that I looked exactly like her."

"I knew it!"

"Knew what?"

"Seamus, don't you think he and Mom were once in love?"

"Seth," he sighed, "stop it."

"Stop what?"

"Telling dumb stories."

"Seamus, come on. Her second marriage ended twenty-seven years ago. Do you think she just stopped being interested in men?"

"Yes."

"What?"

"Yes, considering the men she was married to, that's what I think."

Didn't he know about Jimmy Conroy? Or did he pretend not to know? I wondered if I could have scored a knockout by telling him all about Jimmy, but then thought better of it.

"Well, I don't believe such a thing," I said. "I even think I remember seeing Mom and Elijah together. Remember that time we went to a Christmas party at Alice's house, circa 1966?"

"I don't know. I would have been six years old then."

"That was the day a cop pulled us over because Mom ran a red light. She had drunk too much eggnog at the party, and when the cop accused her of being intoxicated, she told him that she was Jewish and hadn't realized that eggnog had alcohol in it."

Seamus glared at me. "Seth, is there anything you don't remember?"

"No, I don't think so."

I recalled that the cop actually let my mother go after she pleaded with him that if she lost her license she wouldn't able to drive to work and support her children. He called a cab and then graphically told her about all the drunk-driving accidents he had seen, many of them involving children. He told her a story about a little girl who had gone hurtling through a windshield. The little girl's mother had had an open bottle of beer next to her. "What type of mother would do something like that?" the cop had said, just as the taxi pulled up.

"John Coltrane's version of 'Ev'ry Time We Say Goodbye' was playing on the phonograph," I continued. "Mom and this black man were dancing together, holding each other very closely. Mom was smiling and her eyes were closed. She looked like she was having a nice dream. I'm sure that man was Elijah." I also remembered how her bare arms had gleamed with a thin film of perspiration, but I decided to leave out this detail.

"Seth," Seamus said, "you were ten years old in 1966. How did you know you were hearing John Coltrane?"

"Seamus," I replied, "some things you just know."

"You don't know," Seamus said. "Elijah was our mailman."

"I know he was the mailman. But they still could have been lovers."

"Elijah is a religious man. He has a family and goes to church every Sunday. Sorry to disappoint you."

"I'm not disappointed. They still could have been in love."

Seamus gestured dismissively with one hand and straightened his hat with the other one. "You know, Seth, I came here with you because I thought you wanted to have a heart-to-heart. But I have to go now."

"Wait! I did. I do," I said.

"Then how come you're going on like this about Mom and Elijah? Why do you always have to turn everything into such a megillah?"

"Just hear this," I said, putting my hand on my brother's arm. The John Coltrane version of "Ev'ry Time We Say Goodbye" was already on the record player because I had played it about fifty times over the last two days.

I turned it on and the music, velvety and mournful, actually appeared to calm Seamus. He closed his eyes and his rigid posture relaxed. My brother and I had not embraced in years, not even on this day, the day we had buried our mother. I put my arms around him and began to sway with him to the music. Seamus held me tightly; I felt my brother's wet, bearded cheek against my own. "Oh, Seth," he whispered, "I can't believe she's gone."

AT SIX O'CLOCK, I left to get Rachel at her hotel. I brought my mother's old copy of *Pride and Prejudice* with me. Driving to Seamus's house, Rachel asked if I had had a good visit with my brother.

"Yes. We slow danced to John Coltrane's version of 'Ev'ry Time We Say Goodbye.'"

"Oh, all right," Rachel replied.

"I'm totally serious," I said. "But I guess you had to be there."

The front door to the house was open when we arrived. Rhoda and a clutch of my elderly second cousins were standing just inside the door. The cousins included Marcia from Great Neck, Milton and Pearl from Hempstead, and the twins, Jenny and Jeanette, of Rockville Centre, who had lived together for the last thirty-five years, ever since Jenny's husband had died and Jeanette's had fled. I introduced Rachel by name but not by relationship. All my cousins said it was nice to see her again, presuming they had probably met her at some point. Then Marcia marveled at how much I looked like my mother. I replied that I thought Seamus looked more like Mom than I did, and this sparked a five-minute debate about who looked more like Ruth. Then Jeanette said the person I really looked like was Zeyde Jacob. Jenny told her she was completely out of her tree—how could she remember what Zeyde Jacob looked like when she couldn't even remember to turn off the lights inside the house? Jeanette pressed her lips into an angry line. Rhoda interjected that different people remember different things, but Jeanette wasn't about to be mollified and she proceeded to describe how my face was an exact reproduction of Zeyde Jacob's. While all this was going on, I noticed my grandfather sitting in a chair on the other side of the room. I asked Rhoda if I ought to go over and say hello to him.

"Sure, doll, go ahead."

"Do you think he'll remember who I am?"

"Who knows? I live with him day and night, and it's a complete mystery to me what goes on inside his head."

I excused myself, seized Rachel's hand, and went over to my grandfather. I pulled up a chair. He stared vacantly past me, his mouth wide open, rivulets of saliva running down his chin. I reached in my pocket, pulled out the yarmulke supplied by the funeral home that morning, and dabbed the saliva away.

"Hello, Poppa. How are you?"

He stared at Rachel and me.

"How's the family?" he asked.

Behind me, I could hear Jenny and Jeanette still arguing over nothing.

"The family's great, Poppa. Couldn't be better."

"How many children do you have now?"

I was my grandfather's only childless grandchild.

"Two, Poppa. A boy and a girl."

The old man's eyes went out of focus for a moment. Then he fixed his sight on something just over my shoulder. I turned around and saw that it was a mirror draped with black cloth.

He bent close to me. "Did someone die?"

I could have said anything. I could have said that nobody had died, or I could have named one of the dead from long ago— Esther or Samuel, Jacob or Dvorah.

I took hold of his hand.

"Poppa, do you remember your daughter Ruth?"

"Sure, I do!" he said, his dentures gleaming. "How is Ruth? I haven't seen her in so long."

"She's fine, Poppa. Couldn't be better."

I planted a kiss on his cheek and Rachel and I headed for the drinks table.

"It's strange to think that's the same man who tyrannized my mother for so many years," I said.

"He's so sweet now," Rachel commented.

"Just imagine. We'd be the happiest family in the world if no one remembered anything."

I spied Avi and Zipporah sitting at the kitchen table, looking at a book.

"Come," I said to Rachel, "I'm going to try to get my brother's children to like me."

"You go yourself, sweetie. I need to just be myself for a couple of minutes."

They were looking at a book of illustrated Bible stories. I

squeezed myself in between them. "Who remembers me?" I asked. They exchanged shy, uncomfortable smiles.

"Zipporah, you know who I am, don't you?" I said.

"Uncle Seth," she replied quietly.

"Yes!" I said brightly. "The one and only Uncle Seth. So, who's your favorite uncle?"

She looked puzzled for a moment. "We just have one uncle," she answered.

I wondered if she was referring to Aaron, but I brazened it out and exclaimed, "Then it must be me!" I clapped my hands against my cheeks.

Her lips pursed into a coy smile.

"Avi, am I your favorite uncle?"

He looked to his sister for an answer. A small knitted disk of a yarmulke was fastened to his short hair with a bobby pin. A choo-choo train motif ran around its border.

"That's a nice kippah," I said.

"You know kippah?" Zipporah asked.

So I had been described as some type of apostate, a family member who did not live by the Torah. They might read their book of Bible stories and think of me as a Cain or an Esau, a wayward, bitter brother.

"Of course I know kippah," I replied, and placed the one that was still damp with Poppa's saliva on my head. "I never go anywhere without one."

The children laughed at me and then returned to their book. I went back into the living room and saw Seamus bent over Poppa, whispering in his ear. I was standing by a table laden with scotch. I poured myself a drink and waved Seamus over.

"Does Poppa know who you are?" I asked him.

"It's difficult to tell."

"But you speak to him anyway?"

"Sure. Might as well. You never know what gets through to him."

"Sort of like praying to God?" I said.

Seamus eyed me warily, then seemed to decide that my comment was sincere, that I really was interested in how he prayed.

"Yes, you could say that," he answered.

I pulled Mother's battered paperback copy of *Pride and Prejudice* out of my back pocket.

"Here, Seamus," I said, holding the book out to him. "I want you to have this."

Seamus turned his head sideways to read the title. "What? Is this supposed to have some big message for me?"

"No, no message at all. I know you don't want to keep anything from the apartment, but Mom read this book from cover to cover during a game at Yankee Stadium in 1968. The Yankees beat the White Sox four to two. Mel Stottlemyre pitched into the seventh inning, when he was relieved by Jack Hamilton. Here. It would mean a lot to me if you took this."

"Thanks," he said, accepting the book. "I'll try to keep all that in mind."

Then I added, "I also thought Zipporah might like to read it when she's older. You can tell her it was Mom's favorite novel."

"Why can't you tell her yourself?"

"I can? You mean that?"

"Yes, of course."

"Oh, Seamus, thank you! Thank you very much!"

Seamus stared at me as if I were some intractable mystery.

"Seth, can I tell you something that I've always wanted to say?"

"Sure, of course."

"You're my brother, and I love you, but you are a very strange man."

I burst out laughing. "Oh, Seamus, thank you. Thank you very much."

"Well, you are," he said, laughing back. "Why can't you come right out and tell me you want Zipporah to have this book? Why do you have to do some song and dance about a baseball game almost thirty years ago? Or like the way you were playing games with Sandy and Selma at the cemetery this morning, or creating this big megillah about Mom and Elijah. I don't even know how to explain it, Seth, but you do things like that all the time."

"You mean like acting funny when I'm really sad?"

"Exactly!" he exclaimed, as amazed as if Poppa had suddenly become lucid. "So you know you're doing it?"

"Usually, yes."

Seamus's face went slack with sorrow. "Seth, I know we've had our problems, but you don't have to keep me at arm's length at a time like this."

I could feel the vein between my eyebrows beating violently.

"Tell me what's on your mind," Seamus said.

"I really wanted to eulogize Mom this morning," I replied, my voice trembling badly. "How could you not have trusted me?"

Seamus pressed his lips together and bowed his head. I placed my hand against the side of my brother's face.

"I would have given a beautiful eulogy!" I cried.

"I know you would have, Seth. I know you would have. I apologize."

Just then the doorbell rang. From where I was standing, I could see out the picture window. Alice, Freddy, and Elijah were standing at the door.

"You better go, Seamus. Elijah is ringing your doorbell."

"Not just yet," he said. "Deborah will get it. I have something for you too. In my study."

I followed Seamus to a small room with a desk and a computer. On the walls were photographs of his children and his ornate ketubah, or marriage contract. He opened a box on his desk and a pulled out a thin paperback book. I needed a moment to register the title.

A STRANGER ON THE PLANET
By Seth Shapiro

ON THE COVER WAS AN illustration of a boy in his bar mitzvah suit and tallis, looking out at the ocean. A woman, his mother, was standing several feet behind him.

Seamus could see that I was flummoxed.

"Mom wanted me to have copies of this story privately printed," he explained.

"How many copies?" I asked.

"One hundred twenty."

"One hundred and twenty? Is that a Jewish thing? Mom used to say she hoped I'd live one hundred and twenty years."

"Yes, it's a Jewish thing. Moses lived for one hundred and twenty years. So it's a hopeful number. We all hope that we can attain the longevity of Moses."

"So . . . ," I said. "Did you read the story?"

"Yes."

"What did you think?"

"I think you treated Mom much better in that story than you did in real life."

"My ex-wife—remember her? the one you never met?—said something very similar to me one time."

He lightly raked his fingers through his beard and sighed.

"Seth, I owe you an apology. It was bad of me not to have called you when you lost your baby."

"Thank you, Seamus. That means a lot to me. It truly does."

I paged through my story. It was actually bound and typeset like a book, on book-quality paper.

"Do you think Zipporah might like to read this too, when she's older?" I asked.

"Yes, I think she would like that very much."

WHEN WE RETURNED TO THE LIVING ROOM, I saw that Rachel and Sarah were sitting next to my grandfather. Both women were crying. I went over to them.

Poppa fixed his gaze on me. "You! What are you doing here?"

For a moment I was dumbfounded. Then I realized that Poppa had mistaken me for the person I most closely resembled.

"Oh, no, Poppa," I said. "I'm not Elliot. I'm Seth, your grandson."

Poppa looked at the ground and put his hand on top of his head. Then he looked back up at me.

"You know what your father did?" he asked in a whisper.

"Yes," I said. "I know everything."

Poppa turned to Rachel. "My poor Esther never recovered. Did you, darling?"

"That was a long time ago," Rachel replied. "I'm doing much better now."

Esther had died before my father abandoned us. I wondered if, over time, my grandfather had conflated the two events in his mind, refashioning family history so that his wife's death was caused by the great injury done to his daughter.

"We're all doing much better now," Sarah said.

"What about Ruth?" Poppa asked. "I didn't think she would recover from such a shock. She was always so anxious."

"She's fine, Poppa. Just fine," I said.

"Oh, I hope so. I haven't seen her in so long."

"I'm going to visit with the grandchildren now," Rachel said to Poppa.

"All right, Esther, sweetheart," Poppa said. Sarah stood up too.

"Rose, my dearest," he said to Sarah, "come back soon."

"I will, darling."

As we walked away, Rachel said, "He thought I was his wife Esther. He kept telling me how much he had missed me."

"He thought I was Rose," Sarah said.

"You don't look bad for a woman who's been dead for nearly thirty-five years," I commented to Rachel.

"Don't, Seth," Sarah said. "It was so sad."

I looked at Sarah and Rachel.

"I'll tell you what's really sad," I said to them. "I'm looking at the only two women in the world I really love and I can't sleep with either of them."

"Don't get Freudian on me, Seth," Sarah replied.

Rachel laughed, then said to Sarah, "I think the comment was meant mainly for me."

"Am I that transparent?" I said.

Both women answered, "Yes!"

"Do you know what your mother said to Seth after he told her I was gay?" Rachel asked Sarah.

"Oh, God, " I said, putting my face in my hands.

"She asked him if it was because he hadn't sexually satisfied me."

Sarah laughed loudly. "That sounds exactly like Mom." Then she turned to me and said, "Actually, I remember you saying the same thing."

"I plagiarized the line from Mom."

Seamus came over and asked what we were laughing about.

"Just telling Mom stories," I said.

He appeared concerned.

"You don't want to hear them," Sarah added.

"Good," Seamus said.

Rachel looked at the three of us with a big smile on her face.

"What?" I said.

"Your mother really did do something right."

Sarah's eyes welled up and she embraced Rachel tightly. "Thank you," she said when she pulled back. "Mom would have been so happy to hear that."

Sarah said she was going to step outside for a moment. Rachel said she needed to pee. I said I needed another drink. I went over to the drinks table and poured myself a scotch. Alice cast me a reproving look from across the room. She and Freddy had become born again about twenty years ago and they no longer drank alcohol or danced. Freddy made his way over to me and clapped me affectionately on the back. "Seth, my man, you feel like some company?" This was Freddy's style when he thought I was in trouble. Freddy had been one of the men my mother had enlisted to help me when I younger. Freddy would stop by the apartment with a basketball under his arm and say to me, "Can you run with me, my man?"

"Sure, I'd love some company," I said. "Can I pour you something to drink?"

"Maybe some club soda."

I handed him his soda and held up my glass of scotch. "Cheers," I said.

Eyeing my glass, he said, "That's a helluva way to live, brother."

"Look, Freddy, I appreciate your concern, but I'm fine."

"Don't tell me you're fine. None of us is fine."

"All right, all right," I said. "I hear you." On the other side of the room, Alice was putting on her coat.

"I think I'm on your wife's bad side," I commented.

"You know Alice loves you. You just worry her, that's all. But you come to Manny's tomorrow, usual time, and she'll be glad to see you."

Freddy gave my arm a light squeeze, then went to join his wife.

I went outside, looking for Sarah. She was standing in the back-yard, leaning against the railing of the porch, holding a burning cigarette in her hand. I leaned back next to her. It was a clear night with a numinous moon. For a minute we both looked at the sky. I watched a star blink on and off, like the very pulse of the universe.

"Since when do you smoke?" I asked.

"I don't. This is just my private way of remembering Mom."

She then did a spot-on imitation of Ruth, placing half the cigarette in her mouth and inhaling until her eyes bulged.

"Give me that," I said. I took a deep drag on the cigarette and then exhaled Ruth style: head turned, one eye shut, blowing the smoke out of the side of my mouth.

We both laughed.

"This is the first time in my life I've tried a cigarette," I said, coughing.

"Congratulations."

"Did you know that Mom had Seamus privately publish one hundred twenty copies of a story I wrote in college?"

"Yes."

"Did you read it?"

"Yes, it's beautiful, Seth. It really is."

"Why didn't she tell me she was having it privately published?"

"She had this strange idea that you stopped writing because of a letter she sent you about that story. I think she was always hoping you would write again."

I inhaled deeply on the cigarette and then handed it back to Sarah.

"Seamus said I was a lot nicer to Mom in that story than I ever was in real life. Do you think so too?"

She let the cigarette fall to the ground and meditatively ground it out with her shoe.

"I remember one time when we were eleven," she said, "and we were fighting in the backseat of the car somewhere on the turnpike. Mom pulled over to the side of the road and ordered you out. We came back about ten minutes later—that was about how long she needed to go to the next exit and turn around. It was the middle of summer, but you were shivering from fright, and you had peed in your pants."

Sarah's eyes were filled with tears.

"I have absolutely no memory of that," I said.

"I remember it like it was yesterday."

"I can't believe I don't remember something like that."

"Maybe your memory is more selective than you realize."

We looked up at the night sky, mainly, I think, to avoid eye contact, but perhaps we were also wondering if Ruth was somewhere out among the stars, looking down on us.

"Can I say something really strange?" I asked.

"Everything you say is strange," my sister replied.

"I know, you've told me that maybe a zillion times. . . . But I miss Dad," I said. "I feel like we're really orphans now."

"I know what you mean," she said.

"Do you think about Dad at all?"

"Not much. But sometimes I think I'd really love for him to see my children. Maybe because they're the one thing in my life I'm really proud of."

I looked back up at the stars to hide the fact that I was crying.

"Oh, Seth. I'm sorry."

"Forget about it. . . . I actually ran into Dad in Cambridge."

"You did?" she exclaimed. "When?"

"Years ago. After Molly and I split up."

"How was it?"

"Strange. I had sent him a condolence note when Hortense died, and he scolded me for writing just two sentences."

"Jesus! What did you say?"

"I told him he had miscounted. I wrote three sentences."

Sarah let out a mirthless laugh. "Let's go in. I'm getting cold."

INSIDE, I WENT OVER TO the couch where Zipporah and Avi had moved with their book. When I sat down between them, Zipporah's brow furrowed.

"What's the matter, honey?" I said. "Don't you want me to sit next to you and Avi?"

She looked anxiously around the room, as if she were afraid of being seen with me. Then she cupped her hands to my ear and whispered, "Uncle Seth. You're not supposed to sit on the couch."

I cupped my hands to her ear and whispered back, "Why not?"

She sighed with frustration.

"Because," she whispered, "you're in *mourning*. You have to sit on one of those wooden boxes."

Feeling left out, Avi put his mouth to my other ear. He didn't have anything to say and just breathed warmly into my ear.

"Can't I mourn after I visit with you and Avi?" I asked.

I said this lightheartedly, but she looked deeply vexed. Was she afraid that if I violated Jewish tradition I would be banished again back into the world of the dead, or wherever she thought I had been until six months ago?

"You're right, sweetie. I'm going to sit on that box and mourn properly. Can you and Avi join me? I really don't want to sit on a box all by myself."

"OK," she replied.

The three of us moved to the other side of the room. I sat on a crate, and the children stood on either side of me. I opened their book to read to them from the story of Ruth, a story of loss and love, of living among strangers.

I noticed Rachel standing over us, holding a crate in her hands too.

"Do you mind if I join you?" she asked.

"Sit," I said.

She set her crate down and sat on it. Avi stared at her. "Hello," Rachel said. "What's your name?"

Avi turned to me and said, "Is this your wife?"

"No, that's my friend, Rachel."

"Are you Jewish?" he asked Rachel.

"Yes," she answered. "Are you?"

Avi was tongue-tied, but Zipporah laughed. "She's kidding with you, Avi. She knows you're Jewish."

I began reading to them, but after just a page or two I realized that Zipporah was looking out the big picture window. I looked out too and saw Seamus deep in conversation with Elijah. Alice and Freddy were standing nearby. Under the moonlight, my brother's tzitzit glowed luminously against his black trousers. I looked around the room. Rhoda was whispering into Poppa's ear; Sarah and Aaron were sitting on crates, their children on either side of them; Jenny and Jeanette were eating off each other's plates. Everyone was here except my mother. For the first time all day, I missed her in a way that made me dizzy with dread. I was here and she was in the cold ground, sealed inside a pitch black coffin. It was the same dread I had felt so many years before on the night of my bar mitzvah, the night I held my mother in my arms, kissed her on the lips, and told her I loved her, because I was afraid she would disappear down a deep, dark hole and we would all be sent to live in different places.

I looked back out the window. Seamus was nodding, apparently in agreement with something Elijah was saying. Then he bowed his head and placed a hand over his face. Elijah pulled him close and the two of them embraced, rocking and swaying in each other's arms.

Zipporah leaned casually against me, extending an arm across my back. I prayed that she would live another one hundred and twenty years, and that she would always remember this night, remember all of us who were here.

Date: October 18, 2002

Subject: Bat Mitzvah, Books, Stories, etc.

To: zippyjew@yahoo.com

From: sshapiro@BBA.edu

Dear Zipporah,

Well, I hope your father doesn't stroke out when all
the boxes are delivered to your house later today. He
didn't want any keepsakes from Nana Ruth's apartment
when she died, but I'm sending you all of her books now.
I read them all by the time I was your age, so you better start reading. Anyway, the books aren't my actual
bat mitzvah present for you. I'm also sending you a
story I wrote many years ago. That's my real present.
Nana Ruth would have wanted you to have her books, and
I know she would have wanted you to read this story.
It's a story about our family, a story about longing for
solace and connection with something that's been lost.

Much love, many kindnesses—

Your Favorite Uncle (AKA Seth)

A STRANGER ON THE PLANET

By Seth Shapiro

Three months before my thirteenth birthday, I persuaded my father to sue my mother for custody of me. This was in late August, near the end of a two-week visit with my father. I wrote my mother a letter informing her of my decision. I told her I knew she might be disappointed, but I wasn't rejecting her; I only wanted to spend more time with my father, to know and love him as well as I knew her. I also told her not to call me. We could discuss this when I returned home, if she wanted to.

She phoned the second the letter came. Phyllis, my father's wife, answered the phone. "Hold on, Sandra," she said, and held the phone out to me, her palm covering the receiver. I shook my head. Phyllis gave me an exasperated look and told my mother I was busy. She called three more times in the next hour. I had known this was going to happen, but I was not even thirteen, and I wanted to forget how well I knew my mother. Phyllis agreed to relay her messages to me: How long should she preheat the oven for my lemon chicken recipe? Should she run hot or cold water when scrubbing the sink with Comet? What should she do if the washing machine stopped in midcycle? I had typed out three pages of instructions before I left, but the calls kept coming right through dinner. Could she use ammonia on Formica surfaces? Should she use tap or distilled water in the iron? Finally, Phyllis exclaimed, "Jesus, Sandra, we're eating. He'll be home in two days." Then I watched her face darken and imagined the blast my mother was delivering. *Don't you tell me when I can talk to my own son. I'm his mother, and when I tell you to get him, you jump—understand?!* Phyllis hung up the phone and sat back down at the table, her lips drawn across her face like a thin white scar. Ten seconds later the phone rang again. My father and Phyllis looked at each other. I felt like Jonah hiding in the bowels of the ship, knowing the storm above was all his fault. No one moved. "Mommy, the phone is ringing," said Leah, my little stepsister. "Maybe you should answer the phone, Alan," my father said. I stood up from the table very slowly, giving myself every chance that the phone might stop ringing before I reached it.

"What's the problem, Mom? I wrote everything down."

"You little bastard! Don't bother coming home. If I never see you again I'll die happy!"

My father wasn't enthusiastic when I asked him to sue. "Lawyers? Court? Not again." My parents had divorced when I was five, and the episode still bothered him. He had wanted to work things out quietly, but my mother staged a grand opera. She asked for an exorbitant amount of alimony and minimal visitation rights for my father. She accused him of being an adulterer and wife beater. My father was a rabbi in a small town on the New Jersey shore and brought in many members of his congregation as character witnesses. My mother had no witnesses on her behalf. She lost every point she argued for.

"But, Dad," I implored, "she's driving me *crazy!*"

He and I usually didn't have much to say to each other, but I expected the word crazy to explain everything, as if I were revealing to him that we shared the same inherited trouble, like gum disease or premature balding. I pitched my case to him, describing how she complained about her haywire menstrual cycle when I was eating, how she slept on the couch every night, sometimes with a cigarette still burning in her hand.

"Do you know how dangerous that is, Dad?"

He pressed his palms up his cheeks, a gesture that always led me to imagine he was trying to stretch his beard over his forehead. I envisioned him doing the same thing the day he met my mother. When I had asked her, the year before, how they came together—a far more mysterious question to me than where I had come from—she answered, "In the shower." Both were on an archaeological dig in Israel. My father, recently ordained, was covered with soap in the primitive communal shower when my mother walked in, nineteen, naked, enthusiastic about everything. Several months later they were married, but my mother was bored by the life of a rabbi's wife. She had no interest in charity work or Sisterhood meetings. She saw an analyst five times a week and signed up for classes on Sanskrit and criminology. Once she planned a lecture at the synagogue on Gurdjieff's centers of consciousness. Three people came.

I told my father I was fed up with cooking and cleaning, washing and ironing.

"I thought you liked doing housework," he said.

"Not all the time. I want to have a normal life, Dad."

He touched his beard lightly, thoughtfully. I had found the right word.

"Sometimes her boyfriends sleep over. I see them on the sofa bed when I get up in the morning."

"All right. All right."

"Dad, I'm telling you this is an open-and-shut case. I'm old enough to live with whomever I want. That's the law."

I knew about the law from my mother. She sued everyone. Landlords, universities, car dealers, plumbers, my father. She stayed up all night researching her cases and planning her strategies. In the mornings I would see her asleep on the couch, openmouthed, beneath a blanket of law books and the sheets of paper on which she outlined her complex and futile arguments. Years later, after I graduated from law school and returned to New Jersey to practice law, many of the older lawyers around the courthouse told me my mother had a reputation as a compulsive but knowledgeable and creative litigant. "I always thought the law was a metaphysical exercise for her," one of them said to me. "I can sue you: Therefore I exist."

I also learned the art of exaggeration from my mother, the art of how to invent something when the truth is boring or makes you anxious. I had seen her on the sofa bed with a man only once. The year before, she had come into my bedroom very early one morning to tell me that Sidney, her sometime boyfriend, had spent the night. "You don't mind that he's here?" she asked, sitting on the side of my bed. Her weight was comforting, as were her warm, heavy sleepy odors. I told her I didn't mind. "I slept in the other room," she said anxiously. "But I'm going to lie down next to Sidney for a couple of minutes."

"All right," I said, and went back to sleep. I knew she liked Sidney. She had told me that he had always wanted a boy to raise, and that he was personal friends with Joe Namath. He bought me books, bats, tickets to ball games. In two years he would go to jail for fraud and income tax evasion, but that morning my mother and I both believed in him. When I went into the living room he was asleep on his side. My mother was awake, pressed up against his back with an arm around his chest. She smiled at me as if Sidney was some wonderful secret between us.

My mother's explosion of telephone calls came on Thursday night; late Sunday afternoon I took the bus from my father's town to the Port Authority bus station in New York. My mother usually met me inside the terminal, but I didn't see her anywhere. I called home six times in the next hour, counting twenty-three rings on the last attempt. The next local bus across the river didn't leave for two hours. I found a bench at the far end of the terminal, and, sitting with my suitcase between my knees, watched everyone going home, everyone except for the panhandlers, the proselytizers, the old men sleeping against walls, teenagers who had run away.

My mother wasn't in when I arrived home. She hadn't left a note, and by ten o'clock I still hadn't heard from her. I knew what she was doing. She was letting me know how it felt to be abandoned. I knew she would return the next day, but I was still in tears by the time I was ready for bed. My room felt like the loneliest place in the world that night, so I pulled out the sofa bed. I had never slept in the living room before, and I couldn't orient myself, couldn't gauge the black space around me.

Gradually the darkness lightened into a dull grayness. When I could see everything in the room clearly, I began preparing for the first day of school. I kept thinking, *Now he's brushing his teeth, now he's deciding which shirt to wear, now he's pouring milk over his cereal....* as if, without my mother in the house, I were inhabiting someone else's life. I was all ready by six thirty. I lay back down on the couch and watched the clock for the next hour and forty-five minutes.

At eleven thirty, during biology, the school secretary came to the class-room to tell me that my mother had phoned. She told me that I was to go right home because of an emergency. The year before, I'd been called out of class about once a month because of an "emergency" at home. Usually my mother had fought with a patient, or a married man she was seeing had stopped answering her calls, or her father had sent her another sanctimo-nious letter, or some judge had treated her in a cavalier manner.

I declined the secretary's offer of a ride and walked home. When I let myself into the apartment, my mother was sitting at the kitchen table. She held the letter I had written to her in one hand and was burning holes in it with her cigarette. She looked like a curious child torturing a small animal.

"I thought you saw a patient now," I finally said.

She was a psychologist but had only four regular patients. She used her bedroom as an office, though she longed to have one in town. "Someplace beautiful," she would say. "Someplace where I can really be myself."

"I canceled," she said, burning a chain of holes through my name.

"Canceled! What for? That's thirty-five dollars!"

She looked at me for the first time. "Would you please explain this, Alan?"

"I explained everything in the letter."

"Everything? Really? I can think of any number of things you didn't explain. Why you're leaving me, for instance. Can you explain that? Am I really that bad of a mother?"

"I told you I wasn't rejecting you."

"Look, Alan. Let's agree on one thing. Let's agree you're not going to treat me like I'm stupid." She said this slowly and rhythmically, as if I was the stupid one.

"Mom, I just don't want to live here anymore. That's all."

"That's all? You think it's that simple?"

"I explained. I want to live with my father."

"Tell me the last time he called."

"Maybe he doesn't call because he's afraid you'll sue if he says something you don't like over the phone."

"Oh, I see. Now it's my fault. I'm to blame because your father has no interest in you."

"I didn't say that."

"Then what are you saying? That I'm a failure as a mother?"

"No, Mom. You're not a failure. All right?"

"Then why? Why are you doing this to me?"

"Jesus, Mom. I just want to have a normal life."

"*Normal!*" she cried. "What's not normal about the way we live?"

"Everything! The cooking, the cleaning, the shouting. Everything!"

"Who shouts?"

"You do. You're shouting now."

"Of course I'm shouting. My son tells me he doesn't want to live with me anymore. Can't I shout about that? Isn't that *normal*?"

"Mom, this conversation is retarded. I'm going back to school."

"And who asked you to cook and clean?" she shouted after me. "Not me. You love to cook. Or is that another thing to blame me for?"

"Good-bye, Mom," I said, walking out the door.

"Don't come back, you lousy child! Just see how well you can get along without me!"

Before I began cooking and cleaning, my clothes always came out of the wash shrunk and discolored, sending me into fits most mornings because I was embarrassed to wear wrinkled shirts to school and my mother refused to iron them.

"You iron them," she would say. "They're your shirts."

"But I don't know how!"

"Neither do I."

"Yes, you do! You're supposed to know!"

"I am? Where is it written that I'm supposed to know? Tell me? Where?"

For supper she usually boiled pouches of frozen food, and even that gave her problems. "Oh, puke!" I'd say, pursing my face and coughing up a mouthful of half-frozen meatloaf.

Once, on her birthday, I bought her a cookbook and pleaded with her to learn some recipes.

"Oh, honey, I can't deal with recipes."

"But why?"

"Because nothing ever turns out the way it's supposed to for me."

I began with simple dishes—baked chicken, broiled lamb chops and rice. Then I moved on to lasagna, curried shrimp, veal scallops with pro-sciutto, Grand Marnier soufflés, and poached peaches with raspberry puree. I prepared some of my most inspired meals when my mother entertained Sidney.

"I don't know how you do it," she would say, anointing herself with perfume as she watched me work in the kitchen.

"It's easy, Mom. All you have to do is follow the directions."

"Directions," she replied, "bore me."

When my first day of school ended, I returned home as usual to begin dinner. Mrs. Gutman, my mother's four thirty patient and close friend, was

sitting on the couch. She was a stout Romanian woman with a collapsing beehive of rust-colored hair held vaguely together with hundreds of
bobby pins. "Hello, darlink," she greeted me, her accent falling with a
thud on the "darlink." I could tell by the sad cast of her eyes that she
knew all about my letter.

Mrs. Gutman had been seeing my mother longer than any other patient.
Her fifty-minute sessions sometimes lasted for two hours and she would
call at three and four in the morning when her nightmares frightened her
awake. The ringing phone always exploded in my ears. I would sit up in
bed, my heart beating violently, as if it were connected to the phone with
jumper cables. I couldn't hear my mother's words very clearly, but I would
lie awake for hours listening to the dim, low murmur of her voice, a sound
as comforting as the patter of rain after an electrical storm.

Mrs. Gutman was the last scheduled patient of the day because her
sessions went on so long. Usually I would be preparing dinner when they
finished, and Mrs. Gutman would crowd into the tiny kitchen to sample
and advise. Pressing her bosom against my rib cage, she stirred, tasted,
lifted covers off pots, and inhaled deeply. "No, darlink, you must do like
dis one," she'd say, sprinkling paprika into a stew that I had delicately
seasoned and simmered for hours. "Great! Now you've ruined it," I'd say,
hurling the wooden spoon into the sink.

"No, darlink, was too bland. Taste now."

"Don't call me that. I've told you my name is Alan."

"Yes, Alan, darlink."

Later, after Mrs. Gutman had left, my mother would say, "Why do you
have to be so mean to her? Because she's my friend? Is that why?"

"I've told you not to analyze me. I'm not your patient."

"You can't give me credit for my successes, can you? You know how
important I am to Mrs. Gutman, but you won't give me credit for it."

"Mom, she's your patient. She shouldn't be wandering into the kitchen.
It's unprofessional."

"Mrs. Gutman is one of my dearest friends."

"Well, she shouldn't be. You're her therapist. You're not supposed to be her best friend too."

"Where is it written that I can't be both? Tell me! If Mrs. Gutman values my friendship, who are you to tell me I'm wrong?"

That afternoon, Mrs. Gutman stayed only for her scheduled time. When my mother came into the kitchen, I was already eating my dinner, poached turbot. She joined me at the table with peanut butter on stale white bread.

"That smells delicious," she said.

"It is."

"Can I have a taste?"

"No."

"Why not?"

"I'm seeing how well I can get along without you."

"Oh, really? Who paid for that?"

I pushed my plate over to her.

"Look, honey, I'm sorry I said that. The truth is I can't get along without you either."

"Mom, I just want a change."

"But you don't have to leave. I can change. I'll change. You want me to cook? I'll learn to cook. I'll be the best cook in the world. You don't want me sleeping on the couch? I won't sleep on the couch. I'll rent an office in town. How's that? You'll never have to see any of my patients again. Just tell me what you don't like."

I was staring down at the table. Without looking up, I replied, "Mom, I've decided."

She yanked me by the elbow. "You really think some judge is going to send you to live with your father because you say you want a change?"

"Do you think there are any judges who don't know about you?"

"What is that supposed to mean?"

"I mean all the lawyers you've spent the night with."

She slapped me across the face. She had never hit me before, and she began to cry, holding her hand as if she had burned it on something.

"You're just like everyone else," she cried. "You're all the same."

I had hoped my mother would just boot me out, hurling suitcases and insults at me, and when she thought to call me back, to apologize and argue some more, I would already be ensconced at my father's house, too far away to hear a thing. But after my father sued, I barely heard her voice. At dinner, she would occasionally glance up from her plate and look at me oddly, as if I were a stranger she had just found sitting at her table. If I attempted conversation, she'd either ignore me or say, "Ask your father." I felt sure her silence was purely strategic; I felt certain that if I told her I was changing my mind, tears would well up in her eyes, all would be forgiven, and she'd vow to change. Some nights, though, after I was in bed and she called up Mrs. Gutman, her voice sounded extremely faint, more so than usual. I kept changing the position of my head on the pillow, but I couldn't tune her in, and after a time she faded out like a voice on the radio during a long drive in the middle of the night.

At the end of September, my mother and I visited her father in Florida. He was a dentist and we saw him twice a year to have our teeth fixed and to be reminded of things we were not supposed to do. I was not supposed to eat sweets because my teeth were low in calcium. My mother was not supposed to "use" cigarettes in public or tell anyone she was divorced. For some reason, he thought it was less embarrassing to introduce her as a widow.

"Your grandfather doesn't know about our problems," she said to me on the plane, "and I don't plan on telling him."

We always went to Florida at the wrong time—either in May or late September, when the air in New Jersey was most delicious, when the perspiration on your face was cooling as a breeze. Usually we stayed only for two or three days, sunning by the pool of his condominium or accompanying him on the golf course for his daily 6:00 a.m. game. My mother didn't play, but he was adamant she come with us, as if she might get into trouble if she was left alone. By the thirteenth hole she was desperate for a cigarette. She'd quickly light one up as my grandfather was bent over the ball. He'd catch a scent of it and stop his stroke. "Sandra, how many times have I asked you to refrain from doing that in public?" Once the cigarette was lit, she would become calmer, drawing deeper into herself with each drag. "Sandra!" She'd let a long, elegant ash drop to the green.

"Sorry, Daddy," she'd say in a bored voice, as she grasped my shoulder for support and twisted the cigarette out against the bottom of her shoe.

On this visit, we went straight from the airport to his office because a tooth had been bothering her for weeks. My grandfather ushered her into the chair and instructed her to remove her lipstick. She pressed her lips against a tissue, leaving a red O-shaped print, and then she gave it to my grandfather as though she were handing over her mouth. "Sandra," he said, over the whine of the drill, "have you heard from the Yoskowitzes' son?" Both his hands were in her mouth and she moved her head from side to side. I sat in the dental assistant's chair (my grandfather thought he might inspire me to become a dentist), where I had a direct view of the bloody saliva swirling around underneath my mother's tongue. "No? Maybe he'll call you when you get back. I gave your number to Jack and Bea to give to him. He lives in Jersey City and sells hospital equipment. They showed me a copy of his tax returns, so I know for certain that he earned $81,000 last year. He thinks you're a widow so don't say anything to disappoint him." Her eyes widened with hurt. I wanted to do something. Unclasp the towel from around her neck, give her back her mouth and tell her, Run, I'll meet you at the airport. "Let's just hope," he continued, "he doesn't mind that your teeth are so stained with nicotine."

She raised her hand for him to stop. "Daddy, I really don't want to hear this today. My life has been really shitty lately, and I just don't want to hear this."

My grandfather held the drill in the air and looked up, like someone about to begin conducting an orchestra. "Some days," he sighed, "I'm almost relieved that Rose is gone." I watched my mother's eyes brimming with tears. When my grandfather noticed, he reached for a needle and asked her if she needed more novocaine.

A month before the hearing and two weeks before my bar mitzvah, I went to see a court-appointed psychologist. Florence Fein's office, in a red Victorian house, was a large room crowded with old furniture, Oriental rugs, stained glass, and antique lamps. She served me lemonade and asked me what I would like to talk about. I told her I couldn't think of anything.

"Why do you think you're here?" she asked.

"Because I have an appointment?"

"Perhaps you can tell me why you don't want to be here."

"Because there's nothing wrong with me."

"You don't have to have something wrong with you to go to a psychologist, Alan. Most people come here just to figure things out."

"I don't have anything to figure out. I know I want to live with my father."

"No one is keeping you here. You're free to leave."

"Then you'll tell the judge I have to live with my mother."

"Alan, my job isn't to penalize you for anything you say. If you really don't have anything you'd like to discuss with me, I'll just write in my report that I couldn't draw any conclusions."

I was uncomfortable with Florence Fein because I could never say a bad word about my mother to a stranger.

"If I go right now, is my mother still going to have to pay for the time?"

"Yes. How do you feel about that?"

"Bad. She's spending a lot of money for nothing."

"Do you always feel bad about your mother's actions?"

"Sometimes."

"Do you think that's going to change if you live with your father?"

"I don't know. . . . Don't you think people can change?"

"Of course. I wouldn't be in this business if I didn't think so."

I understood then why Florence Fein had a more successful practice than my mother. Florence Fein really did believe people could change. The word didn't hold the same meaning for my mother. When I thought of her pleading, "I can change! I'll change!" the words sounded to me like "I'm in pain! I'm in pain!"

"Alan, you probably know that your parents' divorce was very bitter."

"Yes. So?"

"Do you think your father has put any subtle pressure on you to come live with him?"

"Did my mother say that?"

"Not at all. As a matter of fact, she argued that your father wasn't all that interested in having you live with him and that you might be deeply hurt once that became a reality for you."

"What else did she say?"

"She said she's failed at everything she's ever tried and doesn't want to fail as a parent."

The day before my bar mitzvah, my mother informed me that she planned on coming. I acted surprised, but deep down I had expected it.

"You're not religious," I argued.

She was driving me to the Port Authority to catch the bus to my father's town.

"You know this isn't about religion. You just don't want me to come. Admit it."

"But you're always saying my father's friends are against you. You'll have to face all of them if you come."

"And so why should they be at my son's bar mitzvah and not me?"

"Mom, that's not a reason to go."

"Oh, and are your reasons any better? You just want all your father's friends to think you're more your father's son. You want them to think, 'My, hasn't he turned out so nice and polite despite his mother.'"

"I've told you not to analyze me. I'm not your goddamned patient!"

We entered the Lincoln Tunnel, and I was truly afraid she would order me out. We hadn't talked that way in months. But she didn't say anything until we pulled up to the terminal. "Talk to your father that way sometime," she said, "and see how long he lets you live with him."

That evening Phyllis fixed a traditional Sabbath meal. My father invited six couples from his synagogue to join us. They were too interested and too familiar with me, as if I were a disfigured child and they were pretending not to notice. Before we had finished the soup and melon, they asked me which subject I liked the most in school (social studies), whether I was a Yankees or a Mets fan (neither—the Dodgers), whether I, too, planned on becoming a rabbi (no—either a lawyer or a chef). Everyone gave me a pained smile. I was thinking of the last elaborate meal I'd prepared for my mother and Sidney, and how I loved standing in the kitchen with her, minutes before he came to the door. My mother and the pots rattled with expectancy: Would this be the man to stay with her, to adjust our haphazard course? The kitchen smelled rich with promise, as if the scent of her perfume and the odors of my cooking held the power to transform our lives, to transport us from our crowded, chaotic apartment into a large house where we all had our own rooms, where my mother would be calm, secure, loved.

After we returned from services that evening, I told my father and Phyllis that my mother would be showing up the next morning. They looked at each other.

"Oh, Alan," my father sighed. "Couldn't you have done something?"

"No, Dad, she wants to come."

"Doesn't she know how uncomfortable this is going to be?" Phyllis added.

"Mommy, who's coming?" Leah asked.

"Nobody, dear. Nobody."

The next morning I stepped up to the Torah and saw my mother sitting in a row of empty seats. She waved at me like someone in a lifeboat attempting to flag a distant ship. Everyone's eyes moved from her to me. I brought my tallis to my lips and began chanting in a language I didn't understand. After the service, she rushed over to the receiving line and reclaimed me with a long embrace. She had not held me or kissed me for months. Several people waiting to congratulate me formed an uncomfortable semicircle around us. She tightened her hold, as if I were a charm to ward off bad spirits. People began to file away and then we were standing alone, like two people who had wandered into the wrong celebration. Then Phyllis came over to tell me that the photographer was set up for a family portrait. My mother squeezed my elbow.

"You stay right here, Alan."

"We'll only be five minutes," Phyllis said impatiently. "Come, Alan."

She reached for me and my mother slapped her hand away. Phyllis looked at her hand as if it didn't belong to her.

"I'm his family," my mother declared. "If the photographer wants a portrait, he can come over here."

"Crazy woman," Phyllis murmured, and turned away.

My mother caught Phyllis on the side of her head with her purse. Phyllis whirled around, crying, "Oh! Oh!" more in disbelief than in pain. My mother lunged. Each woman grabbed at the other's hair and face. They teetered back and forth in their high heels. I could hear nylons whispering against nylons. My father rushed over, his hand raised and his black robes billowing. I ran out.

I kept running until I reached the beach, breathless. Each gulp of the November air stung my lungs. I wrapped my tallis around my neck and walked rapidly through the sand. Then I heard my mother shout my name. I turned around. She was perhaps a hundred yards behind me, her shoes in her hands. She crossed them over her head, signaling me to stop. I walked down to the shoreline.

I recalled how she and I used to come to this same beach on winter afternoons when my parents were still married. She liked the remoteness of the beach in winter. Once we came with a helium balloon she had bought me at a nearby amusement park. At the shoreline she had bent down beside me and we placed our fingertips all over its shiny red surface. "We're sending a message," she said, "to your Nana Rose." I let go of the balloon and watched it sail up into the brilliant blue air and disappear high over the ocean. She explained that when the balloon reached heaven, Nana Rose would recognize our fingerprints. Perhaps I looked at her quizzically, because she then said, "Trust me, sweetie. We're already on the moon."

I watched the waves explode and dash toward me, watched the froth top my shoes, and at almost the same moment felt my socks turn to ice.

"Alan, dear, why are you standing in the water?"

She was right behind me. I didn't turn around or answer.

"Honey, doll, you'll ruin your shoes."

"Good."

"You'll catch pneumonia."

"Even better."

"Won't you at least step out of the water?"

"No."

"No?"

"Maybe I want to go for a swim."

I really didn't want to swim. I just wanted to lie down in the surf and close my eyes and drift, like a toy boat or a bottle, to the other side of the ocean, washing up on the shore of a country where nobody knew me.

"Darling, it's too cold to swim. Wait until the summer. Then you can go in the water."

"Don't talk to me like that!"

"Like what, sweetie?"

"Like I'm crazy. Like I'm about to jump out a window. You're the one who's crazy, not me."

"Oh, Alan, don't criticize. Not now. Not after what I've been through. Don't be like all the others."

I turned around, ready to shout, "Why can't you be like all the others?!" Then I saw how bad she looked. One eye was half closed and her nostrils were rimmed with blood. Angry red welts laced her windpipe. She dropped to her knees and began crying, her tears falling into the sand.

I was only thirteen that day, but I knew my mother would never change. She would never have a beautiful office like Florence Fein's. She would never have more than three or four patients, people like Mrs. Gutman, who were as chaotic and pained as she was. I knew she would always feel like a stranger on the planet.

Two weeks later a judge sent me to live with my father. The fight with Phyllis and the depositions provided by nearly everyone in my father's congregation weighed heavily against my mother. I was sullen with the judge, though he was kind to me. Perhaps I could have said something nice about my mother, but I was only thirteen and didn't know that love can be as obdurate as the changes you long for. Perhaps I could have told him that after I turned around and saw her bruised face, I lifted my mother to her feet. I pressed my tallis against her bloody nose. Then I rolled it up into a tight little ball, and we trekked back up the beach together.

ACKNOWLEDGMENTS

Michele McDonald and Eileen Pollack read every draft of this book, always providing me with crucial advice, encouragement, and support. I owe them my deepest thanks. I'd also like to thank Katie Herman, my editor at Soho Press, for her brilliant editorial guidance, and Jim McPherson, my teacher and friend, for teaching me that imagination is the medium through which we invent our best selves.